This Kind of Forever

BOBBI MACLAREN

THIS KIND OF FOREVER

A KIP ISLAND NOVEL

BOBBI MACLAREN

This Kind of Forever

Copyright © 2025 by Bobbi Maclaren

All rights reserved.

No part of this book may be reproduced in any form or by any electronic or mechanical means, including information storage and retrieval systems, without written permission from the author, except for the use of brief quotations in a book review.

This is a work of fiction. Any names, places, and incidents are a product of the author's imagination or used in a fictitious manner. Any resemblance to actual people or events is coincidental.

Paperback ISBN: 978-1-7383063-3-6

Cover by Sam at Ink and Laurel

AUTHOR'S NOTE

Please note that this book does contain: mentions of parental neglect and an ensuing no-contact relationship, discussions of cheating regarding FMC's parents, discussions of feeling abandoned by a parent, very brief mention of pancreatic cancer and treatment, very brief mentions of parental death and a house fire relating to side characters, and sexually explicit material.

If you would like to avoid the explicit material, the chapters to skip are: 27, 30 and 33.

PS. If you're part of my family, it's not too late to close the book. Seriously, I mean it.

ONE

GABE

 my
skin itch.

Or maybe it's just setting foot inside the school I hated for the decade I had to attend. Although we're twins, my sister Clara and I had very different elementary school experiences. As the only girl in the family, she stood out on her own. But me? I was Luke Bowman's younger brother. I love my brother, and I look up to him in a lot of ways, but constantly being compared to him got old the day I started kindergarten.

The school gym looks no different than it did the day of my grade eight graduation fourteen years ago. At the time, it hadn't improved much from when my parents had attended as kids—the same white brick walls, covered in colourful handprints from each graduating class that had come before, and banners from various sports competitions hanging from the rafters.

"You look like you could use a drink."

Delilah presents a small paper cup to me. In the few months it's been since my brother's girlfriend moved to the island, we've become good friends. My daughter and her sister are attached at the hip now, so we weren't given much of a choice. It helps that I like her, though. Especially because she doesn't put up with Luke's shit.

I take the offered cup and peer inside. "Fruit punch?"

She grins. "The stiffest drink the meet the teacher barbecue has to offer."

There are a lot of things you don't really consider about parenthood until you're thrust into the thick of it. One of those things is having to attend functions at your kid's school and mingle with a bunch of other people who don't want to be there for one reason or another. I'd give my life for my daughter, but I'd rather be anywhere else than this stuffy gymnasium.

"Your first one," I say. "How are you holding up?"

Her smile dims a little. Delilah took guardianship of her siblings last year and abruptly went from older sister to parent figure. The Delacroixes have had their share of setbacks since then, but it seems like things are slowly becoming more manageable.

"Alright," she says. She looks down, picking at the lip of her cup. "It never gets easier having to rehash what happened, but I figured Soph's teacher should have all the details in case it impacts her at school. Just working up the courage to talk to her."

I offer her an encouraging smile. "It'll be a bit of a transition, but Soph will be okay. Kids are tougher than you realize, and you'll be there to help her."

Her expression turns grateful, but then her gaze flicks to something over my shoulder. Turning, I find my older brother striding toward us. He's dressed in his work clothes, so he must have come straight here from the fire station. I would have, too, if I hadn't worked a night shift last night.

"Hey," Delilah calls. "What are you doing here?"

Luke's arm slides around her shoulders, and he presses a quick kiss to her lips. "I know you're nervous about this. Thought I'd come offer some moral support."

She leans into him. "Thank you."

"Where's Soph?" he asks, looking around the gym.

I point to the far corner, where Delilah's sister is standing with my daughter and a few other kids. They've been running around for the past fifteen minutes. "Abbie is determined to bring her out of her shell."

Delilah looks in their direction, worry marring her features. "I hope she makes more friends here. She was pretty upset when I told her Abbie couldn't be in her class because she's in a different grade."

"She will," Luke assures. "In the meantime, she's got Abbs. They'll see each other at recess."

Delilah sighs. "I guess I should go find her teacher now. We'll see you later, Gabe."

They walk away, and I pull out my phone, sending Abbie's mom an update about the uneventful evening. Larissa is usually here to laugh at my misery, but she took another nurse's shift today and is still at work.

Only twenty more minutes. Then I'll tell Abbie it's time to go. I've already met and spoken to her teacher for this year, so I've done my part.

I really shouldn't complain. I like being present for my daughter, and she's a great kid. I just really hate being in this goddamn school.

"Mr. Bowman?"

Looking up from my phone, I find Trina Reynolds standing in front of me. She taught Abbie's senior kindergarten class last year. I remember her a little from when we were in high school. She's a year or two younger than me, but in such a small town, it's impossible not to at least know *of* everyone.

I smile at her, pocketing my phone. "Just Gabe is fine."

Her cheeks pinken, and she flashes me a coy smile in return. "Just Gabe, then."

It takes me a second to register, but the way she's looking at me makes me realize she didn't come over here to talk about Abbie.

My smile falls a fraction. I wasn't trying to flirt with her or anything.

But maybe I should?

It wasn't that long ago when Luke asked if I was seeing anyone. I'm sure it was just a way for him to get the attention off himself, back when he still had his head up his ass where Delilah was concerned, but maybe he had a point. I haven't dated in...a while. Kip Island isn't exactly brimming with eligible bachelorettes. Most of my former classmates left and haven't come back, and those that stayed are already married and a couple kids deep.

Trina is definitely attractive. Her long, chestnut hair sits in uniform curls over her shoulders. She's tall and willowy, and her clothing hints at slight curves. She's pretty, and she's nice. I remember her being kind to everyone, going out of her way to make friends.

"How's the new school year treating you?" I ask.

Her smile widens as she fiddles with the ends of her hair. "Pretty good so far! Though it's definitely that beginning-of-the-year rush. It usually wears off by the end of September."

"I can imagine," I say. "I don't know how you do it. I feel like I've got my hands full with one, let alone a class of twenty-five."

Trina laughs. "It's not easy, but I do love it. Even if I want to tear my hair out from time to time."

That sounds like something Hallie would say.

Instantly, I feel myself wanting to cringe. I hadn't seen my sister's best friend in ten years. Not until she showed up at my parents' house the other night, fresh off the ferry from Tobermory. She barely even looked at me. I haven't laid eyes on her in the week since, but after the way we left things before she moved off the island, she's been on my mind more than I care to admit.

Trina. Focus on Trina.

"I'm sure you know all about that," she goes on. "Being a fire-fighter can't be the easiest job."

It isn't. Not by a long shot. Kip Island, as a general rule, isn't very exciting. The mundanity is a lure to many, and it makes for slow days at the station, especially in the winter. But when we do get called, it's almost always to help someone at least one member of the crew has a personal connection to. A neighbour, friend, loved one. I have a complicated relationship with my job, but at the end of the day, it gave me stability when I needed it.

I shrug. "It has its moments, but that's the name of the game."

She shifts closer, setting a hand on my arm. I fight the pull of awkwardness I feel. "That's so noble. And *brave*. It's amazing that there are such selfless people like you out there. We need more of that in this world."

That awkwardness turns to slight discomfort. There isn't anything blatantly wrong with what she said, but her words make me leery. I don't want to be put on a pedestal. I don't deserve that. I like helping people, yes, but I didn't go into this career with selfless intentions. It's just a job, like anybody else has.

I want to give Trina the benefit of the doubt, though. She seems a little nervous. Maybe she just doesn't know what to talk about. Or maybe she thinks I want to hear flattery like that. That my ego needs to be pumped up.

I chuckle a bit. "You're not wrong there."

She takes her hand off my arm, but she shifts another couple centimetres closer. "Listen, Gabe, I was..." She trails off, and I wait patiently for her to get her words out. "You see, I was wondering if you'd maybe..."

A flash of blonde in my peripheral has my head jerking to the side. *Hallie?* It couldn't be. Still, that hair...

Some part of me recognizes I'm being rude, but the bigger part of me doesn't care. If Hallie is here, then I need to find her. I've had days to think about what her being back on Kip Island means, and I know we can't avoid each other forever. I don't *want* to avoid her.

Turning back to Trina, I say, "I'm sorry. I have to go."

"Oh. Uh, okay." Her cheeks are now flaming, and I feel guilty as hell. "Nice to see you again, Mr. Bowman. I hope Abbie has a good school year."

Fuck. I feel like the biggest asshole alive. I *am* the biggest asshole alive.

But I nod and say, "Thanks. See you around." And then I walk away.

Scanning the gym, I search for the woman that caught my attention. I find her amongst a group of older parents. But when I get close enough to see her face, I realize it's not her. It's not Hallie.

Of course it isn't.

Not for the first time, I feel like a major idiot where Hallie is concerned. Something about her—*everything* about her—makes my thoughts scramble.

With a shake of my head, I turn in the opposite direction. I'm more than ready to go home now.

Luke intercepts me as I'm heading toward where Abbie and Sophia are playing. "You okay?" he asks, brow raised. "You look spooked."

I nod. "I'm fine. I just...thought I saw Hallie."

His eyes narrow. "Why would she be here?"

She wouldn't. That's the problem. There is no logical reason why she would be at Kip Island Public School, so why did I see blonde hair that isn't even the same shade as hers and almost lose my mind?

I wave him off. "Abbs and I are gonna head out. I'll see you at work, boss."

I leave Luke standing there with a worried crease between his brows. He has a bad habit of thinking he's responsible for me and our sister, even though we're grown adults. But whether he thinks it or not, I'll be fine.

Hallie is back. She clearly doesn't want to see me, but she'll be around. That's just something I'll have to accept. And eventually, I'll move on—I'll stop seeing her in every blonde woman that crosses my path.

I'll be fine.

TWO

HALLIE

"RISE AND SHINE, BABYCAKES!"

I groan as sunlight blasts through the living room, thanks to the curtains my best friend just threw open. The light illuminates our cramped quarters, which have been made worse by the piles of moving boxes shoved into the available spaces around the room. Same as when I first left home, I don't have much in the way of belongings, but Clara's apartment is *really* small.

"Too bright," I whine, pulling my blanket over my head. Until it's rudely ripped away.

"Up," Clara demands. In answer to my quizzical look, she nudges my knee. "You're not allowed to wallow on my couch today. This is now a wallow-free zone."

I pout. "But I'm comfy."

"Hallie, babe, I love you, but this isn't you." She shoves my legs aside and perches on the edge of the couch cushion. "Where has my bestie girl gone?"

I lost her, and I'm not sure how to get her back.

I've known Clara Bowman since our first day of kindergarten twenty-four years ago. We've been inseparable since. For the first few years, our teachers had a hard time telling us apart. We were both blonde, and we often wore similar outfits. The only differ-ence was Clara's were new while mine were hand-me-downs and thrift store purchases.

When we hit our teen years, though, things changed. Clara started to stand out while I wanted nothing more than to fade into the background. I worried sometimes that she would tire of me, but she hasn't left my side, even when I left hers.

"She's on strike. Try again tomorrow." I attempt to pull my blanket back up, but Clara doesn't budge.

"I know being back home feels weird, but hiding away inside is only going to prolong the inevitable," she says.

She's right. Returning home and winding up on her doorstep, tail tucked between my legs, is certainly not how I pictured my life going when I set my sights on the city all those years ago. Leaving the island behind for the lure of the unknown—for this big city that wouldn't hesitate to chew me up and spit me out—felt prefer-able to staying stagnant in this town that was slowly bleeding me dry.

I was damned no matter how you sliced it, so I took the coward's way out. But life is a circle, and one way or another, you end up back where you started. For me, that place is Kip Island.

Hemmed in on all sides by the waters of Lake Huron, the island is a popular tourist destination when the weather is warm. Cottagers flock here on the weekends and holidays during the summer months. For the people who live here year-round, the island is home. A community. Family.

That closeness was both a blessing and a curse growing up. Now that I'm back, I haven't yet decided which is most true.

I offer Clara a small smile. "I'm scared."

While I'm not a celebrity by any stretch of the imagination, every resident of the island has a certain level of notoriety among the locals. My family is well-known in that regard, for reasons a lot less wholesome than the Bowmans'. Growing up, my mother was something of a problem child, and as a result, I had all kinds of eyes on me. Waiting to see if I'd follow in her footsteps.

Clara's eyes soften, and she takes my hands in hers. "You're going to figure things out, Hallie. Losing your job and giving up your apartment in such a small span is a lot of change. That would throw anyone for a loop. But as your best friend, it's my duty to keep you from withering away in here while life passes you by."

Guilt churns in my stomach. Clara took me in without hesitation when I came back to town ten days ago. Her apartment is barely a one-bedroom. As it is, she has little space for her home library—an impressive collection of books she has been curating for years—yet she hasn't complained once about sharing it with me. I need to get myself together.

"Can you do me a favour?" she asks. "Just this one thing, and that'll be your accomplishment for the day."

I nod. It's the least I can do. While I've been doing my best to clean up after myself and keep out of her way, I feel a little bad that I've essentially commandeered her living room for the foreseeable future.

"I have a list of things I need from the store, but I need to head to Dockside," she explains. "Can you go for me? You can take my car, if you drop me off first."

Dockside, the restaurant built into the base of the island's old lighthouse, is owned by her parents. Clara has worked there since we were in high school, but she's been managing it for about five years now, and it's effectively her baby. The only baby she'll ever have, according to her.

"Of course I can."

She grins as we both stand up from the couch. Then, never one to pass up the opportunity for a good hug, she throws her arms around me. Settling into the familiar weight, I let out a sigh.

"I've missed you, Hallie girl," she says. "Welcome home."

I blink back the sting of tears. I want to tell her nothing has felt like home in a long, long time, and coming back here makes me feel like a failure. I want to tell her that I'm homesick for something I fear doesn't exist anymore, if it ever did.

But I don't.

The shopping list Clara texted me is a mile long. I know for sure she has enough tampons stocked up to last a year, so it doesn't take a genius to figure out that she sent me on this goose chase to keep me out of the apartment for as long as possible.

I can't blame her, though. Any longer and I'd probably transform into a sad lump of goo on her couch.

It's hard to admit, but walking through the parking lot of the grocery store with the early September sun beating down on me feels...good. Normal. And I needed that—normal.

But normal promptly goes out the window as soon as I step into the cool embrace of the air conditioning.

I've never felt more on display than I do right now. Eyes. So many eyes. Some are strangers simply following a natural inclination to stare at anything new, but some are people I've known since I was a kid. If it isn't already popular knowledge that I'm back, it will be now.

Trying to appear unaffected, I grab a shopping cart and pull up Clara's list. As I head for the produce section, the store manager watches me with a curl of his lip. Gordon has never liked me, even back when I worked for him one summer as a cashier. Then again, I'm not sure he likes anyone. What he's doing in a job that forces him to interact with the public, I'll never know.

Slowly, as I round up food and household items, I can feel those stares fall away. A melancholic woman shopping for groceries doesn't make for good gossip fodder, it seems. I'm relieved.

Until I hear someone loudly calling my name.

"Hallie! Hallie Foster!"

When I turn, my cheeks heat at the amount of people looking

in my direction now. Leave it to Carole Dramus to draw every ounce of attention in the building.

"I thought that was you!" Carole exclaims with a beaming grin. "I missed you at Delilah's exhibition the other week."

The day I got into town, Clara dragged me to Haven House, her childhood home. I hadn't been there in years, long before her parents turned it into the bed-and-breakfast many tourists now know and love.

That night, half the town was at the house because Clara's older brother was trying to grand gesture his way back into the good graces of the woman he had fallen for. When Clara told me about Luke's plan to hold Delilah's photography exhibition there, I stupidly agreed to go.

That decision came back to bite me when I locked gazes with the one person I've been desperate to avoid for the past ten years.

The town, I can...*sort of* handle. Gabriel Bowman? Not so much.

You would think that by now, I wouldn't care this much. That seeing him wouldn't send me into a tailspin. But every time I think about him, I think about that day on the beach.

It isn't like I've been totally cut off from him. Over the years, Clara has told me bits and pieces. I know he has a daughter. I know his life has been steadily moving forward in my absence. But sometimes, that just makes it hurt even more.

"Sorry," I say to Carole. "I was pretty tired from the move. I slipped out early."

Not a *total* lie. Just a small, partial one.

She pats my arm. "No bother! But listen, I've been meaning to talk to you. Clara mentioned you're back for the long haul, and I'm looking to cut back on the amount of hours I spend at the gallery. You wouldn't happen to be looking for some work, would you?"

Ever since my most recent nannying position was made obsolete, I've been trying to make a plan. But as far as plans go, I currently have none. With the tourist season on Kip Island winding down soon, the job options are limited. There is more opportunity on the mainland, but taking the ferry to work every day isn't ideal when I don't have my own car. I could only borrow Clara's for so long.

When I smile, it feels like the first genuine one I've worn in weeks. Months. "Actually, Carole, that would be great."

She claps. "Wonderful! It's unfortunately nothing grand, given the time of year. About fifteen hours a week. Is that alright? I figured I'd ask you first, seeing as you were such a good customer before."

Before. Before I left. Before I tried to pretend I was someone else entirely.

"That works for me," I reply. Fifteen hours really isn't anything grand, but it's better than the aimless nothing I've got going on otherwise. Baby steps.

"Oh, you are a *gem*," she gushes, placing a hand on my arm and giving it a quick squeeze. "Come by the gallery on Monday and we'll get everything sorted."

With a quick goodbye, Carole departs in a whirlwind of neon. As I watch her walk away, I envy her confidence. For as long as I've known her, she has been content to follow her own path, and screw anyone who has anything to say about it. She is unyielding in her right to exist.

I want to be like her—to shed this inherent need to apologize for simply living in my own skin.

My thoughts are scattered as I round the corner into another aisle. When I look up, I startle, meeting a familiar pair of brown eyes. My stomach does an award-winning somersault.

Gabe.

THREE

GABE

HALLIE FOSTER HAS BEEN AVOIDING me.

Ten days ago, I saw her for the first time in ten years. Since then, I've been trying to figure out what I'd say when I inevitably ran into her again. When she wouldn't be able to hide from me.

Try as I may, I haven't been able to completely cut her out of my life. She is my twin sister's best friend, after all. I'd have to move across the planet—possibly even to another one entirely—to escape any mention of her. At first, that's what I'd wanted, to avoid her. To stew in my embarrassment. But soon that just became the dull pang of missing her, and I clung to any scraps I could.

A little of Hallie was better than none of her at all.

But standing here now, she is both everything and nothing like the girl I remember. Her blonde hair falls in rivers of gold over her shoulders, far longer than it was a decade ago. The ends are now a pretty lavender shade, dyed sometime since I saw her at Delilah's exhibition. Her eyes are still that captivating baby blue.

And her body... Hallie has been away from Kip Island for ten years, and in that time she transformed into the physical manifestation of every single one of my dreams. She's always been beautiful, but there's something about the flare of her hips that makes me want to grab hold of them and never let go.

"It's been a long time, Foster."

Her eyelashes flutter as she closes her eyes for half a second, as if bracing against my voice. When they open again, her gaze meets mine. "Gabriel."

"What are you doing here?"

What do you think she's doing, idiot? You're at the fucking grocery store.

She sets a hand on her cart and flashes me a shy smile. "Your sister sent me to do her dirty work. By the time I'm done, we'll be able to feed the whole island for a week."

I chuckle. "Sounds like Clara. Anything to avoid shopping." If there's one thing my sister despises, it's picking up groceries.

"I don't mind," Hallie is quick to say. "She has been letting me crash at her place, so I'll happily be her errand girl."

A beat of silence passes between us. It's insidious, a trap to make us think we're strangers. But we are far from strangers, so I scramble to fill the quiet.

Pointing to her hair, I say, "I like that colour. It's nice."

It's nice? The only thing worse than silence is small talk. That's a death sentence.

"Oh. Thank you."

Hallie touches the ends of her hair, and for some strange reason, it reminds me of Trina. Because the two women truly couldn't be any more different, and I'm beginning to wonder why I ever thought Trina might be a good idea. Not that there's anything wrong with her, but she's...not Hallie.

I rock back on my heels. "I bet Pops is happy to have you home."

At the mention of her grandfather, some of the tension coiled in her body melts away. "He is. Clara and I went to see him a couple days ago. He wiped the floor with both of us when we played cards, as per usual."

"Things have been busy lately, so I haven't had the chance to see him in a while, but he's certainly kept my card skills sharp."

Her lips part, and I try not to let the visual go to my head. "You visit Pops?"

"He didn't tell you?" She shakes her head. "It's not often, but I try to go a couple times a month. I figured someone should."

She stiffens at the implication, and any ease to this conversation has officially been lost. *Shit, shit, shit.* That definitely did not come out the way I wanted it to. My mouth and brain seem to be operating at different speeds today.

"Fuck. I'm sorry, I—"

"It's alright," she says, but it doesn't feel alright. It feels like I've torn open a wound that barely had time to scab over. "I should get going. Lots to do. It was good to see you."

"Foster, wait. I—"

"Daddy!"

Little pink shoes slap against the tiled floor, and then Abbie skids to a stop in front of me, holding up a box of cereal. Or a box of sugar labelled as cereal, but it's all the same to her.

Unaware of Hallie's presence, my daughter waves the box at me. "Can I get this? *Please.*"

My eyes flick back up to Hallie, but all I see is her retreating back. *Damn it.* With a sigh, I turn my focus to Abbie.

Taking the box from her, I eye the packaging. "Does your mom buy this for you?"

She clasps her hands together, staring up at me with an angelic smile. She nods. "Uh huh. All the time!"

I almost scoff at that. Larissa shops exclusively in the organic section. She probably doesn't even buy plain Cheerios, let alone whatever this is.

Arching a brow, I ask, "Are you lying, Abigail?"

To her credit, Abbie doesn't break right away. This isn't the first standoff I've had with her, and it sure as shit won't be the last.

But I take comfort in winning these battles now because I know it won't be so easy in a few years.

Her shoulders drop. "Yes," she admits. "But it looks so yummy! Daddy, please?"

I hand the box to her as I shake my head. "Nice try, dude. Put it back."

With a frown, she snatches the cereal and heads down the aisle. I watch her push up onto the tips of her toes to slide the box back onto the shelf. Then she stomps back over to my side, her little arms crossed.

I nudge her shoulder. "C'mon, let's go pick something out for dinner. I think Mom's coming over after her shift."

Her eyes light up at that. Even though we split custody, Larissa and I make it a point to spend time together with Abbie when we can. The early days were a little rough, but now we have our routines and everyone is happy.

Abbie declares she wants pasta, so we head into the next aisle to find some sauce and the pasta shells. I begin to scan the shelves, looking for our usual brand.

"*Oh*, I want this," Abbie says from behind me, still standing out in the main aisle.

I turn just as she sets her hand on a can of Alpha-getti. At the very bottom of the too-tall display. I suck in a breath, reaching out to stop her, but it's too late.

Abbie tugs on the Alpha-getti, pulling it free. Which sends the rest of them crashing down.

All I see is a flash of blonde and lavender before Hallie swoops in and pulls Abbie out of the path of rogue aluminum as the cans careen to the floor. It's like dominoes, one falling after the other. When they hit the ground, they start rolling, amplifying the mess. And the noise.

"Oops." Abbie, standing safe at Hallie's side, still clutches her can. She finds my eyes. "Sorry, Daddy."

I sigh, taking a second to close my eyes. They pop open when I hear angry footsteps marching down the adjacent aisle. Then Gordon appears. His face is the colour of a radish, and his balding head shines under the fluorescent lights.

He looks from the destruction, to Abbie, to me. "I expect you to pay for the damages," he clips. "We can't sell dented cans."

"I'll pay," I assure him. "And we'll help clean up."

The store manager only crosses his arms, supervising as Abbie and I start picking up the cans. An employee takes pity on us and brings a shopping cart over for the damaged ones to be set aside. Hallie jumps right in without a word, working to build the display back up to its former glory.

"Honestly," Gordon mutters. I wonder if he thinks he's talking under his breath. "I should just ban children from the store altogether."

I bristle at that. Hallie does, too.

"Gordon," she calls. "What happens with the food you can't sell?"

He shrugs. "We throw it away."

Her head shoots up, meeting his gaze. "You don't donate it?"

Gordon's lip curls. "No."

When all is said and done, we managed to save most of the display, but there are more than a handful of cans Gordon deems unacceptable to sell to his customers. He goes to take the cart up to the front, likely to make sure I don't leave without paying, but Hallie grabs it from him.

"If you're making Gabe pay for these, then he should get to take them home," she says.

Gordon sighs. "Fine." He stalks away, barking instructions at another one of his employees.

"Foster, I don't need fifty cans of alphabet pasta."

"I know." She watches Gordon's retreating back, then lifts her gaze to mine. "But the food bank does." She shakes her head. "I can't believe he'd waste perfectly good food like that."

I snort. "Have you met Gordon? It's pretty on-brand for him." Then I soften. "Thank you."

She offers me a shy smile. "You're welcome." Grabbing her own cart, she starts to inch backward. "Well, I'll see you around."

I swallow. "See you around," I echo. Then I watch her walk away. Again.

On our drive home from the store, we stop at the island's small food bank, and it becomes the proud owner of fifty-three slightly dented cans of Alpha-getti.

———

I hear the front door open and shut just as I finish loading the dishwasher.

"Hi!" Larissa offers me a bright smile as she rounds the corner into the kitchen, as if she didn't just get off a twelve-hour shift at the hospital. "Whoa," she says when she sees my expression. "What's with the face?"

A lot of people have trouble co-parenting with their exes. It drudges up drama and hurt feelings, and the kids get caught in the middle. Larissa and I have never been like that. Maybe because we were never together to begin with.

We went to high school together, and we had a few of the same friends. I drove down to St. Catharines to visit some of them one weekend while she was in undergrad, one thing led to another, and about nine months later, I was holding our daughter in my arms. We only slept together that one time, then we both agreed we were better off as friends.

"What happened to you?" I counter. "Did you slip a few of your patients' happy pills when the other nurses weren't looking?"

She rolls her eyes, hip-checking me out of the way so she can pour herself a glass of wine, which she left here the last time she was over. "This is all-natural, honey. Can't I simply be happy?"

She leans back against the counter, glass in hand. That's when I notice the rock on her ring finger.

"Oh, fuck. He finally did it, eh?"

Larissa beams. "Yeah. Last night."

Chris has been in the picture since Abbie was about two. Larissa had been hesitant to start dating again after becoming a mom, but when she and Chris hit it off at the gym one week, I encouraged her to give it a shot. Four years later, here they are.

I pull her against my side for a hug. "Happy for you, Riss. You gonna tell Abbie?"

She nods. "That's why I wanted to come over tonight. I couldn't stand waiting until tomorrow." She offers me an apologetic smile. "I hope you don't mind."

I wave off her concern. "You know I don't." I nod toward the stairs. "She's up in her room."

Larissa sets her wine glass down, turning to leave. But then she stops and studies me. "You sure you're okay?"

I cross my arms, leaning against the island. I know I won't get out of this without spilling, so I might as well get it over with. "Hallie's back."

She shakes her head. "Oh, Gabe..."

No one knows what happened between me and Hallie before she left. No one except Larissa. On one particularly sleep-deprived night when Abbie was a newborn, everything came tumbling out. My daughter's mother seemed like an objective enough third party that wouldn't try to get involved like my family would.

"Don't look at me like that. That's in the past." I wince. "But I saw her at the store earlier and...accidentally implied she's been neglecting her grandfather."

"*Gabe*," she gasps.

Again, I wave off Larissa's concern. "It's fine. I'm fine. Go give Abbs the good news."

After another skeptical look in my direction, she heads for the stairs. With a sigh, I rub a hand down my face.

I thought the island was small before, but having to share it with Hallie when she wants nothing to do with me makes it feel fucking tiny.

FOUR

HALLIE

ALL LAST NIGHT, I couldn't get Gabe's words out of my head. *I figured someone should.* Because I'm all that Pops has, and I left. Just like *her*.

Gabe tried to take it back, but it needed to be said. And I'm glad he's been checking in on Pops in my absence. Now, though, I need to do better. Become someone my grandfather can be proud of. The job at Carole's gallery is a start, until I figure out what I want to do long-term.

Staring at Clara's living room ceiling in the middle of the night gave my mind ample time to fixate on other things, too. Like Gabe.

He still keeps his face clean-shaven, showing off his sharp jaw, but his hair is perpetually messy. He got his first tattoo the moment he turned eighteen, and now his arms are covered in ink depicting different naturescapes. I even saw a lighthouse on one of them. The tattoos suit him, and I can't help but wonder if he has more beneath his clothing. I hope he does.

I had a feeling it would hurt, but bearing witness to just how much I've missed over the years was like taking a white-hot knife to the sternum. And when I saw his daughter, an ache settled in my chest. The way he looked at her, so full of love—it was more than I could've hoped for him. He's a family man, through and through. I always knew he'd be a great dad.

But those tattoos. God, those tattoos... I—

"Checkmate!"

I blink, zoning back into the present. The present where my eighty-one-year-old grandfather has just kicked my butt at chess. Again.

"You cheated!" I accuse.

"Now, Junebug," he says, still insistent on that silly nickname —because I was born in June. His finger wags as the tilt of his grin turns teasing. "I didn't raise you to be a sore loser."

The fact that he had to raise me at all still weighs heavily on me. It's not my guilt to bear, but someone has to hold it, seeing as my mother hasn't felt a lick of remorse a day in her life. Otherwise, she would have never left me behind to chase a life she was happier to live.

And I've never known my father. I'm the product of an affair my mother had with a married man. He moved his family—his *real* family—off the island shortly after she told him she was pregnant.

For so long, it was just Pops and Hallie. Hallie and Pops. Amanda would blow through town, cause chaos, then dip again. My grandfather was my constant.

And I repaid him by abandoning him.

I narrow my eyes. "I distinctly remember that knight being in a different position a couple minutes ago."

Pops shakes his head. "I might have to start worrying about you. Your memory seems to be going."

It isn't funny, the thought of either of us losing our memory, but I laugh anyway. It makes Pops happy, to see me happy. I seem to be a little short on joy at the moment, but I'll borrow as much as I need to keep that warm look in his eyes from fading.

A woman in a set of navy blue scrubs walks up behind Pops

and rests a hand on the back of his chair. "Good game?" Teresa, his favourite personal support worker, asks.

He turns and grins up at her. "Every game with my Junebug is a good one."

I have to actively blink back tears. Standing from my seat, I put my focus into packing up the chess pieces. I clumsily knock one to the floor, and as I bend to retrieve it, I take a moment to steady myself.

"I'm glad you had a good visit, Al," Teresa says.

When she walks away, Pops returns his focus to me. His gaze is assessing. If I had been the kind of kid to get into trouble, I wouldn't have been able to get away with it under his watchful eye. He seems to see everything. But luckily for both of us, I did everything in my power to actively avoid breaking any kind of rule.

"Are you planning to tell me what's wrong?" he asks. "Or do I have to guess?"

I roll the rook between my fingers as I debate what to say. "Gabe Bowman visits you," I decide on.

Pops nods. "Yes. We've had some nice chats over the years."

I swallow as I place the rook back in the box. "I'm sorry I haven't been here."

I used to visit as much as I could. Between school and work, it wasn't a lot. Pops's retirement home is on the mainland, so I didn't even have to set foot on Kip Island when I'd come up from Toronto. Yet the proximity always felt oppressive. Like I was being strangled with my own past.

He grabs my hand. "You have a life, Hallie. I want you to live it. As much as I love spending time with you, I don't expect you to be here every day to keep me company. I'm in a good spot, I promise."

I know he is. Even when I couldn't convince myself to make the trip, I'd call often. He'd tell me stories that he'd heard from his friends, the latest drama on his floor. He is still Forty Acres Retirement Home's reigning bingo champion. By all accounts, he has a better social life than me.

"I got a job," I tell him. "Carole offered me a position at the gallery. It's not a lot of hours, but it's something, and it means I'm staying."

Pops gives my hand a squeeze before letting go. "You'll be phenomenal."

I finish squaring away the chess board as one of my grandfather's friends comes over. They get into an animated conversation about a book they both read recently, and I smile to myself.

"Bye, Pops," I say when there's a lull. I lean down and kiss his cheek. "Try not to cause too much trouble. I'll be back soon."

Now that I'm home, I plan to make use of every second I have with him. To make up for the time I missed.

He smiles up at me, and his eyes crinkle at the edges. "I'll be here."

When I settle into the driver's seat of Clara's Volkswagen Beetle, which she has affectionately named Marv, out in the parking lot, I blow out a heavy breath. Then I force myself to put the car in gear and drive.

Boarding the ferry that will take me from Tobermory to Kip Island is a familiar dance. How many times in my life have I done it? Hundreds, if not thousands. I often went shopping with Clara and her mom on the mainland; Pops would take me down to the city to see a play or visit a museum.

Coming back to the island after a long day was supposed to bring with it a sense of relief, like your head finally hitting your pillow when you're tired beyond measure. For me, the ferry pulling away from the dock was like the lock on a cage engaging.

Today, as I watch the late afternoon sun reflect off the water, I know it still feels the same. Trapped for another day.

When I push through her front door, Clara looks up from the romance book she's reading. "Hey," she calls. She's curled up on the couch in her usual spot. "How was your visit?"

I paste on a smile, not ready to divulge to her all of my worries. They're my burdens to carry. "It was really nice. I've missed him."

"Who won today?"

I roll my eyes. "Pops. But you know he cheats!"

Clara laughs as she stands, setting her book aside. "I was thinking of going to Haven House to eat dinner with my parents. Wanna come?"

Once upon a time, I felt like part of their family. But distancing myself from this place meant distancing myself from them, and now I'm not sure where I stand. As much as I love Maggie and John, the thought of sitting down to eat with them while my head is such a mess leaves a sour taste in my mouth. One look and they'll be able to suss out that I'm feeling off.

Not to mention, there's no telling whether a certain brother of Clara's will be there, and I'm not quite ready to face him again. I'm not sure I ever will be.

"I'm actually feeling pretty tired, so I think I'll just stay here. Tell everyone I say hi, though."

"Are you sure?"

Maybe I'm being entirely too dramatic. Maybe Clara is right and I need to rip the Band-Aid off. Face the music. See the hurt in Gabe's eyes once the shock of seeing me has settled.

I think, more than that, I'm scared of what I won't find. What if he doesn't care? What if he's forgotten all about me—us and all of our almosts? I know I should hope that he has, but the prospect of being the only one still hung up on our past hurts.

"I'm sure."

I don't miss the concern that flits across Clara's face. She's been concerned since I showed up back in town. But she thankfully doesn't let the expression linger for very long before she smiles. "Mom will probably send me home with leftovers. You can have them later."

"Thank you." I blow her a kiss. "You're the best."

Clara slides her shoes on and grabs her purse, then she's out the door. I find a pair of pajama shorts and an old t-shirt to change into. The design is faded, but I know it's the one I stole from Gabe before I left. I purposefully ignore that fact as I slip it over my head.

Once I'm comfortable, I take Clara's place on the couch, my temporary bed. Turning the TV on, I let it play a random nineties sitcom as I get lost in my head. Now that I have a job locked down, it's time for me to figure out a more permanent living arrangement. One that doesn't include springs poking me in the back when I'm trying to sleep.

A plan. I need a plan.

FIVE
HALLIE

AS IT TURNS OUT, Clara isn't too happy about these new aspirations of mine, and she isn't afraid to let me know. Maybe it was a mistake to bring the topic up while she's driving.

"Hallie Foster, you are *not* moving out. I told you to stay as long as you need to get on your feet!"

I sigh. "And I love you for that, but I can't keep sleeping on your couch, Clara." Though where I *will* sleep is still up for debate. The apartment hunt has been slow going.

She huffs, adjusting her hands on the steering wheel. "You were perfectly content there a few days ago."

"And then *someone* declared a wallow-free zone. You can't have it both ways."

That isn't why I need to leave, though. Truthfully, living with Clara has been great. But with each day that passes, it gets harder and harder to keep the dumpster fire that is my life from setting hers ablaze. She doesn't need my problems.

She turns to me. "That was supposed to be your sign to stop wallowing."

"Hey, eyes on the road!" I chastise.

Clara huffs again as she turns back toward the windshield,

navigating down the long road that connects the more rural parts of the island to the town proper. "All I'm saying is my couch will be lonely without you."

I laugh. "Oh, I'm sure, but my back will thank me."

A couple weeks of sleeping in Clara's living room has really done a number on my spine. She originally offered to share her bed with me, but after years of sleepovers, I've learned that isn't conducive to a good night's rest. She gets clingy in her sleep, and I need my space.

She pouts. "Do you really have to leave me again?"

Behind her teasing tone, I can sense some truth to her words. Some long-buried hurt. Clara has always supported me, but I know she's been lonely staying here without me. She's always had other friends, but most of them have either moved away or are at different stages in their lives.

"I'm not *leaving*," I assure her. "I just physically cannot keep sleeping in your living room."

"What if I get rid of my couch and buy you a king-sized bed?"

"Don't you dare!"

She nods. "I would totally do it, you know."

With another laugh, I shake my head. "You're ridiculous."

As Clara guides her car through the familiar gate at the end of the driveway, my nerves come back in full force. I've managed to avoid the infamous Sunday brunch with the Bowmans since I've been back on the island, but Maggie cornered me at the gallery two days ago and strong-armed me into attendance.

I am looking forward to seeing everyone again. It's been a long time since we've all been together, and I would be lying if I said I didn't miss it. But seeing Gabe the other day was hard enough. I'm not sure if I'm ready to spend a whole meal with him.

For ten years, my tactic has been avoidance. I thought about reaching out so many times, but then another day or week or month would pass and I'd make myself sick thinking of the hate I was sure I would see in his eyes.

Coming back here means confronting the mess I left in my wake. The only problem is, I'm not sure how to fix it.

Clara parks, and we hop out of the car. The large farmhouse is just as I remember, with its red brick and the porch that wraps around. The newest addition is a sign in the lawn that reads, *Haven House Bed-and-Breakfast, established in 2021.*

As I head for the front porch, I look over my shoulder. Clara is still standing beside her bright red Beetle, head bent over her phone as her thumb flies across the screen.

"You coming?" I ask.

Her head pops up, and a knowing smile slides across her lips. "Yup! Just confirming something for Delilah," she says, slipping her phone into her back pocket. She skips toward me, looping her arm through mine. "Let's go."

I don't have time to analyze her odd behaviour because as soon as we step inside, a German shepherd bounds toward us. Riot belongs to Luke, and although I've only met him once when Clara took him for a walk, the dog greets me like an old friend. I give him a good scratch between the ears, earning myself a lick on the arm.

When we make it to the kitchen, I pause in the doorway. The Bowmans have made some upgrades over the years, but this is still the same kitchen I used to bake cookies in with Clara and Maggie. Gabe would hang around, too, but only to steal some of the raw dough. His mother would smack his hand lightly with a spatula, then shoo him out of the room. He'd only laugh, throwing me a smile on his way out.

A hand touches my shoulder, and then Clara's father is grinning down at me. "Nice to see you again, kid."

"Hi, John," I say with a smile.

Looking at him, I briefly wonder if I'm glimpsing Gabe's future. While Luke looks the most like their father, Gabe shares a lot of his traits, too. I quickly shake the thoughts from my head.

Before I can say more, Clara's mother swoops in and envelops me in a bone-crushing hug. While Gabe and Luke take after their dad, Clara is all their mom. Maggie's blonde hair has a little more grey in it than I remember, but her eyes are still bright.

"*Oh*, it's so good to have you back, sweet girl," Maggie says. "We missed you."

The affection in her tone makes tears well in my eyes. I furiously blink them back as I return her hug just as tight. "I missed you, too."

She pulls back and then touches a hand to my cheek before turning away. "Alright, go take a seat. The food will be ready shortly."

I know better than to argue. After Clara and her brothers set fire to the oven when we were ten, Maggie has had strict rules about who is allowed in her kitchen. Besides that, I know she likes taking care of everyone, and she shows that love through the food she makes.

I make my way over to the table, spotting two more familiar faces.

"Hey, Hallie!" Delilah says with a smile.

Luke, with his arm slung over the back of her chair, nods. "Morning."

"Hey." I quickly scan the room. "Are Parker and Sophia here, too?"

Since being introduced to her, I've learned that Delilah has custody of her siblings, and I met them briefly at Dockside last night. While her teenage brother had an air of aloofness to him, her younger sister was incredibly shy. I can't blame her. I'm not too fond of strangers either.

"Parker's hanging out with a new friend today. Soph is upstairs playing with Abbie, though."

Abbie. Gabe's daughter. She and Sophia must be around the same age, so it makes sense that they've become friends.

Following Maggie's instruction, I take a seat beside Luke. At their old kitchen table, when it was just the Bowmans and me, we all had our usual chairs. Maggie and John would each sit at one end. Clara and Gabe would be placed on opposite sides, diagonal from one another, because they used to bicker when they sat side by side. Luke would sit to Gabe's left, and I would sit on Clara's. Which meant I was always directly across from Gabe.

But it's been a long time. This table is new, bigger, and there are more people now. With Luke sitting beside Delilah, I'm not sure where that leaves everyone else. Maybe it's a free-for-all every week.

At least some things never change. The faint sound of music in the background is a balm to my soul. If anything reminds me of home, it's that.

When the music changes, Luke sighs. "Do we have to listen to this song every week? We got it the first time, Gabe."

"It's part of the playlist now," he says as he comes into the kitchen. Abbie and Sophia trail behind him.

Delilah laughs good-naturedly. "I like it. It reminds us of our first brunch together," she says to Luke, leaning into his side.

He grunts, but he makes no more complaints as "Hey There Delilah" continues to play.

Maggie and John start bringing plates of breakfast foods over as the girls settle in their seats. Clara sits beside her niece. Which leaves the chair opposite me empty.

Oh, God.

Gabe drops into his seat, letting his gaze settle on mine. "Hey, Foster."

I'm sure it's a figment of my imagination, but I swear all the adults in the room are watching us with bated breath. Waiting to see what will happen now that Gabe and I are stuck in a room together for the next hour.

"Hi," I squeak.

They're definitely staring at me now.

"You're the lady from the store," Abbie says, taking some of the attention off me. She shifts in her chair, sitting on her knees so she can lean over the table, closer to me.

I smile. "I guess I didn't get to properly introduce myself, huh? I'm Hallie."

"She's Aunt Clara's best friend," Gabe adds. "We all went to school together."

"So you're Daddy's friend, too?"

I used to be, I almost say. But explaining our complicated history and what went wrong to a six-year-old doesn't seem like the right move.

My gaze flits to Gabe briefly before returning to Abbie. "Yes. I'm his friend, too."

Thankfully, everyone begins to eat, and conversation moves to other things. Safer things. I manage to sit and observe for a while before I'm forced to talk about myself, something I'd much rather avoid.

"Carole says you've been a great help with the gallery," Maggie says. "But I hope Clara isn't driving you too crazy in that apartment of hers."

"Hey!" Clara says. "I'm the perfect host, thank you."

I laugh. "Clara has been great, and working for Carole has been fun. Now I just need to find a place of my own."

A place that costs me zero dollars, preferably. Though in today's market, I'd be more likely to find a pot of gold at the end of a rainbow. At least I was fortunate enough to finish paying off my student loans a few months ago, and I do have a decent amount in my savings because my recent nannying gig paid well, but that will only stretch so long.

"Any luck?" John asks.

I blow out a breath. "None so far. But it's okay, I'll keep trying. Something is bound to come up."

"Why don't you move into one of the rooms here?" he suggests. "We won't charge you, of course."

While Haven House is more than big enough, I don't want to take advantage of their generosity. I feel bad enough mooching off of Clara.

Before I can come up with an excuse to decline, Maggie interjects. "Oh, John, she can't. We've got that thing happening next week."

He turns to his wife with a raised brow. "What thing?"

"You know, Dad," Clara says, as if it's obvious. "Those guys are coming to rip into the walls. All the rooms will be torn apart."

Maggie nods along. "Yes, honey. Because of the termites. Remember?"

I gasp. "You have *termites*?"

"Really big ones," Delilah adds. She nudges her boyfriend in the side. "Right, Luke?"

It takes him a second, but then he nods. "Right... Definitely don't want to mess with those, Hallie."

"I, uh—" John scratches his chin as he looks from his wife to me. His expression is wary, but he acquiesces. "It appears we do... Sorry, Hallie. I misspoke."

I narrow my gaze, more than a little suspicious of their strange behaviour, but then I shake my head. "It's okay, don't worry about it. I'll find something."

"I think I have an idea," Clara says. We all turn to her, and the gleam in her eye has my stomach twisting into a knot. That look is nothing but trouble. "Gabe, why don't you let Hallie move into your guesthouse?"

My gaze slides to him, and in some cruel twist of fate, his eyes are already on me. They flick briefly to his sister before settling back on me.

He clears his throat. "It's not exactly in the best condition." He palms the back of his neck. "I've been meaning to work on it, but I've been putting it off."

Clara casually pops a sliced strawberry into her mouth. "Hallie can help you!"

"Oh, that's a great idea!" Maggie beams, and I die a little inside. "You were such a big help with decisions when we were renovating, Hallie. I'm sure between the two of you, you'll get the job done in no time."

While the offer is tempting, the thought of being in such close proximity to Gabe has me slightly terrified. I haven't been alone with him in over ten years. I'm not afraid of *him*, per se, so much as the memories he brings up. The memories of all the mistakes I've made.

Besides, like his twin, Gabe has always had this uncanny ability to see straight through my façade. If I move into his guesthouse, he'll be that much closer to unravelling me.

"It's literally perfect," Clara adds, driving the last nail right into my coffin. The coffin she'll have to bury me in when I pass away from extreme embarrassment.

"Gabe?" Maggie prompts. "What do you think?"

Please say no. Please say no.

"It's alright with me," he says, apparently unaware of my inner turmoil. "Foster?"

The whole table is looking at me now, waiting for a response. I can feel myself start to sweat under the scrutiny. They mean well, I know they do, but I also hate them a little for putting me on the spot like this.

"I guess..." I swallow to clear the uncertainty from my tone. "I guess I'm moving in, then."

SIX

GABE

TERMITES.

My family is full of shitty liars. As soon as Mom brought up the supposed termites, I knew she and Clara had been scheming, but I didn't blow their cover. Because I wasn't entirely sure *why* they were scheming until it was too late.

Now I don't know whether to thank or kill my sister for suggesting that Hallie help me fix up my guesthouse. The help is appreciated, but the close proximity is going to be torture.

Because if her being back in town has taught me anything, it's that I'm not over her. Not even close.

"Daddy, why do you keep looking outside?"

I sigh, turning away from the front window. Abbie's kneeling by the coffee table with her colouring books and pencil crayons, looking up at me curiously. "I'm waiting for someone."

"Who?"

"Hallie. Remember, we saw her at Haven House a couple days ago? She's helping me with something."

She's supposed to be, anyway, but she was also supposed to be here fifteen minutes ago. Not that I'm counting or anything.

Did she change her mind? I'd hardly blame her if she did. If she's been actively avoiding me since coming back, living in my guesthouse is probably the last thing she wants to do. But I also know her, and I know staying with Clara for a prolonged period would make her uncomfortable. My sister doesn't mind, but Hallie would see it as a problem, like she's taking advantage.

Abbie seems to accept my answer and returns to her colouring. I return to looking out the window, just in time to see a familiar head of blonde and purple hair.

A soft knock sounds a few seconds later. I give it another few before I leave the living room.

When I open my door to her standing on my front porch wearing an unsure smile, I wish I had the power to wipe it away. But seeing as I'm the cause of her discomfort, that won't be happening.

"Hi," she says, tucking her hair behind her ear. "Um, sorry I'm late. The walk was longer than I thought."

She steps inside, and I move to close the door, but I pause at her words. "You *walked*?"

While Kip Island isn't that big, walking from one end to the next could easily take a couple hours, if not more. The walk out to my place from Clara's apartment is at least twenty minutes.

"Yeah." Her lips twitch. "It's that thing people do where they put one foot in front of the other."

I can't help the laugh that slips out. God, I've missed this. Missed *her*. Her tone is tentative, but it reminds me of how things used to be. The way she would tease me, and I'd tease her right back, earning myself one of her infamous blushes.

"I would've picked you up."

"It's fine, Gabe. I'm used to walking places. It was either that or the TTC down in the city."

"Well, I'll drive you back later."

She shakes her head. "You really don't have to. I'm fine. Or Clara can pick me up on her way home from Dockside. Then you won't have to go out of your way."

I cross my arms. "I'm driving you, Hallie," I say, leaving no room for argument.

She has no choice but to nod.

As she looks around my house—or what she can see with her feet rooted on the mat in front of the door—I let myself look at her. On top of the skin-tight, painted-on jeans she's torturing me with, she's wearing a cropped t-shirt with Dockside's old branding ironed on. Before Clara got her hands on it, the restaurant's logo had been the same since my parents bought it when we were kids.

"Abbie's mom should be here any minute to pick her up. Then we can head out back," I tell her.

As soon as the words leave my lips, the front door swings open behind Hallie. Today is one of the rare days Larissa and I both have off work. Usually, we'd do something together with Abbie, but I have other plans today.

"Mommy!" Abbie shouts, rushing from the living room.

Larissa wraps an arm around Abbie as she crashes into her legs. "Hi, baby girl."

They both turn toward me and Hallie, and I'm hit with how alike they look. Although Abbie has some of my features, she shares the same curly hair as Larissa. It took some trial and error on my part, but now I can take care of her hair like a pro.

"Hi," Larissa says with a grin. "It's nice to see you again, Hallie."

Although the three of us went to the same school, Hallie often kept to herself, and Larissa used to hang out with girls on the volleyball team. Still, I think they had a few classes together.

Hallie offers her a shy smile. "It's nice to see you, too."

"You know, I've heard a lot about you over the years."

This causes Hallie to freeze, and I internally curse. The last thing I need is Larissa making her run for the hills. She's always been a little skittish, but especially since coming back. I don't want to completely scare her off.

"Clara talks about you a lot," I explain. "She missed you."

Larissa's brow arches, as if to say, *Only Clara?* I intentionally ignore her look.

"Yes," Larissa says aloud. Her eyes dance with mischief. "You've made quite the impression on a certain Bowman."

I cut her a glare. "Don't you have somewhere to be?"

She laughs, and Hallie's gaze flits between us, curious. "Sorry, yes. Abbs, say bye to your dad."

After a quick hug, Larissa ushers Abbie out the door. As soon as it clicks behind them, silence blankets the house, and it's then I realize they had been acting as a buffer. With the two of them gone, the full weight of awkwardness bears down on us.

Hallie's wide, blue eyes scream, *I don't want to be here.*

I swallow.

"Larissa is nice," Hallie offers. Her words almost echo in the vast expanse between us. The distance isn't physical, but I feel it viscerally all the same. "And she's pretty, too."

"Yeah," I agree. "She's great."

"Is there something—? I mean, are you and—" She shakes her head, cutting herself off. "Never mind."

My brows shoot up in surprise. "You think I have a thing for Larissa?"

Hallie's blush appears again. Or maybe it never disappeared to begin with. "Forget it, Gabe. I shouldn't have said anything. It's none of my business."

It isn't, but *fuck*, do I want it to be.

"There's nothing going on between me and Larissa," I say anyway. I need her to know. "We're friends. Besides, she just got engaged. Her fiancé is a good guy. Chris treats her and Abbie right."

"Oh."

I chuckle. "Yeah, *oh*." Then I turn, walking down the hall. "You wanna see the guesthouse?"

Hallie readily agrees, and she quickly follows me out to the backyard.

When I first bought my house, thanks to a few years' worth of savings and the inheritance left for me from one set of grandparents, the guesthouse in the backyard wasn't a selling point.

It's small, only big enough to fit a bed, a kitchenette and a bathroom. The outside is painted in shades of green, not dissimilar to some of the other colourful houses on the island. At one time, I'm sure it was in peak condition, but it has become a victim of time. The previous owner was an elderly man, and though the main house was maintained, the guesthouse went by the wayside.

"The plumbing needs some work," I say, stepping through the door. I move aside so Hallie can come in behind me. "You'll have to use the kitchen and bathroom in the main house for a bit. The washer and dryer, too."

She doesn't say anything as she walks the perimeter of the room, inspecting the space. On top of the plumbing being shit, a layer of dust coats...well, everything. I've barely set foot in here in years. The surfaces will need a thorough cleaning, which we can hopefully tackle today.

I rub a hand against the back of my neck. "It's not much, I know, but hopefully it'll work for you. Do whatever you want to it. Make it yours."

Hallie finally turns to me. "Are you sure about this?" she asks. "Clara and your mom didn't really give you much choice the other day, but you do have one. I don't want to...force myself on you."

I shake my head. It's pathetic, really, how much I'd welcome *anything* from Hallie. I want it all, no matter how small a morsel.

"You're not, I promise. This is good for us both. This place needs to be cleaned up, and you need a place to live."

And I want you here.

As soon as the thought hits, I know it's true. I want her here. No matter how painful it'll feel to be close to her, I don't want her moving someplace else. I don't want her to find an apartment across town or on the mainland. I want her *here.*

She doesn't look entirely convinced, but she nods. "Alright, then... Where do we start?"

———

Time passes in stilted silence. I should have brought a speaker out here with us so we could at least have some music to fill the void. Going to get it now would only signal how unsettled I feel.

I can't stand this stillness, I want to say. *Can you?*

Instead, I keep working. Every time we move to a new section to clean, we dance around each other. Not in a coordinated way either, but in a way that makes us look like we're walking on a trail of eggshells just waiting to be broken.

"Sorry," Hallie mutters when our arms brush.

I can't take it anymore. With a sigh, I finally say, "Hallie...this is awkward."

She chews on her lower lip, and then her rag lands on the counter with a smack. "I don't know how to act around you," she blurts. It feels like the first truly honest thing she's said in a while.

I throw my hands up. "So don't act. Be real with me."

As soon as the words are out, a look of terror passes across her face. And damn, does that kill me.

"Gabe, I..."

I hate myself a little for what I'm about to suggest, but I'd do anything to take away her fear. "What happened before you left... We were kids, Hallie. It doesn't matter now." I swallow, working hard to hold her gaze. "So you can stop flinching every time you look at me, wondering when I'm going to bring it up."

The way she visibly relaxes only drives the knife deeper. I didn't think that her agreement would be this painful.

"I'm sorry," she says quietly.

I sigh again. "Don't be. You have nothing to apologize for." At the end of the day, this rift between us is my fault.

Her fingers twist together in front of her. "I do. I'm making things weird."

I shake my head. "We both are. The truth is…Clara isn't the only one who's missed you. It might take us a minute, but I want to go back to how we were before."

Before I opened my mouth and screwed everything up.

She smiles. It's tentative, but it's something. "I'd really like that. I've…missed you, too."

"Then consider us friends again." Before the pit in my stomach can grow, I pull out my phone, distracting myself. "I'm going to order pizza for lunch. What kind do you want?"

Hallie's eyes light up, and I take pride in putting some brightness back into her expression. She's always been a sucker for pizza. "Veggie lover's for me, please."

I pause. "Veggie lover's?"

She laughs, and for once, the sound is unburdened. "Yes, Gabriel. I'm a vegetarian. It's pretty standard."

My jaw drops. "Since *when*?"

She shrugs. "Since I moved off the island. Really, since grade eight."

"Grade *eight*? The Hallie I used to know loved a good pepperoni."

"No," she says. "The Hallie you used to know just wasn't very good at making her voice heard."

Looking back on all the pepperoni pizzas Hallie and I split while Clara devoured her Hawaiian is like a punch to the gut. Did I ever ask her preference? Evidently not.

"Veggie lover's it is, then," I say.

Hallie offers me another small smile, and then she turns back to wiping down the counter in the kitchenette.

Once the pizza is ordered, I pick up my own cloth, but I don't go back to cleaning yet. "Hallie?"

"Yeah?"

"The other day, when I implied you weren't visiting Pops

enough, I didn't mean it like that. I wasn't trying to say you did anything wrong."

When she looks at me, her eyes are sad. "It's fine. You were right. I didn't visit him as much as I should have. I shouldn't have...left."

The air in my lungs disappears, and I struggle for breath. She holds my gaze for another moment before she looks away. I swallow, forcing down every question that sits on the tip of my tongue.

Why did you run?

Are you staying for good?

Why didn't you love me back?

SEVEN

GABE

"ABBS, ARE YOU READY TO GO?"

"One more minute!" she yells down the stairs.

I shake my head to myself with a sigh. She's been saying that for the past half hour. I know she hasn't mastered how to tell time yet, but I'm starting to get the feeling that my daughter is delaying us on purpose.

The back door opens, and I peer down the hall just in time to see Hallie sneak into the kitchen. I have no doubt that Abbie will take longer than a minute, so I follow after her.

"Foster," I say.

She jumps a little at my voice but spins to face me. "Yeah?"

"You don't have to tiptoe. This is your kitchen, too."

At least until the one out in the guesthouse is usable. Then Hallie won't have a reason to come inside multiple times a day. She's probably counting down the minutes, but I'm dreading it.

The past couple weeks since she officially moved into the guesthouse have been nice. More than nice. The awkwardness has been slowly slipping away, and it's starting to feel like it used to between us. Like nothing ever happened.

Hallie's cheeks flush. She turns away and drops her dirty dishes into the sink. She also refuses to use the damn dishwasher. "I just don't want to bother you," she says.

You can bother me. Every day, forever.

"You're not. I want you to feel comfortable here. Make yourself at home."

She nods, but I know she's only doing so to placate me. As soon as I turn around, she'll go back to only partially existing, folding herself in half so she takes up a fraction of the space.

But I want her to take up space. I want her here, in my home. I want *her*, plain and simple. The years and the distance did nothing to make me forget that.

Against my better judgment, I move closer. Being in Hallie's proximity is dangerous on a good day, but especially when she's wearing whatever perfume she's got on today. It invades my nose, mixing with the sweet scent of her shampoo.

The tap is on now, filling the sink with a little water. I wait until Hallie shuts it off to speak. "I mean it. You're not a bother. Alright?"

She offers me a small smile as she scrubs at a plate. "Alright."

"I'm ready!" Abbie calls. I hear her shoes hit the landing, and then she's skipping into the kitchen. She grabs my hand and starts to tug. "Daddy, come on! We gotta go."

Hallie looks over her shoulder, biting her lip to stifle her laughter. "Where are you off to?" she asks Abbie.

"The fair!"

Hallie smiles. "I hope you have fun." She gestures to me with her thumb. "Make your dad buy you *lots* of cotton candy."

My daughter's face turns serious. "I love the pink kind, but blue is really good, too." Then her head cocks to the side as she continues to study Hallie. "Do you wanna come with us?"

Hallie pauses. Some suds from the dishwater drip off her hands and onto the tile floor. "To the fair?"

Abbie nods. "Yeah! Mommy always goes on the rides with me because Daddy gets pukey, but she's gotta work. So you can come, and we can have so much fun!"

"*Hey*," I interject, tugging on her braid. "I do not get pukey."

Abbie looks up at me and arches her brow, looking a little too much like Larissa in this moment. "You do, too!"

Hallie giggles. "You really want me to go on rides with you? Are you sure?"

Abbie smiles as her head bobs enthusiastically. "Yes! Please, please, *please*?"

Hallie dries her hands on a towel as she thinks over her answer. I know her, though. She wouldn't be able to say no to Abbie even if she wanted to.

"Okay," she agrees, "as long as your dad is alright with it. I don't want to crash your day together."

Abbie turns to me, eyes pleading. "It's okay, right, Daddy?"

"Of course." I look up at Hallie. "You're always welcome, Foster."

She meets my gaze, holding it. Years of meaning seem to travel between us. Then she grins at Abbie. "Lead the way."

The Thanksgiving weekend fair is a tradition in our family that started when my siblings and I were little. The fair runs from Friday night into Monday afternoon, and Mom and Dad would take us every year. Since Abbie was old enough to start going on rides, I made it a point to bring her, too.

Sometimes, the weather isn't all that great and some events get rained out, but this weekend is mild and the sky is a clear blue. Still, there's a bite to the air that signals fall is upon us.

Abbie bounces excitedly on the balls of her feet as we wait in line at the entrance. Once I've paid the fifteen bucks for our admission—much to Hallie's disagreement—we get wristbands strapped to our wrists and sent on our way.

Immediately, we're thrust into the throng. A lot of cottagers use this weekend as their last hurrah before they pack up for the winter, so most of the people here aren't locals.

We walk along a stretch full of food trucks and tents, where vendors are selling their wares. Carole has a booth set up for the gallery, and she waves as we pass by. Then Abbie is grabbing my hand, dragging me toward the colourful lights of the midway.

"I've only ever been to the fair once," Hallie says at my side. A scream coming from a nearby ride cuts through the air, and she winces. "I forgot how loud it is."

My brows raise in surprise. "Really? That was your first time, when we went in grade twelve?"

She nods as she fiddles with her yellow wristband, avoiding my gaze. "Yeah. It was too overwhelming for Pops, and my mom..." She trails off. "Well, her idea of fun was anything but spending time with me."

Hallie's strained relationship with her mother is by no means a secret. Still, every time Hallie mentions parts of her upbringing like that, it damn near breaks my heart.

"Strawberries!" Abbie squeals, cutting off our conversation. "Let's do that one first!"

I share a look of commiseration with Hallie as I let my daughter pull me to the back of the line. I hate these damn spinning strawberries, and I know Hallie does, too. After she finished making out with her boyfriend, Clara made us ride them the last time Hallie came to the fair. We both came away with pounding headaches.

Thankfully, Abbie doesn't know that the wheel in the middle of our car can control how fast you spin. I don't volunteer that information as we settle into our seats. Instead, I let her enjoy the default pace of the ride and try to avoid looking outside our car to avoid motion sickness.

"You're looking a little green over there, Bowman," Hallie teases.

I grimace. "The rides are admittedly not my favourite. I don't love being tossed around."

"But you suggested the Ferris wheel last time! Why'd you do that if you didn't want to go on it?"

Simple—I wanted to be close to her. For just a little while. And that led to me almost kissing her. I can't say that, though, so I skirt the truth.

I shrug. "I thought you'd have fun."

Soon after, the ride ends, much to my relief. Abbie is grinning as she hops out of the big, metal strawberry. I'm slow to follow.

Hallie glances at me in concern. "Maybe you should sit the next one out. I really don't mind riding with her."

I arch a brow. "I didn't peg you as an adrenaline junkie."

With a laugh, she points toward Abbie's next ride of choice: a small rollercoaster styled like a dragon. "After this, I might go skydiving."

The rollercoaster is rather tame, but watching the way it makes my baby girl light up, it's worth its weight in gold. And when I look at the woman sitting beside her, my heart nearly stops working altogether. Hallie's smile has always been breathtaking, but right now, she looks so carefree. The tension that seems to always rest in her shoulders is nowhere to be found. She looks so happy with the wind whipping her hair behind her, and damn, is she beautiful.

What I wouldn't give to see that expression on her face every day.

After the roller coaster, Abbie starts tugging us along to our next destination. If she had it her way, she'd tackle every ride and rigged game in the place.

"Oh, can we get *those*?" Abbie asks, stopping short. Her eyes are wide as she points toward the funnel cake stand.

I turn to Hallie. "Apparently we're getting funnel cake. Do you want one?"

She chews on her lip as she contemplates, and then she nods. "Yeah, I think I do."

The line moves quickly, and soon it's our turn. I step up to the window and order a cake to share with Abbie, because those things are almost the size of her head and she doesn't need that much sugar in one evening. Then I step aside and ask, "Which one do you want?"

Hallie shakes her head. "I can get my own."

I hand a twenty to the teenager manning the register. "Don't take her money."

She huffs as she rolls her eyes. "Gabriel."

I grin. "There's a line forming behind you, Foster. Better make it quick."

When she looks over her shoulder and realizes I wasn't lying, she quickly places her order and then steps to the side. She crosses her arms as she bumps me with her shoulder, glaring softly at me. I laugh, throwing my arm around her and tugging her against my side.

We both freeze.

A decade ago, neither one of us would have thought anything of my actions. A decade ago, she probably would have leaned into me, even if she was being stubborn. A decade ago, she could stand to be close to me.

I remove my arm and take a careful step away, putting distance between us. "Sorry," I mutter.

"It's fine," she says. But she refuses to look at me.

Now more than ever, I wish I could go back in time. Back to that day. If I could, I'd keep my mouth shut. As it stands, I want to fully repair things between us. But I worry it's ten years too late, and anything I try will just be in vain.

For the next few minutes, we stand there uncomfortably as we wait for our funnel cakes. Abbie chatters on about the fair and how much fun she's having, oblivious to the tension mounting between me and Hallie.

Fuck, I hate this.

When our desserts are ready, we find a flimsy plastic table to sit at. Abbie climbs onto the chair to my right, leaving the other side of the table to Hallie. She chooses the seat across from me, like always.

We're destined to be on opposing sides forever, it seems.

Voices and laughter float around us as we eat. Usually, I find comfort in the chaos, but now it only functions as background noise to my swirling thoughts.

Abbie giggles, covering her mouth with her hand. "Hallie, you got fluff on your lip."

Her nose scrunches in confusion. "Fluff?"

I chuckle. "Whipped cream."

Hallie's cheeks turn pink instantly. "Oh my God." She searches around for her napkin, but it must've blown off the table in the breeze. Her eyes connect with mine, full of helplessness.

Ah, hell.

Reaching across the table, I swipe the drop of whipped cream off her lip with my thumb. Then I lick my thumb clean. The whole time, Hallie barely breathes, her gaze fixed on me.

I expected her to freeze like she did when I put my arm around her before. Or maybe jerk back. But despite her stilted breathing, she hasn't run away. I take that as a good sign.

"Um, thanks," she squeaks.

I lean back in my chair with a grin. "Anytime."

"Daddy, my hands are *sticky*," Abbie declares. She holds her palms up, showing me how the chocolate sauce from our funnel cake has begun to act like glue between her fingers.

"Let's go to the bathroom," Hallie says quickly, standing from her seat. "I'll help you wash up."

Before I can blink, the two take off. Hallie holds Abbie's chocolate-covered hand so she doesn't get lost in the crowd. I busy myself with tossing our empty plates in the garbage, then start walking in the direction of the bathrooms.

Based on how quick Hallie was to jump up from the table, I spoke too soon. I thought maybe she decided to stay, for real this time, but she didn't.

She's still running.

EIGHT

HALLIE

ELEVEN YEARS AGO

JUST AS I finish tightening the elastic securing my hair in a half up, half down look, my phone pings on my dresser.

CLARA

We're outside!

I'll be down in a minute!

Tucking my phone into my crossbody purse, I leave my bedroom. I bound down the stairs and spot Pops in his recliner in the living room, half asleep. Crossing to him, I place a kiss on his cheek. He startles, waking from his nap.

"I'm heading out," I say.

He smiles up at me. "Did you eat?"

I shake my head, forcing a smile of my own. "Not hungry. I'll probably have something later."

Pops reaches out and opens the drawer of the side table. He pulls out his wallet, which is secured with a rubber band because it's falling apart and he refuses to get another. He carefully unwinds it and then fishes out a couple twenties.

"Here," he says. "Buy yourself something at the fair."

I thank him and take the money, knowing full well that I'll just slip the bills back into his wallet when I get home later tonight. I don't like taking his money, so I only buy things using what I make from my part-time job at Dockside. For now, though, I tuck the bills away in my purse.

"I'll see you later, Pops."

"Bye, Junebug. Have a good time."

Outside, there's a bit of a bite to the air, but it's a relatively mild day for October. Still, I maybe should have grabbed a jacket. It's too late now, though. I don't want to keep my friends waiting.

Clara is hanging out the back window of her brother's truck. I can see her boyfriend, Cooper, sitting beside her. I guess they're not fighting today. That leaves the front seat, right next to Gabe, to me.

"C'mon, slowpoke!" Clara calls as I hurry down the front path.

I stick my tongue out at her as I pull open the door.

When Gabe's eyes land on me, my foot falters on the running board. I catch myself before I fall and look like a total fool, but my cheeks still flame in embarrassment. The colour only deepens when Gabe's lips stretch into a smile.

"Hey, Foster."

I settle in my seat and buckle my seatbelt. "Hey."

"*Hey*," Clara says, poking her head between the front seats. "Let's *go*!"

"Why are you so impatient?" Gabe asks, but he puts the truck in gear and takes off toward the fairgrounds.

"Why are you driving like a grandpa?" she counters. "I think our *actual* grandpa could drive faster than you."

I clap a hand over my mouth to stifle my giggle. He *is* driving kind of slow.

"I just got this truck, thank you very much," he defends. "Excuse me for not wanting to wrap it around a lamppost a week after I bought it."

The fair is busy tonight, so we end up having to park on a side street and walk to the entrance. Within minutes, we're sucked into the fray. There are locals and cottagers alike, making our small town feel bigger than it really is.

It doesn't take long for Clara and Cooper to ditch us. Knowing them, they've found a secluded corner to make out in. It's been like that for the past few months since they started dating —them sneaking away and leaving me on my own.

Except tonight, I'm not on my own.

Gabe is walking beside me, hands in his pockets, as the midway lights dance around us. Kids scream as they're flipped this way and that on the carnival rides, just asking for motion sickness.

"How come you aren't with your friends?" I ask.

Then I immediately cringe. *Great. Now he's going to feel like I don't want him here.*

"Connor has the flu," he replies. "And truthfully...none of the guys are as pretty as you."

When he says this, he looks at me. *Right* at me. One of his signature smiles graces his lips. I don't know what to do, so I slide my gaze to the ground.

He called me pretty.

But he doesn't mean it like that, *Hallie. He's just being nice.*

I try to come up with something to say, but my mouth won't work.

"Are you hungry?" he asks. I let out a silent sigh of relief at the change in subject. "I think I'm gonna get a funnel cake."

The laugh comes easily, and I look up. "I think that's supposed to be dessert."

He shakes his head. "Nah, there aren't any rules at the fair. I'm pretty sure that sugar is an official food group here."

I bite back a goofy smile. "You're ridiculous."

He's still wearing that grin of his when he nods toward the stand. "Do you want one?"

It's tempting, but I don't need to waste the money. I have school to pay for next year. "No, thanks."

I stand off to the side as Gabe walks up to the window and orders his funnel cake. I scan the menu, taking in all the toppings they have to offer. I know that Gabe's will be simple, though—strawberries, vanilla ice cream and icing sugar.

My stomach grumbles at the sight of his plate, but I ignore it. I'll eat something when I get home tonight.

When we sit down at a vacant picnic table, I realize Gabe has a second fork. "You should have some," he says. "Since I probably should save room for some real food."

I take the extra fork with a small smile. "What happened to sugar being a food group?"

"What can I say? You're a good influence on me, Foster."

We eat in silence, but it's comfortable. It's always comfortable with him. And when I spend so much of my life feeling out of my comfort zone, having him around makes things feel less...hard.

After Gabe throws away our empty plate, we start walking around the midway again. It's incredibly overstimulating, with the pulsing lights and varying sounds. Still, my heart aches a little when I see all the kids here with their parents. I've never had that. My father has never been in my life, and my mom is too busy chasing the next thing that will give her a bit of short-lived happiness.

Just once, I wish that would be me.

"You're quiet over there," Gabe says. "What are you thinking about?"

I clutch the strap of my purse as I struggle to think up a response that isn't super depressing. "Just that I'm having fun," I say. "Thanks for sticking with me."

He bumps my shoulder with his arm. "There's nowhere I'd rather be. I think you might be my favourite person, you know."

This makes my tongue tie up. I can't form words. All I can do is focus on the beat of my heart and the way it skips a little when I find Gabe still watching me.

"Do you want to go on the Ferris wheel?" he asks.

I've never been on one before. On any ride, actually. But the Ferris wheel seems like it would be fun, so I agree.

In response, Gabe takes my hand. A thrill runs through me. Gabriel Bowman is *holding my hand*. He's done it before, of course, when we were kids. But it feels different now.

To my disappointment, when we fall into line beneath the ride, he lets go. Then he shoves his hands into the pockets of his pants again, and I fold my arms over my chest.

Then we're up to ride next. A cool gust of wind blows by, causing me to shiver. *I really should've grabbed that jacket.*

"Cold?"

I shake my head. " A little, but it's fine."

Gabe doesn't listen. The next thing I know, he's shrugging out of his jacket and draping it over my shoulders. The material envelops me in his lingering warmth.

"It'll only be colder up there," he says, pointing to the top of the wheel.

"What about you?"

His hands return to those damn pockets. "I'll be okay. I'm a little warm right now anyway."

I'm not sure how that's possible, but I don't argue. When another breeze whips through and he doesn't ask for his jacket back, I slip my arms through the sleeves. Just in time, too, because the ride attendant waves us forward. Once the previous riders exit, Gabe gestures for me to hop on first.

The seats remind me of a ski lift, where you sit side by side. When I sit down on the far side, Gabe slides in after me, and then the lap bar is pulled down to secure us in place.

The ride begins to move almost instantly, but it stops shortly after to exchange another pair of riders. When we get to the top, the ride comes to a halt again.

"I feel like I'm on top of the world up here," I say. Then I blush. "Oh my God, that was so cheesy."

Why can I never just be chill around him? I feel like I'm always blurting out something stupid when I'm in his presence.

Gabe chuckles. "No, I get it," he assures me. "There's nothing that makes your problems feel small quite like watching everything from up here."

It's true. The cars look smaller, the houses, the world. I take a deep breath. It's a perspective shift, one I've been needing.

When I turn back to him, Gabe is studying the fair below us. I study his profile, memorizing his features. His brown hair is a little messy, but I know he uses products to make it look that way. Unlike his brother, he keeps his face clean-shaven. To put it bluntly, he's insanely handsome, and he makes the butterflies living in my stomach flutter nonstop.

Gabe looks over at me just as the wind kicks up again, blowing a wayward strand of hair into my face. Before I can swipe it away, his hand is there. With deft fingers, he tucks the piece behind my ear, and then he...lingers.

He's touching my jaw, so close to my thundering pulse, and his gaze is locked on mine. But then it shifts, and *oh my God*, he's looking at my lips. They part in disbelief. Gabe tracks the movement.

Holy crap. *What do I do?* I've never been kissed before, unless you count when one of the boys in my grade three class was dared to kiss me on the lips during recess. It was over in half a second, and he only caught the corner of my mouth.

"Foster," he says. His voice is strained. "Hallie."

"Yes," I breathe.

I don't know what I'm agreeing to exactly, but *yes*. Obviously yes. Gabe could ask me anything right now and I'd happily agree.

He leans closer, tilts my head back. I'm barely breathing. Then—

The ride lurches, and the Ferris wheel starts spinning. We both scramble back to our respective sides of the bench, startled. I can't look at him, so I stare off to the right. Even in the near dark, Kip Island looks pretty from up here. I focus on that.

And I tell myself Gabe wasn't about to kiss me.

It was all in my head.

NINE

HALLIE

I'VE BEEN SCARED of the wind since I was seven years old.

Back then, Amanda and I lived by ourselves in a small house in town. That night, there was a lot of rain coming down, and the wind was strong. I don't remember much before the tree fell, except calling out for my mother and not getting a reply.

When the tree landed on our house, the loud bang reverberated as the branches smashed through my bedroom window. It sounded like the world was ending, the earth being ripped apart at the seams.

I do remember being terrified. The wind grew louder, howling as it whipped through my bedroom. Glass was scattered all over the floor and caught in my clothing. My hair. My fingers came back bloody when I touched my cheek. And still, Amanda didn't come. Not until much later, when she returned from a friend's house.

Pops was really angry that night. After that, he brought me to live with him. Amanda stuck around town for another month and then she took off. That wasn't the first time she'd run. It certainly wasn't the last.

Tonight, the rain comes down in sheets, battering against the roof of the guesthouse. I can handle the rain, but when the lightning and thunder start, that's when I begin to worry. Soon, all I can think about is that window. That tree.

There are a few towering maples in Gabe's backyard. They look pretty solid, but you never know. I certainly never thought that tree at our old house would come crashing down.

Sitting in the middle of my bed, I tuck my knees up to my chest. The storm has been raging for a while now, with no end in sight. I've already resigned myself to the fact that I won't be getting much sleep tonight, if any, thanks to the howling that's going on outside. Outside, where branches twist and bend and snap.

Nothing bad can happen if I stay up to watch.

I can't be disappointed if I don't expect anyone to come save me.

A bang on the door makes me shriek. I cover my ears and slam my eyes closed, curling further into a ball. The knocking sounds again.

"Foster!" I hear over the shrieking of the wind. "Let me in!"

I scramble off my bed and lunge for the door. Gabe, soaked through with rain, stands on my doorstep. I only allow myself a moment of confusion before I tug him inside and shut out the storm once again.

"What are you doing?" I croak. "You're wet."

The Gabe I used to know would have made a cheeky joke in response, but this Gabe is only looking at me in concern. I cross my arms over my chest, suddenly very aware that I'm not wearing a bra under my t-shirt.

"You don't like storms," he says simply. As if that answers all my questions.

"No, I don't. That doesn't explain why you came out here."

"You're coming inside. I wasn't crazy about the idea of you out here alone in the first place, but especially not when it's storming and I know you're scared."

My heart trips over itself at the look of genuine care on his face. But he has always looked out for me—it's what he does. I need to stop myself from reading more into it.

We're friends. Friends care about each other.

My arms tighten across my chest. "I'm a grown woman, Gabriel."

"Believe me, Foster, I'm well aware." If I didn't know any better, I would say that his eyes trace my body then, lingering on the dips and curves. "Doesn't mean I can't be worried about you."

Another protest is on my lips when thunder crashes above our heads. I cry out as I instinctively clutch Gabe's shirt, pressing my body against his. He wraps an arm around me, a hand trailing up and down my back in a soothing motion.

"Will you come inside with me now?"

I nod as my cheeks flame in embarrassment.

After I find an umbrella in one of the boxes I still haven't unpacked, we make a run for the main house. Gabe holds the umbrella above us, dragging me along behind him by my hand, but it does little to keep us from getting drenched. Once we're inside, Gabe sets the umbrella out to dry and then tugs me deeper into the house.

We ascend the stairs and head down the hallway. Gabe opens the door to Abbie's bedroom and peers inside quickly. She's fast asleep, despite the noise outside, the pink glow from her nightlight casting the shadows away.

I haven't been in this part of the house before. I haven't had reason to come up here. I try to only stick to the spaces that are absolutely necessary, so I haven't explored beyond the kitchen, downstairs bathroom and laundry room.

Gabe leads me to another room and gestures for me to go inside. I step over the threshold, noting the bedside lamp that illuminates the space, and stop short. But Gabe is already slipping past me.

He pulls open a dresser drawer and rifles through it. When he pulls out a dry shirt and sweatpants, and tosses them toward me, I frown.

"You can change in there," he says, pointing to the en suite. I stare blankly at him, my brain caught up on the fact that I'm in his *bedroom*. "Hallie?"

I blink, my brain restarting. *Right.* My pajamas are soaked. He's being nice enough to lend me some before setting me up in the guest room down the hall.

In the bathroom, I quickly strip out of my wet clothes and toss them over the edge of the bathtub. Then I slip the borrowed shirt over my head. It's just loose enough to be the perfect amount of comfortable. I shamelessly bring the collar up to my nose to inhale the familiar scent of Gabe's detergent. It's probably run-of-the-mill, but it reminds me of him.

After I have the sweatpants on, I return to the bedroom. It's then I notice that Gabe has turned down the other half of his comforter.

"You can have that side."

"Gabe—"

"Bed," he says, pointing for emphasis.

"But I can't. This is your room." My voice comes out shaky. "I'll stay in the guest room."

"Get your ass in my bed, Foster."

The command in his tone turns my insides to jelly. Coupled with the shakiness of my limbs from the stress of the storm, I have no choice but to comply.

"Jeez," I mutter as I slide under the covers, instantly wishing I could stay in this bed forever. "You're really bossy."

At this, Gabe smirks. "Baby, you haven't seen bossy yet."

A retort—a really freaking clever one, too—dies on my tongue when he proceeds to *take his shirt off*. Not only are there muscles that eighteen-year-old Gabe did not possess, but there are also tattoos. *Lots* of tattoos, just like I secretly hoped. On the left side of his ribs, I spot Abbie's name.

"Gabriel!" I hiss.

He quirks a brow when he comes back from hanging the wet shirt in the en suite. "Yes, Hallie?"

"Why are you getting naked?"

"Don't you know that's how I sleep?"

"I—" My mouth runs dry. "Wh-what?"

I can feel all the blood draining from my face. But at the same time, the thought makes my insides feel warm.

No. Abort. Shut it down, Hallie Foster.

Gabe laughs at the look on my face. "I'm kidding. Would you prefer if I changed in the bathroom instead?"

Do I *want* him to? No. Do I *need* him to? Yes. Definitely yes.

"Please. If you don't mind."

Gabe gathers a dry shirt and pajama pants for himself, and then he disappears into the en suite, as promised, while I wither away in embarrassment on his king-sized, cloud-like bed. Now that I sent him away, I just look like a prude who can't handle a little bare skin.

When he emerges from the bathroom, fully clothed, I pretend to be asleep. You can't answer questions if you're asleep, and I know he's itching to ask me about my freak-out in the guesthouse. I feel the bed dip as he settles beside me. I hold my breath, afraid it will give me away.

"I know you're still awake."

Busted.

I roll over on my side to face him. He mirrors my position. Since I came into the house, it's been easy to ignore the storm raging outside, but another snap of thunder—louder than all the rest—has my eyes squeezing shut. Gabe's palm slides under mine, and then he interlaces our fingers. He gives my hand a reassuring squeeze, and I take that as permission to tighten my grip.

"Wanna talk about it?" he asks gently.

I shake my head. Growing up with my mother was compli-cated. Most people know there's a story there, but only Clara has been afforded some of the pieces. The last person I want to share all that with is Gabe.

His thumb begins to rub soothing circles across the back of my hand. "What do you usually do when there's a storm?"

Slowly, I open my eyes. My cheeks flush. "Stay up until it stops or until I'm physically too exhausted to keep my eyes open."

"Christ, Hallie." I try to pull my hand out of his, feeling oddly vulnerable, but he refuses to let me go. "Wait. I'm not judging you. I just hate that you've had to go through that alone all these years."

My one shoulder tips up in a shrug. "C'est la vie."

Gabe is quiet for a moment. The wind never ceases, but neither do the concentric circles he draws on my skin.

"Can we try something?" he eventually asks.

"Like what?"

Gabe tugs gently on my hand, guiding me until I'm half on top of him. My lips part as my breasts brush against the hard planes of his chest. And with that, I've lost all my ability to speak.

He pats his chest, just above his heart. "Lay your head here."

This time, I know better than to argue. Or maybe I've just given up pretending that I want to. I rest my head on his chest, my ear turned to his heart. Immediately, I hear the organ's rhythmic beats. It doesn't drown the storm out completely, but it gives me something steady to focus on.

"Better?"

I hum. "Better."

"Good," he says, wrapping his arm around my back. "You're safe, Hallie. I've got you."

I've got you. The words do something to me, stitching up a hole that has been left in my heart from years of my mother's neglect. It isn't Gabe's hurt to fix, but he does it anyway.

I smile. "I know you do."

"Goodnight, Foster."

"Night, Gabriel."

And for the first time in what feels like forever, I fall asleep easily.

TEN

HALLIE

WHEN I WAKE UP, it takes me a moment to realize I'm not in my own bed. Although the new mattress out in the guesthouse is comfortable enough, it has nothing on this one.

I allow myself an extra minute under the covers before I slip out of bed, leaving the warmth behind. Thankfully, Gabe's side is empty. I'm not sure what I would have done if I had to face him like this. It's bad enough that he found me in such a vulnerable position last night.

It's not a secret to my friends that the wind scares me. But I try to keep the extent of my fear to myself. I've been relatively successful—until last night.

Last night, Gabe learned more than I ever wanted him to know. Now I need to figure out how to forget about it so the next time I see him, I can act somewhat normally.

I tiptoe across the floor and into the bathroom. Shutting the door as quietly as possible, I wince when the hinges give a slight whine. I avoid the mirror entirely, not wanting to know how bad the bags under my eyes are. My guess is they're pretty big.

As much as it pains me to part with it, I pull Gabe's shirt off and toss it in the hamper in the corner. Then I grab my shirt and tug it over my head. It's a little stiff from air drying, but I don't plan to be wearing it for long. I only need to get downstairs and out the back door without being seen.

Perhaps I haven't exactly left my cowardly ways behind.

After I switch out Gabe's sweats for my pajama pants, I creep out of the bathroom and into the hallway. I go slowly past Abbie's bedroom. The door is still closed, so I'm assuming she is still asleep. The last thing I need is her finding me sneaking out of her dad's bedroom. That would lead to questions. Ones I don't have good answers to.

I cringe each time the stairs creak beneath my feet. Peering down into the foyer, I see no sign of Gabe, which means I may be able to make a clean getaway after all.

I hit the bottom of the stairs and silently head down the back hallway. Just as I reach my shoes, a voice stops me in my tracks.

"Sneaking out on me, Foster?"

Damn it.

I turn on my heel to face Gabe. He's leaning against the archway into the kitchen, tattooed arms crossed over his chest. The sight makes my brain short-circuit for a second. How can one man look *that* good? Even slightly rumpled from sleep. *Especially* slightly rumpled from sleep.

I shrug and then cross my own arms, still very aware that I'm not wearing a bra. "Just wasn't sure what the morning after protocol was. I've never spent the night in your bed before."

He hums. "Consider it a practice run, then."

Now my brain truly does short-circuit. Because that sounds a lot like flirting—like something the Gabe from ten years ago would say, just to see the blush coat my cheeks. If he's up to his old ways, it sure as hell is working. I can feel the heat rush to my face...and other places.

Friends. We're friends. We agreed. Besides, I was the one who ran away last time. I doubt Gabe has been waiting all this time for me.

I flounder for something to say, but he thankfully beats me to it. "C'mon," he says, turning back to the kitchen. "I made you breakfast."

I glance over my shoulder at the door to the backyard. *So close.* I was so close to making my escape. And now my body is betraying me by listening to his command yet again. I follow him and sit on one of the stools at the island while he crosses to the stove.

I watch the muscles in Gabe's back move as he grabs a plate and starts to arrange whatever food he made.

"Oh," I say, when I see what he's plating. "Bacon. I don't—"

"You don't eat meat. I remember." He turns from the stove and slides the plate toward me. "It's veggie bacon."

My jaw drops. "How did you get that? I asked Gordon if he could order some for the store and he said no."

Dealing with the crotchety manager of the only grocery store on the island is one thing I did not miss while I was gone. When I was a teenager, working for Gordon was horrid. Safe to say he's only gotten worse, if that situation with the Alpha-getti is anything to go by.

Gabe shakes his head. "He said the same thing to me. So I asked my mom to grab some when she was on the mainland a couple days ago."

My heart squeezes inside my chest, and tears threaten to prick at my eyes. Kindness like this was familiar to me at one point in my life. I've been without it—been without Gabe and the rest of the Bowmans—for so long, it feels foreign now. Strange. Like it's too good to be true.

"You can't do nice things like that, Gabriel."

Amusement dances in his eyes. "Why not?"

"Because."

"Because why?"

Because you'll make me fall in love with you all over again.

I shake my head as I bite into a piece of veggie bacon, taking out my frustration. It has the audacity to taste good, too. "Thank you," I say after I've finished chewing.

He chuckles. "You're welcome." After grabbing his own plate, he comes to sit down beside me at the island. "How did you sleep?"

My cheeks heat again. *The best in a long time*, I want to say. "Good. I'm, uh, sorry about all that last night."

Gabe pins me with a stern look. "Don't apologize. I was only asking because I've been thinking about something, and I want to talk to you about it."

I eye him warily. "Okay..."

He sets his fork down, swivelling on his stool to face me. "I don't want you to live in the guesthouse."

My whole body deflates at his words. "*Oh.*" I push my eggs around on my plate, my appetite suddenly vanished. I knew this was a bad idea, that Clara and Maggie were too pushy. "That's okay. I'll figure it out. I can go back to Clara's until—"

"No. *Shit.*" Gabe runs a hand down his face as he lets out an exasperated breath. "I'm sorry, Foster, that's not what I meant. I'm not kicking you out."

"Then what are you saying?"

"I want you to move in here."

My jaw drops. "What about fixing up the guesthouse?" I ask. "I'll really be fine out there, Gabe. Last night was a one-time thing."

"But what if it's not? The guesthouse still needs a lot of work. I wanted you to have your own space, but after last night..." His eyes turn pleading. "Please, Hallie. I can't stand the thought of you being out there, alone and scared."

My breath catches. I was so worried I would come back to Kip Island and find indifference in Gabe. That he had written me off all those years ago and wouldn't care anymore. It's less about me thinking the worst of him than it is my brain preparing me for every reality, even the hard ones. But he has proven me wrong at every turn.

I twist my fork, round and round, between my fingers. "This is really important to you?"

"It is. The room beside Abbie's is a blank slate, so you can move in there and decorate it however you like."

"Will you still let me help you with the guesthouse?"

He nods. "Yeah, we can still work on it. I really have been meaning to fix it up."

"And I'm paying more rent," I add. It's one thing to sleep on Clara's couch for a couple weeks, but we're talking about a longer term situation here. I'd be living inside his *house*.

He frowns. "We'll talk about it."

I take a moment to think. Can I really do this? Staying in Gabe's backyard has been hard enough, but living just down the hall? I'm not so sure I'll survive it. I can't exactly say no, though. The guesthouse belongs to him, and if he doesn't want me out there, I have no grounds to argue.

"Alright," I relent. "I'll move inside."

He smiles in relief. "Thank you."

We continue eating, settling into silence. For once, it isn't uncomfortable. Maybe things are starting to go back to normal. Like before. Which should be a good thing, but I can't help the small seed of disappointment that sprouts from the thought.

I've just gotten off my stool to wash my plate when Abbie bounds into the kitchen. She's still wearing her pajamas, and some of her hair is sticking out of her braid.

"Morning, Abbs," Gabe says.

She beams. "Morning!"

I've never met a kid who likes mornings as much as she does. I wake up because I have to, not because I want to.

She sets herself up in her chair at the kitchen table. Gabe leaves his plate on the island and joins her. "I've got something to tell you. Hallie is going to live inside the house for a while. That okay with you?"

She looks up at her dad. "She's moving in with us?"

"Yes, she's moving in with us."

She shrugs as she kicks her legs beneath the table. "Okay."

After Gabe gets Abbie some breakfast and she finishes eating, he offers to help me bring my stuff inside. Thankfully, I haven't fully unpacked yet. I wanted to finish more of the projects we have planned before I truly settled in.

Quickly, I get dressed and ready for the day, throwing my hair into a bun. Then Gabe and I haul our first load up the stairs. When we get to the guest room, which is at the opposite end of the hallway to Gabe's bedroom, he flicks on the light.

The room truly is a blank slate. The walls are a shade of white a real estate agent would salivate over, and the bed doesn't have any sheets on it. It looks to be the same size as the one out in the guesthouse, though, so my comforter should fit perfectly.

"Clara is the only person who's ever stayed in here," Gabe explains. "I wouldn't put it past her to have left some clothes behind, but it should be empty otherwise."

I set my box on the end of the bed. "Thank you. You really don't have to do any of this for me."

"I want to, Hallie." He pulls something from his pocket. A key, I realize. To his *house*. "For you."

I reach for it, but my stomach does a little dip when I notice the colour. "It's purple." The metal feels cool against my skin. "When did you get this? You didn't just have this lying around as a spare."

"I had it cut last week."

My eyes search his. "What? Why?"

He doesn't look away. "I wanted you to know that I'd always be here, if you needed me. And I didn't want anything to stand in your way, even something as simple as a lock."

The admission leaves me breathless. I feel like that girl who stood on the beach and let her fears override her heart. She couldn't speak when words mattered most, so I don't have a hope in hell of recovering now.

"You can start unpacking," Gabe says. "I'll grab the rest of your stuff."

I'm still clutching the key when he leaves the room. The grooves in the metal have left small indents in my palm.

I am officially in way over my head.

ELEVEN

HALLIE

I HAVEN'T PAINTED in a long time.

Not for myself, anyway. First, it was because I was too focused trying to survive in my university classes, so I let my creative outlet fall to the wayside. After I graduated, I found myself too busy with work.

Now I find myself unsure how to handle a blank canvas. The entire wall is empty, free for the taking, according to Gabe. He put all his faith in me, and I'm trying not to convince myself it was misplaced.

I can do this.

My sketchbook sits on the ground at my feet, full of several renderings of the wall in front of me. I hate all of them.

Maybe I can't do this.

With a sigh, I set the paintbrush on the rim of the paint can. The wall is primed, but I can't decide whether I should paint it the same as the others or step outside the box.

The guesthouse door opens behind me, letting in a cool breeze. It feels good against the back of my neck.

"Foster?"

"Hey," I say, turning to face Gabe.

He's still dressed in his work clothes, and I have to admit, he looks *good*. Too good. I can feel my cheeks turning red as my thoughts travel down that dangerous path.

"It's looking great in here," he says, stepping inside and slowly turning, admiring the work I've done. Three of the walls have a fresh coat of light pink paint. "I could've used you a long time ago."

I blush harder. "Thank you." I tuck my hair behind my ear, then mumble a curse when I get paint on myself.

With a laugh, Gabe grabs the rag I've been using and takes a step closer. I suck in a sharp breath at his proximity, not even daring to breathe as he leans in. With one hand on my chin, he angles my head to the side and wipes the paint from my skin.

"There." For some reason, the word sends a shiver down my spine. "That's better."

I purposefully take a step back so I don't lose all brain function from our proximity.

Gabe sets the rag down before he pulls a white envelope from his pocket. "Clara gave me this to give to you. The letter went to Pops's old place. The Frasers live there now, and they brought it to Dockside this morning," he explains.

With a furrowed brow, I take the envelope from him. I haven't lived at that address for a decade now. Some of my mail still went to Pops's house while I was in school, but I changed everything when he moved to his retirement home.

The penmanship on the front isn't one I recognize. I wouldn't put it past my mother to send me something in the mail asking for money after I refused to answer the phone the last few times she's called, but I know Amanda's loopy scrawl and this isn't it.

"Did Clara say anything else about it?" I ask. Like maybe who it's from.

Gabe shakes his head. "She didn't."

With a fortifying breath, I hook my nail under the flap and rip into the envelope.

Hallie,

My name is Kevin Landell. I don't know if you recognize my name, but in the case that you don't, I'll be direct. I had a short relationship with Amanda Foster about 29 years ago. I'm your father.

Before I get into this, I want to say that I understand you owe me nothing. After almost three decades of no contact, I understand if you want that to continue. I wouldn't blame you. I wouldn't blame you if you decide not to finish reading this letter, but on the off chance that you do, I'm going to say what I need to say. What you deserve to hear.

First, I'm sorry. I know that a simple apology is woefully inadequate, but I am truly sorry for missing out on all these years with you. It is my greatest regret, as is not coming to my senses sooner. I recently went through some health issues that made me see my life through a different lens, and I have come to understand just how wrong I have been.

I am far from a perfect man, but I am trying to be better. I know I have no right to ask this of you, but would you talk with me? I want to explain as best I can, and get to know you, if you are willing. I'll leave that in your hands. And once again, I'm sorry.

My phone number is written at the bottom, in case you ever feel like reaching out.

Sincerely, Kevin

"Hallie?"

It takes me a second to realize my hands are shaking. When

Gabe pries the paper away from me, I finally look up. The amount of concern in his expression makes me wonder if he called my name more than once.

"Are you okay?" he asks.

"I…" *Am* I okay? I shake my head. "That letter is from my father."

"Your *father?*"

He sounds as shocked as I feel. The last thing I expected to be inside that envelope was…that.

"He wants to see me." My tongue is dry, scraping against the inside of my mouth. "He wants to see *me.*"

Gabe scoffs. "That's the least he could do."

Like I'm in a trance, I drift across the room and practically fall back onto the end of the bed. It's just a bare mattress now, stripped of its sheets when I moved into the main house. Gabe follows warily, stopping to stand in front of me.

"When I was little, that was all I wanted," I say quietly, gesturing to the paper in Gabe's hand. "So many times, I wanted him to take me away. Because he had to be better than my mom."

Gabe's eyes soften. "Foster…"

"That was my birthday wish for at least ten years. I'd blow out my candles and wish he'd show up at the door. And now he's reaching out, and I— I can't—"

My resolve shatters, and tears start to fall. Then the sob works its way up my throat, getting caught before it springs free. I clap a hand over my mouth, trying to stifle the sound, but it's no use.

Gabe sits beside me on the bed. The next thing I know, he hauls me into his lap, wrapping his arms around me like it's the most natural thing in the world. I want to pull away, to keep a healthy distance between us, especially after I've already spent a night in his bed, but I can't. Instead, I press my face into his neck and let him comfort me, despite how guilty it makes me feel.

Stop using him, Hallie. You're exactly like the mother you claim to hate.

The voice is right, of course. I'm a hypocrite. I shouldn't be seeking comfort from the man whose heart I stomped on all those years ago. Still, I cling to him. His ever-steady presence is the only reason I haven't fully succumbed to my emotions, which roil inside me, just waiting to spill free.

Sadness. Relief. Anger. Hope. Desperation. They all fight for dominance. Why *now*? Why now, when I'm a mess who feels like she's simply floating through life with no real direction, does he decide to reach out?

When the tears eventually slow, I pull back, swiping at my cheeks. My eyes feel puffy and swollen, and I'm sure I look like a disaster, but Gabe's gaze is void of judgment. Regardless, my face flames.

"I'm so sorry," I say, disentangling myself from him. "I didn't mean to do that."

The last thing I wanted was to fall apart on him. To burden him. It's already bad enough I'm living with him, taking up his space.

When I try to stand, his arms keep me trapped in his lap. New conflicting emotions swirl inside me—the urge to curl up against his chest and beg him to never let me go versus the panic brought on by our closeness.

"You don't have to do that with me, Foster."

"Do what?"

"Run when shit gets hard."

It has always been more difficult with Gabe. Clara is my best friend, sure, but I've always been able to balance opening up to her while keeping her far enough away so as not to witness the depths of my dysfunction. Her brother, on the other hand, managed to find a way to slip past all of my defenses. All of my safeguards.

This time, when I try to slide off Gabe's lap, he lets me go. I cross the room, dragging in a deep breath now that it won't be full of his cologne. My heartbeat settles, but I find that in the stillness, there's a hollow ache.

"What do you want to do with this?" he asks, folding the letter back into neat thirds.

"I have to do it," I say, eyes darting from the paper to Gabe's waiting stare. "I have to see him. Right?"

His fingers tighten on the letter. "You don't *have* to do anything. You have every right to start a bonfire with this and never think of the man again." His grip loosens, and he sighs, giving me a soft smile. "But I know that's not what you want to do."

He tries to mask it, but I can see Gabe's frustration. He's never been happy about the relationship—or lack thereof—I have with my parents. Of course he wouldn't be. Maggie and John are the best parents you could ask for. They're not perfect, but they beat my own by a long shot. And Gabe's a dad himself. A great one. He'd never in a million years abandon Abbie the way my father abandoned me.

There is a part of me that wants to hang on to my anger. My hurt. But the bigger part of me is curious. Is this what it is to finally be wanted? After twenty-eight years, I want to truly know what that feels like.

"Is that stupid?" I ask. With everything I do, there's always a seed of doubt that takes root.

Gabe shakes his head. "You're allowed to feel however you feel about this, and you're allowed to do what feels right to you. No one, least of all me, can tell you any different."

I wish someone *could* tell me what's right. Which path will carry the least amount of heartache. I'm not good with the unknown. In that liminal space, my brain is free to make up whatever scenarios it sees fit, to prepare me for the worst. And then I spiral.

But Gabe's gaze, warm and trained on me, lends me strength. I may not know what will come of this, but if I don't try, I'll only be left wondering. Do I want to live with that for the rest of my life?

"I want to meet him," I finally say.

Gabe nods as he holds the paper out. "Then you should reach

out. You're not obligated to do anything beyond that, but at least you'll know."

I take a step closer, back to him, and take the letter. I run my finger over the surface. "Thank you. I didn't mean to fall apart on you, but thanks for holding all my pieces. Helping me put them back together."

He stands from the bed, and his familiar scent invades my senses again. "As long as I'm around, that's never something you'll have to do alone."

I don't deserve this. You. Your kindness. He would only refute it if I tried to tell him, so I don't. But the guilt wraps around me anyway, like the comforting embrace of an old friend.

TWELVE

GABE

FOR THE THIRD time this morning, I knock on my daughter's bedroom door. "Let's go, Abbs!" I call. "I have to get to work."

"I'm going fast, I promise!" she calls back. "One more minute!"

Abbie has been dressing herself for school for the past couple years, which is great. Except it often leaves us running late because she changes her outfit countless times and refuses my offers to help.

I sigh as I check my watch again. My mom is supposed to be bringing her to school this morning, but for that to happen, I need to drop her off at Haven House before I go to work.

I head back downstairs, double checking Abbie's lunch bag is packed. Mornings have certainly grown more chaotic since she started school, but I wouldn't change them for anything. In fact, on the days she's with her mom, I miss it. The only thing I would change is her being able to stay with me full-time, but I know that's not fair on Larissa. It's for the best Larissa and I aren't together, but it sure does burn not having my kid home with me every day.

When Abbie still hasn't made it out of her room a few minutes later, I jog back up the stairs. Standing outside her door once more, I raise a hand to knock again when, down the hall, the bathroom door swings open. Turning, I'm met with the sight of Hallie. In absolutely nothing but a goddamn towel.

Slowly, my fist lowers to my side, and my mouth runs dry.

"*Oh.*" Her cheeks flush as she freezes in the doorway, clutching the fabric to her breasts. Her hair is tied in a loose bun atop her head, purple and blonde strands overlapping. She still has a sleepy look in her eyes, like she isn't fully awake yet. "I...thought you were gone already."

Thank fuck I wasn't.

Words escape me as my eyes rove her body. From her bare legs up to her exposed collarbone. The towel does little to hide her curves, and I'm doing little to stop myself from drinking her in. From thinking about how beneath that threadbare towel, Hallie is naked.

So incredibly naked.

For a moment, we both stand there, at an impasse. My brain is woefully empty, my tongue tied. Even after ten years, after her rejection, she still manages to have this effect on me. I should be over this, over her. But every second I spend in her presence is a reminder that I'm not. I'm not sure I ever will be.

"I, um, forgot something in my room," she rushes out. And then she darts down the hall and slams her door closed behind her.

Hanging my head, I brace my hands on either side of the door-frame in front of me and stifle a groan. No matter how hard I try, I can't get her image to leave my brain. It's now a permanent fixture, like so many of the memories I have from before. Including the day I told her I loved her and she ran away.

Abbie's door swings open then, and she chooses this moment to appear, finally dressed for school. "I'm ready, Daddy!"

With a sigh, I push away from the wall, letting her slip by as I pull my shit together. She bounds toward the steps and then grips the rail, skipping downstairs. I spare a final glance in the direction of Hallie's room before following after Abbie.

What sweet fucking torture.

Call me whatever you want, but if this is the price I have to pay to have Hallie in my life again, I'll pay it happily. I've always been greedy when it comes to her.

———

Somehow, I managed to only be five minutes late for my shift. I hate being late, but it has been happening more frequently as Abbie decides to take liberties with our morning routine. On days like today, it's inevitable. Luke doesn't say anything, but I can tell he doesn't like it, and that's almost worse. If I were anyone else, he would've already lectured me about being more punctual and not making this a habit.

I know it's natural for him to want to cut me some slack, given I'm his brother, but I don't want that. A part of me wonders if it's his guilt rearing its ugly head again. I've never blamed him for what happened with his ex—when Kristina was supposed to be watching Abbie and instead held a party, resulting in a fire—but it has been a point of contention for him. Hell, it nearly cost him his relationship with Delilah. But I don't want him walking on eggshells with me.

Connor finds me in the kitchen, brewing a pot of coffee. One look at his face tells me I'm not going to like whatever he plans to say.

I've known Connor since the beginning of grade nine. The Lees moved to the island that summer, and we met in gym class on the first day of school. Back then, we were both a couple of scrawny, barely pubescent boys. Now Connor rocks a killer mustache and can bench-press more than me.

Wordlessly, I take two mugs down from the cupboard, then lean against the counter, waiting for the caffeine to brew.

Connor takes up a spot beside me.

I raise a brow in question.

"So…" he begins casually. "How's it going, living with Hallie?"

He's certainly not pulling any punches. But that's Connor. Subtlety has never been his forte.

"It's…" *Slowly making me lose my mind.* "Fine."

He scoffs as he crosses his arms. "Fine? That's all you're gonna say?"

I shrug. "It's good. She has a safe place to stay, and Abbie likes having her around."

"And so do you," he adds.

I say nothing. We both know he's right. Having Hallie back on the island is amazing, but having her in my home? It's a dream. And if I don't think about it too hard, I can pretend, just for a moment, that she's there to stay. That she isn't going to leave again, without so much as a goodbye.

Avoiding Connor's watchful gaze, I rub at my chest. The phantom ache there. It's ridiculous, I know—I need to move on. Except I'm not sure how to do that when I couldn't even manage in the ten years she was gone. Now that I'm in her orbit again, I'm finding it difficult to extricate myself.

"Look, just be careful, Gabe," he says. "You know I like Hallie, but…"

But he hasn't hidden his disapproval of our current living situation. I get it, I do. It's not exactly conventional, and it's borderline agonizing at times—like when I catch her in nothing but a towel— but I can't do anything about it now. I meant what I said about hating the idea of her out in the guesthouse alone.

The truth is, I never want Hallie to look at me again like she did that day on the beach. I put my heart on the line, and I made her so uneasy, she *ran*. Away from me, away from the island. So as much as I want her, I'm not going to jeopardize our slowly returning friendship. I can't.

A little of Hallie is still better than none of her at all.

"I'll be fine," I assure him. "We're friends, and I'm helping her out. That's what friends do."

He sends me an unconvinced look, but he thankfully doesn't push.

A small knock has us both turning toward the door. Hallie stands in the threshold, a sheepish smile on her lips. Instead of a towel, she's wearing a black overall dress with gold buttons running down one side. It's a little looser on top, showing off her white t-shirt beneath, but it hugs her hips perfectly. My hands curl around the edge of the counter behind me to keep from reaching for her.

Without conscious thought, a smile tips my lips. "Hey," I say.

She tucks a strand of hair behind her ear. "Hey."

Connor steps forward, grinning, like our previous conversation didn't even happen. "Hallie Foster, in the flesh. Good to have you back! How are you?"

"I'm good, Connor. How are you? Your parents?"

He nods. "They're alright. Driving me nuts now that they're both retired. They need to get a hobby or something."

Hallie laughs. "Pops went a little stir-crazy when he retired, too. They'll get used to it. They might even have a better social life than you before long." Which would be a feat, considering how much Connor loves to socialize.

I push off the counter, crossing to her. "What are you doing here?" I ask. "Is everything okay?"

"You left your phone at home." She digs around in her purse and pulls the device out, handing it to me. "I figured it was pretty important you have it."

"Thanks." I take the phone and pocket it. "I was in such a rush to get out the door, I must've forgotten to grab it."

Hallie grins. "Abbie was giving you a run for your money this morning, huh?"

I sigh, rubbing at my jaw. "My mom says it's payback for how I was as a kid."

"You did cause your fair share of trouble." Her eyes cut to Connor. "Both of you did. I still have nightmares about those worms you put in Clara's bed that one summer."

Connor throws his hands up in surrender. "Hey, I'm innocent. That was all Gabe's idea."

I snort. *Innocent* and *Connor* don't even belong in the same vicinity, let alone the same sentence.

Hallie glances at the clock on the wall. "I should head out now. Carole wants me at the gallery."

I step forward. "I'll walk you out."

It's not necessary—the station is only so big, and this isn't the first time Hallie has been here. Still, once she waves goodbye to Connor, I take the opportunity to set a hand on the small of her back and guide her through the building to the lobby.

When we make it to the front door, she turns to me. "About earlier..." Her cheeks turn pink. "I'm sorry if I made things awkward. I didn't mean— I shouldn't have—"

I take her fidgeting hands in mine, and she abruptly stops speaking. "It's okay," I assure her. "We're good. No awkwardness here."

She searches my gaze. "You're sure?"

I reluctantly release her hands. I stuff my own into my pockets so I don't take hold of them again. "Positive. I'm an adult. I can handle a little bare skin."

Or a lot.

I force the memory of her in that towel out of my brain. I file it away with all the other things I shouldn't be thinking about when it comes to Hallie.

Friends. We're friends.

She looks poised to argue, but footsteps from behind me stop her short.

"Hey, Hallie," Luke says. "How's it going?"

"Hi." Her cheeks are still flushed in embarrassment, but she hides the emotion well, pasting on a smile. "Your brother left his phone at home. I was just dropping it off."

His eyes slide to me, then back to her. "That's nice of you. Good thing he has you around to keep him organized, eh?"

I try to ignore the way that comment makes me feel. I'm sure Luke doesn't mean anything by it, but it irks me all the same.

Hallie laughs nervously as she adjusts the strap of her purse on her shoulder. "I should get going, let you get back to work." She waves. "Bye."

"Wait," I call out. "Did you—?"

But she's out the door in a flash, before I can even finish my sentence. Luke claps me on the back, then retreats to his office.

When I make my way back to the kitchen, the coffee is ready, and Connor is shaking his head. "You, my friend, are fucked."

I don't argue. I can't.

THIRTEEN

HALLIE

TODAY, I'm finally meeting my father.

I probably should have called him when I inevitably decided to reach out, but me and phone calls are mortal enemies, so I chickened out and texted him instead. His response was almost immediate.

> Hi, this is Hallie. I got your letter. I was wondering if you'd like to meet?

KEVIN

> Hi, Hallie. Absolutely! Tell me a time and a place. I'll make it happen.

We settled on Dockside on Monday at three o'clock. Which is today. Soon.

I got to the restaurant early. I wanted to get a good seat. Now I've been sitting so long, my butt has gone numb. Eyes on my hands, I pick at a dried bit of nail polish on my cuticle. I let Abbie paint my nails last night, and now they're a pretty shade of lavender that matches my hair. She mostly managed to keep the polish on my nails and off my skin, which is a plus.

I check the clock above the bar for the hundredth time. Kevin is going to be here any minute.

Oh, God. *He's going to be here any minute.* If I wasn't so worried about making it back in time, I'd bolt to the bathroom and empty my stomach. Instead, I force the nausea down.

Calm down, Hallie. This is fine. Everything is fine.

Except it doesn't feel fine. It feels like I'm about to take a test on a subject I haven't studied before. I see a giant F in my future. Thinking about this moment for as long as I have should have prepared me, but I feel inept. What do I even say? How do I hide the messiness of my current situation?

What do you do for work? I lost my job in the city, so now I work part-time at the local gallery because the owner took pity on me.

Where are you living? In my best friend's brother's spare bedroom. It's not as bad as it sounds, except maybe it's worse because I think I'm still in love with him.

I don't have any significant accomplishments to show off. No accolades from a high-powered job, no house, no kids of my own. I'm just...me. And that's never been good enough.

"Hallie," Clara says, coming up beside me. She touches my arm. "I need to talk to you for a second."

"I'm meeting my d—" I stop myself. *Dad* seems too familiar, and we're the textbook definition of strangers. "My father will be here, like, right now. Can it wait?"

She shakes her head, then quickly glances over her shoulder. I see Carole standing by the bar and give her a wave.

"Not really," Clara insists. "It's kind of important."

"I—" The sound of the door opening cuts me off. My head whips in the direction of the newcomer. *It's him.* I just know it. "He's here. I promise I'll find you after, and you can tell me then."

She grimaces but nods. "Good luck, babe. I'll be behind the bar if you need me. Or a drink."

Clara quickly takes her leave, and I stand on shaky legs. I try not to be obvious about wiping my sweaty palms on my thighs. Then I hold up a hand, gaining Kevin's attention.

I've never seen any pictures of him, but somehow, he looks exactly as I expected he would. A little older, because when I used to picture him, he was still the thirtysomething my mom recklessly jumped into bed with. Now he's in his early sixties, with laugh lines and greying hair, though he looks somewhat gaunt. His health issues must have been pretty serious, then.

"Hallie?" he asks, coming closer.

I offer him a small smile. "Yes. Hi."

We sort of just look at each other for a moment, lost for words. I wonder if he's remembering my mother. I know I look like her. I guess I look a little like him, too, but there is certainly more of Amanda Foster in me than I'd prefer.

He lets out a bit of a chuckle, unsure. Disbelieving. "Wow. I was hoping I would have the chance to do this, and now that it's here, I'm struggling to find my voice."

"Do you want to...?" I gesture to the table, and he nods.

Alright, I can do this. One step at a time. It's not that scary.

Once we're seated, we both study each other again. I return to picking my cuticle. The clock ticks forward.

Kevin clasps his hands on top of the table. "I'm not really sure how to go about this. Where to start. Maybe you could ask me questions? Anything you want to know."

A million different inquiries scream at me. Why did he leave? Why wasn't I good enough? All have varying degrees of pain attached to them. I know we won't come out of this totally unscathed, but I shift directions slightly. Not exactly easing us in, but I need to know.

"What made you change your mind?" I ask. "You said in your letter that you went through some health issues."

He nods. Swallows visibly. "I was diagnosed with pancreatic cancer two years ago. They found it early, and my scans are clear now, no evidence of disease. But going through treatment made me realize, as cliché as it sounds, how precious life truly is. As I got better, I couldn't stop thinking about you. How I should have handled everything differently."

"Why?" I ask, voice cracking on the word.

I don't elaborate, but he understands. "My wife, Dana, and I weren't in a good place. I'd like to say I simply wasn't thinking when I decided to start up a relationship with Amanda, but that isn't the truth. I was looking for a way to express my discontent. I knew what I was doing. Things between me and Amanda didn't last long. I broke it off, came clean to Dana. Then Amanda told me she was pregnant."

Guilt comes, fast and hot, because I know what happens next.

"To put it frankly, I was a coward. Dana was willing to work things out, but only if we left. If I agreed to put everything behind us. Selfishly, I didn't want my world to change, so we moved. And I tried to forget about you."

Hearing that stings. *I tried to forget about you.* Because at the end of the day, I'm inconsequential enough to be forgotten. By him, by my mother.

"When I was sick, I told your siblings about you," he continues. "Caitlyn and Bryan. They were both, understandably, angry at me. They still are. But eventually, we came to the conclusion that I needed to reach out. So I wrote you a letter."

My breath leaves my lungs in a whoosh. *Siblings.* The closest I've had to that is watching the Bowmans as we grew up. Deep down, I longed for an older brother like Luke, a sister like Clara.

"This is...a lot to take in," I say.

Kevin's expression softens. "I know. I'm sorry. We can leave it there for today, if you'd like."

I hardly have time to mull over his words before a riot of colour and chaos descends on us. "Hallie!" Carole exclaims as she steps up to the table. "I hear congratulations are in order."

My brows furrow as I look up at her. "Congratulations?"

I glance over at Kevin, as if he might have some insight, but he's only looking at her curiously. Of course he wouldn't know—he hasn't lived on the island in close to thirty years.

"Yes!" Carole shoves my shoulder good-naturedly. "You thought you could go and get engaged to one of those darling Bowman boys without me finding out?"

I choke on air. "What?" My gaze slides to Kevin. "I, uh—"

"You're engaged?" he asks. His eyes are shining with what I can only describe as joy.

No! I want to shout. But the word gets lodged in my throat.

Carole nods, utterly oblivious to my internal freak-out. "Miss Abigail let the news slip to her teacher yesterday, and you know Melinda and I are yoga buddies. She mentioned it during our sunrise session this morning. Gosh, I'm *so* glad I ran into you! I bet Maggie is simply over the moon."

Words. I need words. Any of them, really.

"Who is Abigail?" Kevin asks.

Bad. This is bad.

"Gabriel's daughter," Carole replies.

"And who is Gabriel?"

She flings a hand in my direction. "Hallie's new fiancé."

This is *so* bad.

Carole looks down at her wrist, where a multicoloured watch rests. "Oh, would you look at the time. I've gotta run. Best wishes to you and Gabe, dear. I'll see you at the gallery tomorrow afternoon!"

Carole sweeps out of the restaurant with a flourish, none the wiser to my struggles.

I turn to Clara at the bar. Based on the expression she wears, she heard everything Carole said. My stomach swims. That's what she wanted to talk about. She wanted to warn me.

Kevin clears his throat, pulling my attention back to him. "I apologize if you didn't want me to know about your engagement," he says. At least someone can read the discomfort on my face, although it's not for the reason he thinks. "But I... Well, I'm glad that I know. I'm serious about doing this right, Hallie. I'd love to get to know you. And your fiancé. If you'll give me the chance."

Do it now. Tell him the truth.

Instead, I smile shakily. "I'd really like that."

———

I pace the length of the living room as I wait for Gabe to get home from work. I messaged him to ask where he was, and he said he was on his way, but that feels like hours ago now.

The pit in my stomach grows steadily bigger.

Finally, the front door opens. I all but sprint into the hall, catching Gabe off guard. He eyes me warily as he removes his boots.

"We need to talk."

"Are you breaking up with me?" he jokes, but it falls flat when I don't smile. My stomach is too twisted up to do that. "Alright, we can talk. Can I shower first?"

I shake my head. "Talk first."

I've been rehearsing what I'm going to say all afternoon. If I don't get it out now, I fear I never will. Then I'll have to think of some other way to get myself out of this mess. This big, messy mess.

Gabe follows me into the living room and sits on the couch. I resume my post in front of the coffee table. I don't pace this time, though. Instead, I cross my arms over my chest, only to uncross them a second later.

What am I supposed to do with my hands?

Gabe leans forward, bracing his elbows on his thighs. I try to ignore how hot he looks in that position. "Alright, Foster. What's up? You're starting to worry me."

"It's nothing...bad." Or is it? It's arguably not *good*. "I suppose you haven't heard who the gossip mill's latest victims are?"

He raises a brow. "No. Who is it?"

"Us."

"*Us?*" He points between us. "You and me?"

"Yes, Gabriel. It turns out your daughter said something to her teacher that has been making the rounds."

He sits upright at that. "What did she say?"

I sigh. "For some reason, she told her teacher that we're going to get married."

"You're sure she said us? Not Larissa and Chris?"

Shrugging, I say, "Carole was pretty convinced. She does yoga with Abbie's teacher, so she was all too thrilled to learn about this and then run into me at Dockside."

Gabe runs a hand down his face as he leans back against the couch cushions. "I'm sorry. She probably got confused because her mom and Chris are moving in together, too. I'll talk to her. And Carole. She can undo whatever damage she's done in the past twelve hours."

I bite my lip as I look down at my feet. "About that..." Inhaling a deep breath, I meet his gaze. "My father was there when Carole dropped the bomb."

He grimaces. "*Shit*. At least you could have a good laugh. Break the ice."

"Um, yeah, we would have. If I had told him it was a mistake."

Gabe's eyebrows shoot halfway up to his hairline. "You didn't tell him? Why?"

"Because I froze," I admit. Saying it out loud sounds even more pathetic than I already knew it was. "You should've seen his face, Gabe! He looked so hopeful, like he hit the do-over jackpot. Getting to know me in time for me to get married? He was so happy."

"Hallie, I'm sure he'll understand," Gabe says. "Hell, he doesn't have a right to be mad about anything when it concerns you."

"But what if I didn't?" I whisper. "What if we just...pretend?"

He shoots out of his seat then, looking at me like I have ten heads. It would explain my wooziness—too many heads, not enough blood.

"You want me to *pretend* to be your fiancé?"

The expression on his face makes my stomach twist again. He looks pained, like the very thought of being engaged to me is too much to bear. That stings, but I swallow the hurt.

"Would that be so bad?" I ask. "Being with me." My voice comes out quiet, and despite my effort, some of that hurt seeps through.

It's not a fair question to ask him. It's not, and I know it.

His eyes soften. "I don't mean it like that. I—" He runs a hand through his hair, mussing up the dark strands. The tattoos on his arm shift with the movement. "*Fuck.* I want to help you, I do, but I'm not sure this is the answer."

The first tear falls without my permission. I've been crying too much lately. I don't *want* to cry. But I build situations up in my head, picturing the worst, and then when they're over, my anxiety all rushes out in the form of tears. Like my body doesn't know any other way to rid itself of the toxicity.

I sobbed on the way home from my first driving test. Same with my first university exam. And now here I am, crying over the meeting with my father.

Gabe doesn't hesitate to gather me in his arms. "Hallie, baby, why are you crying?"

I shake my head, swiping at my wet cheek. "I'm sorry, I don't mean to. It's just been an...overwhelming day. And—" I take a deep breath, trying to stop my tears. "I want him to love me, Gabe. I want him to accept me."

"You don't think he will, just as you are?"

No, I don't. He didn't before.

I swallow as I close my eyes. I hide my face against his chest when I admit, "I'm feeling a little unmoored right now, and I want to put my best foot forward. I don't want to come off as aimless.

Having a successful relationship would at least give me *something* to show for myself."

Even if it was all smoke and mirrors.

Gabe sighs, his chin resting on top of my head. He pulls back, looking down at me. "Are you sure about this?"

I nod, catching the last tear as it cascades down my cheek. "I am."

"Then I'll do it."

"Really?"

He offers me a small smile. "Yeah, Foster. Just tell me where and when, and I'll be there."

"Thank you." I clutch his arms, giving them a grateful squeeze. "I promise it won't be forever. Just until I can find my footing with Kevin and his family. Then I'll stage a breakup, and you'll be off the hook."

He takes my chin in his hand, tilting it up. "Just promise you'll go easy on my heart," he says. My breath hitches. "You know, when you stage that breakup."

"Yeah, of course." I smile shakily. "It just didn't work out. We've always been better off as friends."

He takes a step back, clearing his throat, and his hand falls away. "Friends. Right."

Friends. The safest thing we can be.

The *only* thing we can be.

FOURTEEN

GABE

AS I HELP her down from my truck, Abbie waves her shopping list in the air. "Daddy, I did such a good job. Didn't I do a good job?"

I chuckle. "You did. You'll be acing those spelling tests before we know it."

Now that Abbie is in grade one, she has gotten very serious about learning how to spell things. After school today, she insisted on copying the list I had made of groceries we need, and now she's on a mission to find them all.

As soon as we enter Sunnyside Market, I spot Hallie. She's a hard woman to ignore, but even then, I find myself looking for her in every room, even if I know she won't be there.

She's talking to someone I haven't seen in years. Ethan doesn't look much different than he did back in high school. Same shaggy blond hair and bulky build. He's got one ankle crossed over the other as he leans against a shelf, laughing at whatever Hallie said.

A little bit of something that can only be described as envy sprouts, and I start toward them before I even realize what I'm doing.

"Daddy, we gotta go that way," Abbie protests, pointing behind us.

"We will. But Hallie's talking to an old friend, and I want to say hi," I reply, steering her in their direction.

Hallie's back is to us, so she doesn't see us approach, but Ethan does. "Gabe," he says with a grin. "What's up?"

Hallie turns then, her gaze full of surprise. She always looks a little bewildered when I seek her out. As if she can't quite believe I'm standing in front of her, asking for her attention. Little does she know, I'd do a whole hell of a lot for it.

"Hey," I say to Ethan. "It's been a while."

He holds out a hand to shake, then slaps me on the back with the other. When I step back, his eyes drift down to my daughter, who isn't shy about returning his curious stare.

"And who's this?" he asks.

"Abigail Mae Bowman," Abbie replies proudly. Her smile reveals the gap from the front tooth she lost two days ago.

"Nice to meet you. I'm Ethan." He smiles at her, then looks between me and Hallie. "You've got yourselves a cute kid."

"Oh, no," Hallie says, her cheeks instantly turning red, "it's not like that. I mean, she's not— *I'm* not—"

"Abbie is my daughter," I supply, rescuing her. "Hallie is a... friend." The word tastes sour, the way it always does when I'm forced to use it.

Ethan's brows raise. "Shit, eh? My bad. Everyone thought for sure you two would get together. Especially after you turned me down, Hallie."

My teeth grind together at the reminder. Not that she said no, but that he even asked her out in the first place. He had every right to—Hallie and I were never together, despite how much I wanted us to be—but it annoys me all the same.

Hallie laughs awkwardly. "Sorry to disappoint."

He shrugs, clearly not bothered about the past, then turns his attention to me. "What are you doing now? You still at the fire department?"

I nod, grateful for the subject change. "I am."

"Heard your brother's the chief now. Good for him. I never expected him to climb the ladder, but it makes sense."

And we're back to the teeth grinding. These conversations always come back around to Luke. I get it, he's impressive. He's the youngest chief Kip Island Fire Department has seen since its inception, but he's not a god.

"Yup." I force a polite smile, and Hallie sends me a concerned look. "What are you up to now?"

"I work for the coast guard out of Tobermory," he says. "We do a few different things, but a lot of search and rescue."

This genuinely piques my interest. "We've coordinated with you guys on some rescues over the years. You do good work."

As annoyed as I may be, I can respect what Ethan does. Lake Huron is a beast, and with as many cottagers as there are in the summer, I'm not surprised at the need for search and rescue crews. They've always intrigued me.

"You ever think about doing something like that?" he asks. "We can always use solid people like you on our crews."

I shake my head. "I haven't given it much thought."

Ethan quickly checks his watch. "Listen, I've unfortunately gotta run. It was great seeing you both. If you ever are looking to try something new, Bowman, you know where to find me."

He says goodbye to Abbie, and then he heads toward the cash.

Abbie tugs on my hand. "Daddy, can we go now? You were talking *forever*, and I'm hungry!"

"Yeah, let's go. We just have to grab a basket."

"You can put your stuff in my cart," Hallie offers, patting the handle. "If you want."

"Sure. And to pay you back, I'll be driving you home."

She shakes her head, like I knew she would. "That's not necessary."

"It's very necessary."

Impatient, Abbie drops my hand and marches off, consulting her list. Hallie and I follow after her.

"Just because I'm living in your house doesn't mean you're responsible for me," Hallie says as we turn down the aisle with the canned goods.

I grab the vegetables we need before Abbie can, flashbacks of our last shopping trip together assaulting me. We don't need to give Gordon a reason to instate that ban on children he muttered about.

"I don't think I'm responsible for you. But we're going to the same place, Foster. Why *wouldn't* I drive you?"

She looks down at where her hands grip the cart handle. "I don't want to burden you."

"It's not a burden if I'm offering." I smirk. "Demanding, really."

Her lips quirk upwards. "You have grown rather bossy."

"*So* bossy!" Abbie agrees.

Hallie outright laughs. I shake my head, but I can't hide my own amusement. It quickly dies, though, when I pin Hallie with a stern look. "You have never been, nor will you ever be, a burden to me." I raise a brow. "Got it?"

She nods sheepishly. "Got it."

"Good. Now that that's settled," I say, gently nudging her out of the way so I can take over pushing her cart, "let's finish this list and get out of here."

Hallie purses her lips, but she doesn't object. Instead, she moves to my daughter's side, helping her check the items off. I can't help but notice that Hallie's pile of items is lacking, so I end up adding a few things to my pile that I know she likes.

And for a minute, I let myself think about how this scene looks from the outside. A family doing their weekly shopping. My hands tighten on the cart handle. It's a damn good scene.

Too bad it's not real.

After a while, Hallie falls back to my side. "Did something happen between you and Ethan? You seemed a little...irritated back there."

I sigh. "It's nothing. He brought up Luke, and I'm just...sick of all my conversations with people revolving around my brother." *And I hate the fact that he liked you back in high school.* "I've always been compared to him, but working in his shadow has somehow made it worse."

"And you want to shine on your own," she says.

"I don't need to *shine*." I shake my head. "I'm not looking for glory or anything. It'd be nice to be seen as me first, instead of Luke's brother first. That's all."

"Are you gonna say yes?" she asks. "To Ethan's offer?"

"You think I should?"

Hallie shrugs. "You kind of lit up when he mentioned search and rescue. And...I don't know, you've never seemed that enthusiastic about being a firefighter." She glances at me, a blush rising in her cheeks. "But what do I know? I've been gone a long time."

"And you still know me better than anyone else." She blushes harder. Even after all this time, that pink colour remains my favourite. "I'm not sure. Leaving the department..."

Hallie sets her hand on top of mine. "It's hard when you're a legacy," she says. "But you owe it to yourself to consider all the opportunities you're given, not just the ones you think Luke or your dad want you to take."

How do you admit that maybe you made a mistake? That the path you're on isn't the one you want to be walking? I don't necessarily regret following in my dad's and brother's footsteps, but if I were given the choice to do it all over again, I'm not sure that I would.

"I'll think about it," I finally say.

She smiles. "Whatever you end up deciding, I support. Not that you need my approval or—"

"Hallie." She looks up at me expectantly. "Thank you. I might not *need* it, but your opinion matters to me."

We turn out of the aisle, and Abbie starts leading us toward the cash. Hallie's phone pings, and she digs it out of her purse. I watch the expression on her face as she reads the screen. It's a mixture of excitement and nerves.

"Good news?" I ask.

She looks up to find me watching her. "It's Kevin. He invited me—well, I guess *us*—to dinner at his house on Saturday." She chews on her lower lip. "Are you still alright with...*you know?*"

We both glance at Abbie, but she's too busy looking through the Halloween candy on display to listen to our conversation. Hallie and I agreed to keep the engagement talk to a minimum around her. Especially after I set Abbie straight—that just because Hallie is living with us, it doesn't mean we're getting married like her mom and Chris—I don't want to confuse her.

"Yeah," I reply. "Saturday works for me."

To be truthful, I'm not in any rush to meet the guy that's supposed to be her dad. I know his experience with cancer gave him a different outlook on life and made him realize the errors of his ways, so he claims, but him skipping out in the first place is unforgivable to me. Doesn't matter what I think, though. This is about Hallie.

And for whatever reason, she wants to give Kevin a chance. If she needs me to pretend in order to feel more comfortable, then of course I will.

"Thank you," she says softly.

I shrug. "That's what I'm here for."

Her eyes sparkle in amusement. "You mean to tell me you have prior experience with fake betrothals?"

"No." I shake my head with a grin. "You're getting the Hallie Foster Special."

She ducks her head at that, trying to hide her flustered expression.

At the register, Hallie loads her groceries onto the belt first. Abbie grabs the plastic divider and slaps it down, then starts adding the items I hand her.

When I glance up, I find Gordon watching us from near the front doors. I fight a scowl.

"I swear, he's only gotten grumpier since I've been gone," Hallie says, eyeing the store manager. "I wonder why he's so miserable."

"Maybe he's sad," Abbie offers. "Sometimes people are mean because they don't know how to say they're sad."

You never truly know if you're doing a good job as a parent, but moments like these remind me that Larissa and I must be doing something right. The fact that she can empathize with someone like Gordon makes me proud.

I wrap an arm around Abbie's shoulders, hugging her to my side. "You're absolutely right."

Maybe this is my sign to cut Hallie's father some slack, too. He's obviously trying to set things right, and while that will never erase the pain Hallie was caused before, she deserves a good relationship with at least one of her parents. If Amanda can't be that for her, maybe Kevin can.

We make idle chitchat with the cashier as he rings up our purchases. Then we load them back in the cart and head for the doors.

As we pass by the manager, Abbie waves. "Have a good night, Mr. Gordon!"

The grouchy look on his face transforms into one of shock. I bite back a smile. *That's right. Try banning my kid from the store now. I dare you.*

"Did you see that?" Hallie asks once we're outside. She pushes the cart so I can hold Abbie's hand in the parking lot. "You totally threw him off."

Abbie beams, swinging our joined hands. "Maybe now he'll be happy more."

I don't think Gordon will be changing his entire outlook on life after one interaction with my six-year-old, but it's a start.

"You never know how being kind might turn someone's day around," Hallie says. "And it makes you feel good, too."

"I like feeling good," Abbie says with a nod.

When we get to my truck, I start loading the groceries in, and Hallie helps Abbie into her seat. My daughter takes the opportunity to regale Hallie with the story of the made-up game she and some friends played at recess this morning. And Hallie listens to it all with a smile, asking questions when it's appropriate.

My old feelings for Hallie don't need any help resurfacing, but if they did, watching the way she interacts with Abbie would be enough. She doesn't treat her like an annoying kid who's just hanging around; she treats her like a full-fledged person who's curious about the world.

Hallie loves my daughter, and I love her.

FIFTEEN

HALLIE

TWELVE YEARS AGO

GROW UP, *Hallie. Stop being a wimp.*

No matter how many times I tell myself to stop being afraid, it doesn't work. My brain won't let go of the memories. It was nine years ago now when that tree smashed into our house, but it feels so *recent* every time a branch scrapes against my window.

I squeeze my eyes shut as another bout of thunder rolls in. The wind is howling, and I can hear the trees swaying. Panic grips me. Pops is fast asleep down the hall, just like everyone else in this town. With nothing to distract me, I'm left sitting here in the lamplight, waiting for the storm to pass.

On my nightstand, my phone buzzes. For one, shining moment, I forget about the roaring wind. And when I see Gabe's name on my screen, my heart trips over itself.

GABRIEL

you awake?

I stare at the words, thinking of a response. A whole five minutes goes by before I work up the courage to text back.

> Yes. :(What's up?

Lame. That is literally the lamest thing I could have said. *Ugh.* Gabe is going to—

GABRIEL

> can I call you?

To this, I don't waste a second saying yes. My heart is firmly in my throat now. Then my phone buzzes in my hand again, and I hit the button to accept.

"Hello?" I whisper. It's unnecessary—it would take a lot more than me talking at a normal volume to wake Pops from a dead sleep.

"Hi," Gabe says. "What do you want to be when you grow up?"

I can't help but laugh. "Um, a teacher?" At least, that's the program I plan to apply to university for.

Gabe groans on the other end of the line. "Everyone else has things figured out, and I don't."

I roll onto my side, curling one hand beneath my chin as the other holds my phone to my ear. "That's not true."

"Isn't it? Clara wants to take over Dockside, you want to be a teacher. Connor's basically already signed on to the fire department. Luke was the same when he was our age."

"What about those career aptitude tests we took at school last year? What did yours say?"

"Some bullshit like a lawyer or a dentist. I wasn't really paying attention."

"Gabriel!"

He laughs, and my heart flutters. It's one of my favourite sounds. "I don't think those tests are accurate anyway. Or maybe they are. Who knows. I was a little distracted that term."

"Oh, yeah? And what was this distraction that kept you from your studies?"

"There was this girl who sat in the chair beside me," he says, and I can hear the smile in his voice. "Maybe you know her. Blonde hair that falls halfway down her back, bright blue eyes. She's always blushing, and her nose crinkles in the cutest way when she's confused."

My cheeks grow hot, and my heart begins to thump wildly. Dangerously. I feel like I'm always on the verge of cardiac arrest around Gabe. But what a way to go.

Poor girl. She was only sixteen, but her heart couldn't handle such a big crush.

"Hmm, I don't know. She sounds kinda boring."

"No way. She always steals my attention."

I bite my lip against a smile. "Ah, so she's a thief."

"Yeah, but I don't mind. I'd give her anything she asked for."

I feel like I'm floating. We've talked like this before, but tonight feels...different.

What would Clara think? If she knew Gabe and I are having a secret phone call in the middle of the night. We're not doing anything wrong, technically, yet the familiar worry begins to set in.

She wouldn't like this. You can't be with her brother. She loves her brother. She wouldn't want you to hurt him.

Quickly, I come crashing back to reality. Another crack of thunder, followed by tree branches scraping the side of the house, has me letting out a small whimper.

"Foster? You okay?"

"Yeah," I reply. My voice comes out a little breathless. "I just stubbed my toe."

The last thing Gabe needs to know is exactly how much of a baby I am. Sixteen years old and still scared of the wind. It's totally irrational. Nothing like what happened when I was seven has happened again. I need to get over it.

"Damn, that rain is really coming down out there," he says. "I wonder if we'll lose power."

That panic is back. *God, I hope not.* The one thing that would make this situation worse is darkness. It was dark the night that tree came through my window. It was dark, and I was all alone.

"Maybe," I say weakly.

Thankfully, Gabe changes the subject back to something safer. "Should I be a firefighter?" he asks. "My dad has mentioned it."

"If you want to. Because that's the cool thing. You can do anything you want."

"*Anything* is too many things."

"Well, despite what you think, *I* think it's okay that you don't know yet. You're only sixteen. You've got time. We don't graduate for another couple years."

He sighs. "What's it like being so smart all the time?"

I giggle. "Stop it. You're smart."

"Maybe, but not school smart. I can't stand that place."

That's true. Gabe has never looked more miserable than sitting through math class last semester. He likes to *do* things, work with his hands.

I think about telling him he should look into some kind of skilled trade when the yawn hits me. I try to hide it, but it can't be disguised.

"Sorry. I should let you get some sleep," Gabe says. "Goodnig—"

"Wait!"

"Yeah?"

I squeeze my eyes shut, my cheeks flaming. At least he can't see me. "Would you stay on the phone for a bit?" I ask. "Just until I fall asleep."

"Of course," he says. Because Gabriel Bowman is too kind for his own good. "Anything particular you want me to talk about?"

"No," I say. "Tell me anything. I just want to hear your voice."

So he does. He tells me about Connor's newest obsession with starting a band, even though he can't carry a tune to save his life. He complains about the five-page essay he has to write for his English class. After a while, I can't even distinguish what he's talking about. All I know is the sound of his voice is soothing as my eyes droop.

The storm fades into the background as my breathing evens out.

I can't be sure, but before I fall asleep completely, I swear I hear him say, "Man, I really like you, Foster."

I really like you, too.

SIXTEEN

HALLIE

I'VE NEVER BEEN MORE terrified of dropping a pie plate in my life. A pie I didn't even make.

It wasn't hard to convince Maggie to help me with the apple pie, but the whole time I was at Haven House with her, guilt churned in my stomach. Because I was *lying*, and using her son to do it. Sure, I wasn't lying to *her*, but I also wasn't being outright about Gabe pretending to be my fiancé. About him coming with me to the dinner that requires this pie.

"You ready?" Gabe asks beside me.

I take a deep breath, then nod. "Ready."

Or not. But it's too late. Gabe has already rung the doorbell, and Kevin is already standing in the threshold, a cautiously optimistic smile on his face.

"Hi," I say. "I brought pie!"

Tone it down seven hundred notches, Hallie. You sound like you sucked on a balloon full of helium.

"Looks delicious," Kevin says. "Come on in."

Gabe and I step inside, and then we do the awkward shuffle of removing our shoes and shedding our jackets. Somewhere along the way, the pie transfers to Kevin, and I realize I have nothing left to hold on to for support.

"It's nice to meet you," Kevin says, holding out a hand. The other safely holds the pie. "You must be Gabriel."

Gabe returns his handshake. He's wearing a button-up, but he has the sleeves rolled up, which means his tattoos are on full display. "Gabe is fine. Nice to meet you, too."

Kevin gestures to the woman standing off to the side. She's tall and slender, dressed in slacks and a cashmere sweater. Her light brown hair, threaded with some grey, is fastened into a neat chignon. Her lipstick complements her fair skin.

"This is my wife, Dana."

I offer her a sheepish smile. Awkward tension hangs in the air. Still, I push through it. I want to make this work, so I exchange pleasantries with her.

"And your daughter?" Dana asks Gabe.

"She's at her mom's house this week," he replies.

And thank goodness for that. I love spending time with Abbie, but the last thing I want is to drag her into this mess. It's bad enough I've got her dad tangled up in my web of deceit.

My eyes drop down to my hands. There, they latch on to the ring on my left hand. Cubic zirconia looks surprisingly real—if you don't look too closely. But I don't have the money to waste on a real ring, and I certainly wasn't going to ask Gabe to get me one.

I know you're already lying to strangers on my behalf, but can you buy me a diamond ring, too?

"Can I get you both a drink?" Kevin asks.

Gabe sets a hand on the small of my back. "I'm alright with water," he says. "Foster?"

"Hmm?" My head snaps up. "Oh, I'm good with water, too. Thank you."

While Kevin heads to the kitchen, Dana leads us into the living room. Scratch that, a *sitting* room. There doesn't seem to be much life in here.

The furniture is pristine, as if it were delivered from the store today. Merely stepping into the room feels like an affront to it. I might have even retreated if not for Gabe's steady presence at my side, his hand guiding me forward.

Gabe and I sit side by side on a tan-coloured love seat, leaving the couch for Dana and Kevin.

"You have a lovely home," I say to Dana, to break the awkward silence. Everything about this situation is *awkward*.

"Thank you," she replies. "We were lucky it came on the market when it did. Serendipitous that we were leaving Kip Island at the time."

Her gaze couldn't be more pointed if it tried. My stomach drops. Clearly, I don't have a friend in Dana. But can I even blame her? I'm the product of her husband's affair. It can't be easy having to interact with me. I'm nothing more than a reminder of a painful period in her life, one I'm sure she thought was far behind her.

Thankfully, Kevin returns swiftly with our waters. He sets them on coasters on the glass coffee table, where they already have glasses of wine. I reach for mine, taking a wobbly sip. Then I clench my fingers around the cup to stop them from shaking.

From the front hall, the sound of the door opening echoes. Three voices carry through the rooms, and I stiffen in preparation.

They round the corner into the sitting room, stopping short. Two women and one man. Instantly, I recognize the blonde woman and the man as siblings. They look alike, and they both resemble Kevin enough for me to know who they are. The second woman, with tight black curls and umber skin, is holding the blonde's hand.

"Hallie, Gabe," Kevin says, "this is Bryan and Caitlyn. And Caitlyn's fiancée, Amara."

Amara offers me a smile, but my half siblings are studying me. I fight the urge to squirm. They're both a few years older than me, and for a brief flash of a second, I wonder if this feeling is what it would've been like if I'd grown up with them.

Constant scrutiny because of the decisions made by their dad and my mom.

I swallow. "Hi."

Caitlyn is the first to approach. Her smile is a little unsure, but it puts me somewhat at ease. "Hi," she says. "I really love your hair."

I relax a fraction. "Oh, uh, thank you."

"The food should be about ready," Kevin says. "We can head to the dining room."

The dining room that turns out to be equally as fancy as the living room we were just in.

As the food gets passed around, I begin to realize something. Almost everything has some kind of meat in it. Even the Caesar salad. The bacon bits aren't those artificial ones either. They're real, crispy pieces of bacon.

"Honey, where is the quiche?" Kevin asks. "Hallie doesn't eat meat."

"Oh, *gosh*," Dana says. She shakes her head forlornly, looking anything but sincere. "I'm so sorry, I forgot to make it. It totally slipped my mind."

Beside me, Gabe goes rigid. It appears her tone isn't lost on him either. He tightens his grip on his fork as he looks over at me, a silent question in his eyes. I set a hand on his knee, giving it a quick squeeze.

"That's okay," I say with a small smile. "I can stick with salad."

I'll have to eat around the bits of bacon, but it's fine. I don't want to cause a scene. It's not a big deal anyway. It's just food, and I have options. It's not like I'm going to starve. Besides, it isn't like I *can't* eat meat. I'm not allergic. I've just been opposed since one of my teachers showed us a documentary about beef production in elementary school.

"I'm sorry, Hallie," Kevin says with a frown.

"It's really alright. I'm super easy."

Dana offers me a razor sharp smile. "Of course you are."

Gabe shifts in his seat, looking even more agitated. It takes me a moment to register what just happened—the double entendre—and then I blush furiously.

Caitlyn sends me an apologetic look, but she doesn't say anything. Bryan stares at his plate.

Beneath the table, Gabe takes my hand, forcing my attention to him. I'm thankful for it—it gives me a second to collect myself after Dana's verbal jab.

She's uncomfortable. My presence makes her uncomfortable. And when people are uncomfortable, they lash out.

Kevin clears his throat.

"So," Caitlyn says, changing the topic, "you can say no, but Amara and I have been talking, and we'd like you and Gabe to come to our wedding in a couple weeks."

My mouth pops open. I notice Dana is wearing a similar expression, which means this is news to her, too.

I fiddle with my napkin. "That's very kind. Are you sure? I don't..." *Want to ruin anything.*

My half sister nods, a small smile on her lips. "Yes. I know it's short notice, so it's alright if you can't or don't want to. But I thought I'd offer." She glances at Kevin, then turns back to me. "We've all missed out on so much, and I don't want to miss any more."

You're a terrible person, Hallie. She's so sweet, and you're so awful. How can you sit here and lie to her face? Lie to all of them.

"I'll be there," I say. "I'm not sure about Gabe's work schedule, but—"

"I'll make it work," he declares. Because he knows going alone would be too much for me.

The guilt sinks its claws in deeper. But of course, I won't refuse his help.

"Perfect." Caitlyn smiles fully now. "I'll get your number from Dad and send you the details."

Her casual use of *Dad* throws me off, and I'm unable to form a reply.

"How did you two meet?" Gabe asks her, saving me. Always saving me.

Amara smiles, and Caitlyn's eyes dance. They both look so happy and in love. For a moment, I'm envious, but I stuff those feelings down. I don't want to feel any bad emotions toward my half sister. It's certainly not her fault I messed things up with Gabe and haven't been able to move on since.

"We were assigned as roommates when we were both in residence our first year at Queen's," Amara replies. "We got along well and became friends, but we went our separate ways after graduation."

"Then by chance, three years ago, we were both attending the same work conference," Caitlyn continues. "We spent all our free time together that weekend, and the rest is history."

"What about you?" Amara asks us.

Oh, God. I begin to sweat a little. Of all the things I thought about, I didn't think to create a cover story. How stupid.

"My sister claims Hallie as her best friend," Gabe says, "but I like to think she was mine first."

Mine, mine, mine. The word plays on a loop in my head.

My gaze swings to him, trying to catch his eye. I have no idea where he's going with this.

"We met the first day of kindergarten. Clara, my twin sister, was sick the first week, so I had Hallie all to myself. That quickly changed when Clara came to school, but Hallie was always there as we grew up. She moved to Toronto when we were eighteen, and we lost touch. She was never far from my mind, though." He turns to me, a soft smile on his lips. "I tried to move forward, and I did for a while. We both did. But when she came back to Kip Island, it was like no time at all had passed."

They say a good lie is rooted in truth, but I hate hearing these words pass his lips. Because while Gabe has my father and his family fooled, I think he may have me fooled, too. I want so badly to believe him. Believe he means what he says.

But he didn't tell them how I broke his heart.

"That's so sweet," Caitlyn gushes, hand on her chest.

"Do you have any wedding plans yet?" Kevin asks.

"Not yet." I can feel my smile wobbling, but I hold on to it for dear life. "We're enjoying being engaged for now."

Until my lie has run its course.

"Well, when the time comes, I'm here if you need any tips. Mom and I spent *months* ironing everything out for ours," Caitlyn says.

My stomach twists, and I'm struck with how sisterly her offer feels. How badly I wish I could actually take her up on it, for no other reason than to know what it feels like to have an older sister giving me advice. Maybe one day, I'll be engaged for real, and have an actual wedding.

It just won't be with Gabe.

The conversation shifts then. Bryan talks a bit about his work as a veterinarian, and my siblings and father ask Gabe what it's like working for the fire department. I know that part is nice for Gabe. They have no idea who his brother is, so the conversation doesn't get pulled in that direction for once.

I try to engage as much as possible, but it's hard when I feel Dana's eyes boring into me, and the weight of my lies threaten to bury me.

You don't have to lie forever. Just a little while longer.

SEVENTEEN

GABE

SILENCE SUFFOCATES us as soon as we get in the truck. That dinner was something else. I'm trying not to judge, but *fuck*, Dana made that hard not to do.

I kept my mouth shut because I know Hallie wouldn't have wanted me to start anything. But there were a few times I almost snapped. I know Hallie wants to get to know these people. I just wish they wouldn't treat her like shit. As far as I'm concerned, them not standing up to Dana is just as bad as what Dana said and did.

Once I'm sure Hallie has her seatbelt on, I peel away from the curb. The sooner we get home, the better. Then I can try to undo whatever damage has been done tonight.

Except when I hear her sniffle a couple minutes later, I instantly pull over again. I can't stand to have her burying her emotions.

"Foster, look at me." She refuses, continuing to stare out the window. I hear another sniffle, and my heart cracks. "Hallie, *please.*"

Finally, she lifts her head. The streetlights shining through the windshield illuminate the tears lining her lashes. As far as I can tell, none have fallen yet, but they shouldn't even be there in the first place.

My fists tighten in my lap. I want to reach for her, comfort her. Only, I'm not sure I'd be able to let go if I did.

"I'm okay, Gabe," she says. Her smile is sad.

"I'm sorry things went the way they did," I say. "But you handled that well. I'm proud of you."

Her smile instantly drops. "You shouldn't be. I'm a liar."

Fuck it. I reach across the centre console, taking her hand in mine. She looks a little startled at the gesture—maybe because there's no one to pretend in front of right now—but she doesn't pull away.

"I'm proud of you for doing something outside your comfort zone. For being kind enough to give Kevin this second chance, despite how much his absence has hurt you."

With her free hand, she covers her face, hiding herself. Always hiding from me. "This night was such a *disaster*. Dana clearly hates me. So I'm not sure it matters much if I'm willing to give this a shot."

I could tell her to forget about them all. They don't deserve to know her—not if they won't cherish her. But if I did that, I'd be no better than everyone else in Hallie's life who has ignored her needs.

"It does matter. Dana aside, Caitlyn and Bryan seem like they want to get to know you. Kevin clearly does. If this is what you want, keep going." I stroke the back of her hand with my thumb. "Having siblings can be a pain in the ass, but you deserve to decide that for yourself."

She lets out half a laugh at that, finally uncovering her face. "Your siblings are great." She squeezes my hand, and I let go. "Thank you for coming with me. I'm not sure I would have made it through without you."

"You would have, because you're stronger than you give yourself credit for. But I'm happy I could make things a little easier for you."

She checks the time on the dash. "Let's get back. There should be another ferry soon."

Instead of driving away, I pull out my phone and make a quick search. Once I've found what I'm looking for, I put the truck in drive again and pull away from the curb. Hallie doesn't seem to notice that I'm not heading in the direction of Tobermory.

When I pull into a parking spot, she looks to me in confusion. "What are we doing here?"

I unbuckle my seatbelt, then reach across to unclick hers. "We're getting you food. I'm not letting you go to sleep hungry."

She shakes her head. "It's fine, Gabe. It's getting late. I'll make a peanut butter sandwich or something when we get back."

I scoff, opening my door. "You're not eating a peanut butter sandwich for dinner, and I'm not asking. Ass out of the truck, Foster."

With an adorable little huff, she jumps down and follows me across the parking lot. A bell above the door chimes as we enter the restaurant. Though it isn't as much of a restaurant as it is a small shack known for its burgers and fries. According to their website, they have vegetarian and vegan options, too.

Hallie's eyes scan the menu board hungrily, and I know I made the right call. My girl needs to eat. Something more substantial than a picked-over Caesar salad.

"Hey, what can I get for you?" the teen standing behind the register asks.

Hallie steps forward, telling him what she wants. He rings it up. Then before she can pull her wallet out, I slip a twenty into the guy's hand.

"Gabe," she hisses. "You need to stop doing that!"

I grin. "Never."

Once he counts out my change, the employee directs us to sit at a table. There is only a few of them, so pickings are slim. I hold a hand out, letting Hallie lead the way. She shakes her head, a disapproving frown on her face.

"I'm going to pay you back," she declares as I settle across from her. "For this and the funnel cake."

"No, you're not."

"*Yes*, I am." She crosses her arms.

"Then I'll just keep finding more things to buy for you."

She throws her arms up. "*Why?* You already refuse to let me pay a fair amount of rent."

I'd charge her nothing if I thought I could get away with it.

Leaning back in my seat, I let an amused smile settle on my lips. She's cute when she tries to be angry. "Because I like to make you smile."

Some of the fight leaves her then, and her eyes soften. "You're sweet. Too sweet for your own good."

"What kind of fiancé would I be if I wasn't?"

She sighs at that, and I instantly wish I could take my words back. I'm trying to make her less sad, but that ring she's wearing keeps drawing my attention. It's not real, I know. But it damn well looks like it could be.

"The fake kind," she replies. Then she twists the ring off her finger and deposits it in her pocket.

The employee appears at our table, setting a plate in front of Hallie. I'm not too keen on the idea of veggie burgers, but even I have to admit, it smells good. The sweet potato fries heaped beside it do, too.

Reaching out, I steal a fry off her plate and dip it in the cup of chipotle before popping it in my mouth.

She gasps. "Thief!"

I grin. "The fries are good."

She glares at me, but it has no real heat. "I wouldn't know. I haven't had the chance to taste them yet." She picks up a fry and lets out a satisfied hum at the taste. "Are you just going to look at me while I eat?"

I shrug. "Maybe. It's a damn good view."

Her cheeks turn pink, and she ducks her head.

"So." I lean on the table. "I never asked before, but...what made you come back home?"

Hallie looks down at the cup of sauce in her hand. "I was nannying for a family in the city. I'd been with them for a couple years by then. It wasn't my dream job or anything, but it paid the bills." She shrugs, looking up at me. "Then one of the dads changed jobs a few months ago, and they decided they no longer needed a nanny. The kids are older now, so..."

My brows raise. "They fired you?"

She tips her head side to side. "Not in so many words. They gave me time to find something else, and they gave me a generous payout at the end. But once I stopped working for them, I realized I felt a little...lost. I had for a while. And when my job search in the city was proving fruitless, I decided maybe it was time to come back."

"Do you regret it?"

I'm not sure why I ask. Maybe because I need to know she's not entirely miserable, being here with me. Because I'm the furthest from miserable when I'm with her.

She shakes her head, a soft smile on her lips. "No, I don't think I do."

"Good." Needing something to do with my hands, I grab the salt shaker and spin it between my fingers. "You said you were nannying. What happened to that teaching program?"

"I graduated, but finding a permanent job was hard. Lots of subbing. Then one day, I realized I actually kind of hated it." She laughs, and I smile. "It wasn't the kids. As hard as they can be sometimes, I loved working with them. It was more so the school environment I wasn't a fan of. Nannying seemed like a logical step."

"And did you like the nannying gig?"

"Much more than the teaching gig. I mean, I helped them with homework and stuff, so it was kinda like teaching. But being in a home setting was much more relaxed and comfortable for me. It made me more comfortable around kids in general."

I keep spinning the salt shaker. "You're great with Abbie. She loves you."

I don't miss the way her eyes light up at the mention of my daughter, and that sits on my chest, making it hard to breathe. The few times I've thought about dating, settling down with someone, I knew she'd have to be the right kind of person. The kind who adored my kid almost as much as I do. Hallie certainly does.

"I love her," she says. "She's so funny, and I love the way she sees the world. And she's so caring. You and Larissa are great parents, Gabe. I've always thought you'd make a great dad."

Emotions I can't quite explain wash over me. A mix of pride and feeling validated, maybe. "Thank you. I figured I'd have a family one day. Didn't exactly expect it to start the way it did, but I wouldn't change it for anything."

A comfortable silence settles between us as Hallie continues to eat. It feels familiar, the way it used to be when we were teenagers. We're far from the people we were then, but I catch glimpses every so often that remind me of a time when it was just me and her, and an infinite amount of possibilities.

"What do you want to be when you grow up?"

Hallie laughs as she swipes another fry through her chipotle. "What?"

I nudge her free hand. "Don't think about it too hard. What do you want to be?"

Her lips purse. "Content," she finally says. "I want to be content."

"You deserve that." And so much more.

"Your turn, then. What do you want to be?"

I remember back in high school, it felt like whatever path you set for yourself then was the one you'd be walking for the rest of your life. Like you had to have everything figured out at eighteen.

But as I creep closer to thirty, I can confidentially say that's bullshit.

"I don't know yet," I reply.

Hallie's expression is warm. Gentle. "That used to scare you."

Does she remember that night I called her at sixteen, worrying I wouldn't amount to anything meaningful? Because I do. I stayed on the phone until she fell asleep, talking about nothing of importance. I knew she was scared of storms back then, but I hadn't known the extent of her fears. I don't think she realizes how much she helped me that night, too.

"I'm learning to be okay with it."

Hallie finishes her food just as the employees start mopping up, getting ready to close. We clear off the table and head outside, where the air has grown noticeably colder. Hallie laughs as she hurries to the passenger side of my truck, tugging on the handle while she shivers. I unlock it, and she slips inside the cab.

When I'm seated beside her, she turns to me. "Thanks for feeding me. You're...a really good friend, Gabe."

Friend. There's that fucking word again.

I swallow my distaste, but I tell her truthfully, "I'd do just about anything for you, Foster."

And I would. More than I want her to be mine, I want Hallie to be happy. So if I have to pretend to be her fiancé or find a way to wrangle the stars into submission just so she can see them up close, I'll do it with a smile.

EIGHTEEN

HALLIE

CAITLYN

Here are the wedding details! Seriously no pressure, but I'd love to have you there.

THE GALLERY IS SO QUIET, I can hear the clock ticking on the wall. I worry my bottom lip as my thumb hovers over my keyboard. I've typed ten messages and deleted them all.

As it turns out, figuring out what to text your half sister who you just met for the first time the night before is no easy task. I tend to overthink on a good day, but right now? I'm way out of my element. I need a step-by-step guide, but unfortunately, I don't think one exists.

The sound of the front door opening startles me. I quickly lock my phone and set it aside. I'll force myself to reply later, when I can read the message a hundred times to check for embarrassing typos.

A moment later, a redheaded woman steps inside. I don't recognize her, so she's either a tourist or someone that has moved to the island in the last ten years. My guess is tourist—one of the last of the season, now that we're closing in on November.

"Hi," she says when she sees me. "I'm looking for some post-cards. Do you have any?"

Definitely a tourist.

I take a breath, putting on the mask I wear when interacting with customers. It's me, only not. This version of Hallie is much more outgoing, and by the time I get home after work, I'm exhausted from having to maintain it.

"I think so," I reply, stepping around the counter to enter the shop space. "I'm new, so I'm still learning where everything is. But I'm pretty sure Carole keeps them over there."

I show her the rack of postcards that feature both illustrations and photos of the lighthouse and the wildlife you can find in the area. Carole has curated a broad selection of local artists and photographers, including some Anishinaabe friends of hers from Manitoulin Island, a neighbouring island on Lake Huron. I'm sure she'll convince Delilah to add her photography to the mix before long.

I point to a postcard with the lighthouse on it. "This one is my favourite."

The customer smiles as she takes one off the rack. Then she gestures to me. "That's a beautiful ring."

My eyes snap to hers, then down to my left hand. *Crap.* I was so tired, I forgot to take the fake engagement ring off last night. After we got back to the house, I slipped it back on so it wouldn't accidentally get put through the wash in the pocket of my pants. It should probably worry me how natural it feels to wear, even knowing what it represents.

"Oh, um, thank you," I mumble.

She laughs. "I sometimes forget, too," she says, mistaking my alarm for surprise. "My husband and I got married two months ago, but I still find myself calling him my fiancé. When did you get engaged?"

Double crap. Either I keep lying or I backtrack and make both of us feel awkward. At this point, the only way is through.

"Uh, last week. The ring is...very new," I say, then chuckle nervously. "You're right, I'm still getting used to it."

Thankfully, I'm saved from the conversation and a steadily growing pile of more lies when the door opens again. This time, a man steps inside, and he makes a beeline for the woman.

"There you are," he says. "I thought you were going to the post office?"

"Sorry, baby," she says with a sheepish smile. "I saw this place and thought I'd try my luck here. Look." She holds up a few postcards. "I think Sam would like this one, and this is *perfect* for Opal and Thiago. I also found these for Jamie and Mia, and Nate and Paige. Do you think we should send one to Margaret?"

He chuckles. "Hadley, all she'd do is wonder why the hell you wasted a stamp on her."

Hadley grins. "That's true, she would. We should send it anyway." She turns back to me. "We'll buy these."

I take her back to the counter and ring up the handful of postcards. As she pays, I slide them into a protective envelope.

"Thank you," I say, handing over the receipt. "I hope you have a good rest of your trip."

"Thanks! This island is so cute. The downtown reminds me a little of home. If you and your fiancé ever find yourselves in BC, we'd love to have you in Sugar Peak," she says. "I manage a ski resort there, and Brooks owns the bar in town."

As soon as Hadley and Brooks leave, I let my head sink into my hands. I highly doubt I'll ever end up on a trip across the country with Gabe. As it is, it'll be a miracle if he doesn't hate me by the time this engagement charade is through.

As I stew, the metal of my ring brushes against my cheek, and I pick my head up. It slips easily from my finger, and I shove it into my purse. Maybe if I can't see it, I'll be able to forget the guilt. Until I have to put it on again.

When the door opens for a third time a few minutes later, I find myself dreading having to interact with more strangers. Or worse, locals. All this lying is making my stomach churn, and it feels like I'm living a double life. To Kevin and his family, I'm happily engaged. To the people of Kip Island, I'm the woman who couldn't hack it out in the big, bad world and had to come running home.

Briefly, I thought maybe everything in my life was going to click into place. I'd come back here and find my footing. Now I know that was just an illusion. Because everything is messier than before, and I have no idea how to make it *un*messy.

Thankfully, I'm able to release a small sigh of relief when I find Carole standing in front of me.

"Hi, Buttercup," she says. "You doing alright? You look a little sad."

I take a deep breath, then paste on a smile. "I'm okay, just tired. How are you? I didn't think I'd see you today."

"I'm just peachy! But listen, I have a small proposition for you."

This makes me somewhat wary. Carole's *proposition* could be anything. "Yeah? What is it?"

"I have some friends who are looking to commission a painting. Their mom is heading to a nursing home, and they want to gift her something to give her comfort. A painting of her childhood home." Her head cocks as she assesses me. "Do you think you'd be up for it?"

I blink. "*Me*?"

Carole laughs. "Don't sound so shocked, Hallie." She taps her temple. "I remember exactly how talented you are."

I've never aspired to turn my art into a career. It has always been something that is simply for me. A way for me to express myself—something my mother couldn't touch or taint. That hasn't changed, but for the right circumstances, I don't mind creating for someone else.

"I'll do it," I tell her. "But I don't want to be paid."

Carole takes one of my hands between both of hers. "You are a gem on this earth, Buttercup. Don't forget that."

If only she knew the truth.

———

As the day drags on, the temperature begins to dip and the sky turns grey. After locking up the gallery and starting my walk to Gabe's house, the rain begins. Thankfully, it's just a sprinkle, so it doesn't soak into my clothes too much. Still, I find myself shivering as I draw my sweater tighter around my body. Summer is firmly in the rear view now, and it won't be back for at least the next seven months.

I don't mind, though. I've always loved the fall. There's something about the changing leaves and the cooler temperatures that comfort me. The guesthouse has become my favourite place lately, in part because I've been working on it, but also because it's nestled amongst the colourful trees at the back of Gabe's property.

When an Audi slows and comes to a stop beside me, I look over. The window rolls down, and Delilah leans over the centre console. "Want a ride?" she asks.

It takes me a second, but I nod. I don't know Delilah all that well yet, but I already know I like her. Her personality feels like a balance between mine and Clara's, and it's easy to see how much Luke loves her.

Quickly, I open the passenger door and slide inside her car, trying not to let the rain in. The heat is on, and I relish the warmth as I buckle my seatbelt.

"Thanks for this," I say.

She smiles as she puts the car in gear. "It's no problem. I'm passing by anyway. Did you just get off work?"

"Yeah, Carole asked me to work a little extra this week because she got a big order for some art prints." Along with selling art, the gallery also has the means to print out customers' pictures and wrap canvasses. It's the island's one-stop shop for art and photography of any kind, essentially.

"Oops, that's my fault. I'm trying to make our house feel more like *ours*, so I've decided to start a gallery wall in the living room." She grimaces. "The only problem is, I can't decide what prints to use until I see them all in the space. Luke tried to help, but he just doesn't have the vision, you know?"

I laugh. "Hey, I don't mind. More hours is a good thing for me."

As we continue to drive, the rain picks up, and Delilah's grip on the steering wheel tightens.

For a moment, I debate saying anything, but my concern wins out. "Are you okay?"

"Yeah." She takes a deep breath. "Rain freaks me out these days. I don't know how much Clara told you, but my parents died in a car accident last year. They hydroplaned."

"Oh my gosh, I'm so sorry," I say automatically. "You didn't have to go out of your way to drop me off! You probably want to get home."

Delilah shakes her head. "It's okay. Really. I'm trying to work through it. Can't avoid the rain for the rest of my life."

"Well, if you need to take a break, I don't mind. I'll wait. Storms are...tricky for me, too, sometimes."

She throws me an appreciative smile.

A couple minutes later, Delilah pulls into Gabe's driveway and puts the car in park. In the cup holder, her phone lights up with a text. I catch Luke's name on the screen.

She reaches for it as I brace myself to head into the onslaught. The relieved smile that stretches her lips makes me pause.

"Everything good?"

"Oh," she says, looking up. "Sorry. Luke was just checking in because of the weather. It helps me, knowing my people are safe."

My own phone chimes then. Looking at the screen, I see a text from Gabe.

GABRIEL

Need me to come get you? The rain is coming down pretty hard.

It's okay, I'm outside. Delilah gave me a ride.

The front door swings open a moment later, and Gabe fills the doorway. He waves to Delilah. She waves back.

"Looks like he's checking on his person, too," she says. Gone is the worry in her expression. Instead, I find something akin to mischief.

"What?" I squeak.

"You know, his person. His go-to. His girl—"

"I know what you mean, but that's not— We're not—" I cut myself off. "Gabe and I are friends."

She laughs. "I get it, Hallie. I'm sorry, I was just teasing."

My cheeks heat, but I offer her a smile so she knows I didn't take offence. "Thanks again for the ride."

"You're welcome." Delilah holds out her phone. "Here, give me your number. I'm surprised Clara hasn't added us to a group chat yet, but we can fix that."

I type my number in, then hand her phone back. A quick glance out the windshield shows the rain isn't letting up anytime soon. "Are you okay to get home? I'm sure Gabe wouldn't mind if you came inside for a bit."

She nods. "Thanks, but I'll be okay. I have to relieve Sophia's sitter anyway."

"Text me when you get there?" She agrees, and I throw open the door and step out. "See you later!"

As I hurry up the walkway toward the front door, toward Gabe, I decide maybe things aren't as bad as I thought. I may not have my life figured out, but at least I'm making a new friend. I had a few acquaintances in the city, but no one came close to Clara. I could see Delilah becoming equally as important to me, though.

"Hey," Gabe says, closing the door behind me, "how was work?"

For a second, I bask in the domesticity of this moment. It feels so *normal* to come home from a long day and find Gabe waiting for me. To have him ask me how my day was.

I want that.

"It was good," I reply. "Caitlyn texted me this morning. She gave me the wedding info."

"Do you still want to go?"

Slowly, I nod. "Yes, but...will you still come with me?"

The look Gabe gives me feels like a caress. "Of course I will. You don't even have to ask."

And I know that he means it. Gabe has always been like that—dependable. You couldn't want for anyone better to be in your life.

My stomach tightens with guilt. Because it's only a matter of time before I ruin things again.

NINETEEN

GABE

THERE IS nothing Kip Island loves more than Halloween. The township holds a house-decorating contest, and most residents observe it like they would any other important holiday. The island as a whole tends to go all out, and as a result, so does the fire station.

We've spent the past week decorating. Now that the big day is finally here, Connor and some of the other guys are going to hang out and hand out candy.

Despite how surly he can be at times, I have to hand it to my brother, he's good at community-building. Besides the obvious aspect of putting out fires, the fire department has many responsibilities, including public safety education. Luke's good at finding opportunities to make that happen without it feeling like school. I may get annoyed by his role at times, but I respect the hell out of him as my boss.

Poking my head into Luke's office, I say, "Hey, Connor's going to take my shift on the second. I'm going with Hallie to her half sister's wedding."

While my family doesn't know that Hallie and I have been pretending to be engaged, they're all aware of Kevin's recent presence in her life. And like me, they're a little wary. Whether she knows it or not, they've fully embraced Hallie as one of us, and that means their protectiveness extends to her, too.

"How's Hallie doing with all this?" my brother asks. Worry lines his brows. Though the expression isn't uncommon for him, it's nice to know that there are other people looking out for her, too.

I sigh. "It's a lot, but you know her. She's trying to focus on the good." Even if she has to set aside Dana's disdain to do it.

"And you're going to the wedding as her what? Date?" This time, there's a hint of a smile on Luke's lips.

"Her platonic plus-one," I say. "And what about it?"

He shrugs, returning his attention to his computer. "Nothing, just curious."

I shake my head. "You're a shit liar. If you're trying to get information so you can report back to Mom or Clara, you can fuck off."

Luke only chuckles, and I leave him to his paperwork. Outside the front of the station, I find Connor digging into a box of chocolates.

As I walk by, I pluck the mini Coffee Crisp out of his hand. "Save some for the kids, asshole."

He snatches the chocolate back and quickly unwraps it, stuffing it in his mouth. "Kids don't even like coffee," he says with his mouth full. "Ergo, they're free game. I've had, like, ten already."

"Don't come crying to me when you get a tummy ache, Lee," Jodi Booth, our deputy chief, calls.

Connor pats his stomach. "I've got intestines of steel, don't you worry."

She sends me a flat look. "I wasn't."

I grin as I help Connor finish setting out the candy. Luke certainly didn't skimp on the sweets this year. Knowing him, it's probably because Delilah and her sister will be swinging by.

"Daddy!"

Abbie comes running toward me, already dressed in her costume. I pick her up and spin her around before setting her on my hip.

"Where's Aunt Clara?" I ask. "You didn't leave her at home, did you?"

Abbie giggles. "No, silly. She's over there."

She points down the sidewalk. Clara, like Abbie, is dressed in some elaborate costume, complete with shiny wings. But I'm more drawn to the woman walking beside her. When my eyes settle on Hallie, my mouth runs dry. I'm not sure what she's supposed to be dressed up as, but whatever it is, I am a fan.

Her dark purple dress is long, the hem hitting her ankles, and the sleeves flare out at her wrists. The bust is fitted, and it's cut low enough at the front to give a hint of cleavage.

Fuck, she's pretty.

When Clara and Hallie reach us, Clara sets a crown made of flowers on Abbie's head. "There, now you're complete."

"Guess my costume, Daddy!" Abbie demands. She and my sister have been scheming for months now, and they both refused to tell me what they picked. Even Larissa doesn't know.

I make a show of inspecting her pink dress and multicoloured wings that resemble stained glass. Clara must have spent hours making them. "Hm. A butterfly?"

She giggles again. "No! Me and Sophia are *fairies*! We've got matching dresses. And Clary is the fairy grandmother."

"*God*mother," my sister corrects. She taps Abbie's nose with the tip of her flower wand. "And Abbs and Soph are my protégés."

Behind me, Luke comes out of the station. He waves to Clara and Hallie before crossing the parking lot to greet Delilah and Sophia, who have just pulled up in Delilah's car. Sophia is wearing a dress identical to my daughter's, and Delilah appears to be dressed as Wednesday Addams, the total opposite of Clara's sunshiny persona.

"And what are you tonight?" I ask Hallie.

She sets a black, pointed hat atop her head. "A witch."

Abbie gasps. "But witches are bad, and you're so nice."

"I don't know, I think witches can be good," Hallie replies. "Just like regular people, they're not all the same. Even if they look the part."

My daughter thinks for a moment. "I think you should be a good witch," she declares.

Hallie nods. "That's what I was thinking, too."

When Abbie spots her mom, she wiggles to get out of my hold. She hugs Larissa's waist and slaps a high-five to Chris's palm, then drags them both over to us by the hand.

"Happy Halloween," Larissa says. "Hallie, I love your costume. You look *hot*."

I've never agreed with Larissa on anything more.

Hallie smiles, her cheeks pink from the compliment. "Thank you. I love yours!"

Upon closer inspection, I realize Larissa and Chris have come dressed as Daphne and Fred from *Scooby-Doo*. They're definitely the type of people to go for a couple's costume.

Connor ambles over and throws an arm around Clara. "Lookin' good, girl of my dreams."

I slap the back of his head. "Don't hit on my sister."

Clara pats his chest. "Sorry, Con. You know you couldn't handle me."

"But you could handle me," he says with a wink.

Thankfully, Abbie has migrated over to Sophia, where she stands with Luke, Delilah and Jodi, so she isn't present for this overly suggestive conversation. I'm not sure how I'd explain if she had questions.

"Where's your costume, Gabe?" Larissa asks.

I gesture to my work clothes. "Right here."

Normally, I make an effort to wear some sort of costume, because it makes Abbie smile. But with everything that's been going on lately, the end of October crept up on me, and now it's too late to find something.

"I've got a cowboy hat in my truck," Connor offers, because of course he does. "Then we could slap a sign on your chest that says, *free rides*. Problem solved."

Chris snorts, and Larissa lets out a laugh. Clara rolls her eyes as she disentangles herself from him. Hallie stifles her giggle with a hand over her mouth.

I cross my arms as my lips flatten into an unamused line. "I'm not going trick or treating with my *daughter* wearing a sign offering free rides."

He shrugs. "I thought it was a good idea. What about you, Hallie? Don't you think our boy Gabe would make a good cowboy?"

I expect Hallie to be embarrassed, being put on the spot like that, but a streak of mischief shines in her eyes instead. She makes a show of dragging her eyes up my body, from my feet to my head. I don't move a muscle, letting her drink her fill. I like her eyes on me.

Finally, her gaze meets mine. "I imagine you'd have a pretty long waitlist for those free rides."

Connor whistles, grabbing me by the shoulders and giving me a shake. "*Oh*, boy! Giddy up!"

I shove him away from me as he dissolves into laughter.

As the group gets ready to head out for trick or treating, my eyes can't help but trail after Hallie. It's not even the way she looks —though that is undoubtedly part of it—but the way she interacts with my family. Like we've been working on a puzzle for years, and now that she's home, we finally have that piece we've been missing.

Connor slaps me on the back. "You are down *so bad*, dude. It's not even funny," he says.

I glower. "And here I thought you'd be helpful."

He throws his hands up, though his lips twitch with a grin. "Hey, I can do both. But *someone* has to give you shit."

"I don't need shit. I need..."

What do I need? *Her.* Always her.

———

One of the houses on Hawberry Lane, just down the street from where Delilah and her siblings live, sets up a haunted house in their garage every year. Like the rest of the town, they spare no expense, building an addition to their garage in their driveway to make the haunted house as big as possible.

The family that lives there has been putting this together since I was a kid, but they change it up slightly so you don't know what exactly to expect. It isn't overly scary, but it can make you jump.

"We'll sit this one out," Delilah says, taking hold of Sophia's hand at the entrance to the haunted house. While Abbie has loved this since she was a toddler, Sophia is visibly apprehensive. "Have fun, guys!"

Luke stays back with them, but the rest of us keep going. I'm a little surprised Hallie didn't choose to opt out. When we used to go out on Halloween, she would stay outside, holding our bags of candy for us.

As Abbie charges forward, holding Larissa's hand, I hang back with Hallie. Bumping her shoulder, I say, "First rollercoasters, now a haunted house. Maybe you really are turning into an adrenaline junkie."

She shrugs. "I figure it can't be *that* bad now. I mean, we were, like, twelve the last time we came here."

We round a corner, and Hallie immediately runs face-first into a giant fake spider hanging from the ceiling. She lets out a shriek, jumping back. Then she trips over her boots and slams into me, and I grab her waist to steady her.

"Careful," I murmur in her ear.

I swear I feel her shiver.

"Thanks," she says, looking up at me sheepishly. "I guess I was a little overconfident, huh? Maybe I should turn back."

"Or you could hold my hand," I offer without thinking. I don't take it back, though. "Would that help?"

There's hardly any light in here, but a purplish bulb casts a glow over half of her face and neck. I watch as she swallows, considering.

"Okay." She clears her throat, projecting her voice a little louder. "Yeah. That would help."

I hold out my palm. Slowly, she slides her hand into place, and I link our fingers. Her skin is soft, a sharp contrast to the roughness of mine. I've held her hand before, but something about this time feels different. Maybe it's the way Hallie instinctively leans toward me when we turn the next corner, bracing for another jump scare. Or maybe it's simply the fact that I don't want to ever let go.

Is it possible to fall in love with the same person more than once? Because every day, I feel like I'm falling for Hallie all over again.

I know I have to push these feelings away, though. The last time I voiced them, I lost her. And I don't think I can go another ten years without her in my life.

TWENTY

GABE

I STARE AT MY PHONE, waiting for a text that isn't coming. It's been over twenty-four hours now, and she hasn't said a word.

> Hallie, I'm sorry.

> We can go back to how we were. Forget I said anything.

I've known my sister's best friend since we were four years old, and I've loved her just as long. Over the years, I've kept my feelings to myself, but recently, something shifted. Maybe it was the thought of graduation and everything that came after—change, both big and inevitable. I couldn't let her move without telling her how I felt.

My brain tried to convince me I was reading too much into things. No way would Hallie Foster love me back. But then I thought about how she would blush when I was around, and the way her smile turned brighter when I made her laugh, and I knew. *I knew* she loved me, too. She had to.

But I was wrong, and I threw away fourteen years of friendship for nothing.

God, Clara is going to *kill* me when she finds out. If she finds out. But why wouldn't Hallie tell her? They tell each other everything, and I'm sure this will be no exception.

Hey, Clara, do you wanna hear how much of an idiot your brother is?

And Connor is going to have a field day with this. He's the only person I've told about my feelings, and he gives me shit every chance he gets.

When my phone buzzes in my hand, it takes me all of one second to realize it's not her. My body deflates when I see my friend's name on the screen instead.

CONNOR

How'd it go?

Ok, considering you're reading this and not making out right now, I'm gonna assume not well

Very bad actually.

She literally ran away after I said I loved her. Now she won't answer my texts.

CONNOR

Damn that's rough, man. I'm sorry

Me, too.

With a sigh, I tuck my phone away. It's doing me no good staring at it. If Hallie wants to reach out in her own time, she will. I just have to be patient. Part of me wants to drive over to Pops's house right now and demand that she talk to me, but I know that's not fair.

God, I'm so stupid.

When I hear the sliding door open behind me, I turn to find my brother crossing the back porch. "What are you doing out here in the dark?" Luke asks. "Mom's been looking for you."

I frown. "Why?"

Our mom is usually the first in the family to head to bed. She should be asleep by now.

"Clara's sad, and she thinks you can cheer her up."

That instantly puts me on alert. "What happened?"

He shrugs. "Hallie left for school today. You know they've been attached at the hip since you guys were little."

The air is knocked right out of my lungs then. I knew she was leaving. Hell, I was the first person she told about her acceptance to her top choice university in Toronto. But she wasn't supposed to leave yet. I thought I had more time to fix this.

"Hallie's gone?"

My brother nods, unaware that his words are having such an affect on me. "She left this morning. Clara has been moping around since Hallie got on the ferry."

The city is only a few hours away. It isn't like she'll be away forever. *But Hallie's gone.* She's gone, and she didn't even say goodbye.

Dread sits at the bottom of my stomach, forming a pit. She didn't only flee the beach—she left the island because of *me*. I never should have said anything. I've kept these feelings to myself for this long already. I should have held out, waited for them to fade.

"Gabe? You coming?"

"In a minute," I reply. Though I'm not sure how much help I'll be, considering I'm feeling the same way our sister is.

Luke heads back into the house, and the quiet of the night settles once again. I run a hand through my hair, frustrated with myself. Frustrated with her.

"Damn it, Hallie," I mutter, letting my head fall back. The stars above seem to mock me. "You didn't let me fix it."

TWENTY-ONE

HALLIE

IT'S safe to say I'm freaking out.

The wedding is tomorrow and I still haven't figured out what I'm going to wear. Usually, I'm not this picky about clothes. Except, like everything that has to do with my estranged father, the urge to appear like I have my life together can't be helped.

The dresses lying on the end of my bed taunt me. I grab my phone and snap a picture, then send it to the group chat I now have with Clara and Delilah. Clara, of course, had to name it something quirky. It's gone through a few iterations, but it's currently titled *Hot Girl Shit*.

Help me!

DELILAH

Those are so pretty!

CLARA

Damn, babe. You've been holding out on us!!

Most of the clothing I own is *nowhere* near this fancy. A majority of the time, I opt for comfortable fashion. But that isn't going to work for Caitlyn's wedding. The dress code isn't black-tie, but it's pretty freaking close, so I had to dig in my closet for the nicer dresses I own. Thanks to the New Year's Eve parties I used to attend with my nanny families back in the city, I had a few options to choose from.

> I can't decide! I've been staring at them for days. I need the decision to be taken out of my hands.

DELILAH

Soph says green and I agree. It complements the purple in your hair.

CLARA

Green. Definitely green.

I stare at the dresses, and the more I think about it, the more I know they're right. Grabbing the black dress, I shove it back into the closet. I'll bring the green dress down to the laundry room later so I can get rid of any wrinkles.

CLARA

On a scale of one to ten, how much are you freaking out about this wedding?

Fourteen.

While I haven't told even Clara about her brother's willingness to lie for me, I've been upfront about the situation with Kevin and what it was like meeting my half siblings for the first time. Clara was none too pleased when I told her about Dana's comments.

> Probably a ten...

CLARA

You know I'd go with you! All you have to do is say the word.

My cheeks heat. I guess I forgot to mention that I already have a plus-one. And while I don't particularly want to tell her that role belongs to her brother, I know she'll keep offering if I don't.

> It's okay. Gabe's actually coming with me.

I brace, waiting for her reaction. It isn't like I told her I'm madly in love with him, but my heart pounds regardless. I've always been worried about what Clara would think if she knew just how deeply I feel about Gabe. In my imagination, all the worst case scenarios end with her not wanting to be my friend anymore, and I'm not sure if that's something I could live with. In a lot of ways, she's the sister I never had, and I don't want to lose her.

CLARA

You're taking Gabe as your date?! And you neglected to tell me??

> I'm sorry!

CLARA

It's fine, I suppose. He'll probably make a better date than me anyway. I can't promise I won't take someone's eye out if they look at you wrong.

DELILAH

Clara! Violence isn't the answer.

CLARA

It is sometimes!!

Really though, I'm glad Gabe is going with you. You need someone in your corner too.

DELILAH

And I'm sure he'll be the *perfect* gentleman. ;)

Now my face *flames*. I know Delilah is teasing, but it makes my palms sweat. Because she has no idea how much I want that to be true—how much I want Gabe to be anything *but* a gentleman and have his way with me. Being in his space, living with him, has been nothing short of torture. Especially when he comes inside after working out with his equipment in the garage…

CLARA

I made a mistake. I take back my friendship.

DELILAH

Too late! You're stuck with me now.

CLARA

Trapped in a hell of my own making.

Please refrain from discussing my brothers and their…gentlemanly qualities. I'd rather not puke today.

But we're just friends!

DELILAH

He doesn't look at you like just a friend.

I suck in a sharp breath.

Thankfully, the sound of the front door opening down on the main level gives me the perfect excuse to hide from this conversation. I toss my phone onto the bed and leave my room. Hopefully by the time I come back, the two of them will have moved on to a different topic.

As soon as I start walking down the stairs, Abbie comes stomping up them. She bypasses me entirely and heads straight to her bedroom, slamming the door behind her.

Yikes.

When I get to the bottom of the stairs, I take in Gabe's pinched expression. "That bad?" I ask.

He shakes his head. "I don't even know what happened. She seemed upset when I picked her up from school, but she won't say why."

I chew on my lower lip as I think. "I might have an idea, if that's okay."

He waves a hand toward the stairs. "Go ahead. I'm clearly not her favourite person right now anyway."

My expression softens, and I close the distance between us, setting a hand on his arm. "She might be upset, but she still loves you. So much. And her expressing her feelings like this is a testament to how safe she feels with you."

His lips quirk slightly up at that. "Luke said something similar a few months ago."

It's true. I was never comfortable enough with Amanda to be so free with my emotions, good or bad. I always felt like I was tiptoeing. Like even if I did express myself, I wouldn't get the care I craved. Watching Gabe with his daughter is healing, in a way.

I give his arm a squeeze, then let go. "You're a great dad, Gabe. Abbie is lucky to have you."

I don't go back upstairs right away. Instead, I head out to the guesthouse. Although I moved most of my belongings into the main house, I left my painting supplies out there. Once I gather what I need, I go find Abbie.

Knocking on her door, I call out, "Abbs? Can I come in?"

I hear a dejected *okay*, so I step inside. Abbie's room is something out of younger Hallie's dreams. She has a shimmery green canopy that drapes around the head of her bed, and her comforter is pink and covered in flowers. Along one wall, she has shelves full of books and toys, and beside them, a large wooden dollhouse that has John and his craftsmanship written all over it. On the opposite side of the room, there's a small table and set of chairs.

Abbie peers up at me from her spot in front of her dollhouse. Her usually carefree expression is guarded.

"I came to see if you wanted to paint with me," I say, holding up the supplies.

That piques her interest. "I like to paint."

I smile. "I had a feeling you might." Setting everything on the table, I pull one of the chairs out and take a seat. "Come see what I have."

Abbie's dolls are forgotten then. She can't resist the temptation. She quickly climbs into the chair opposite me and watches as I set out watercolour paints, brushes, a cup of water. Then I set a piece of watercolour paper in front of her.

"I have those colours in my paint set at Mommy's house," she says, pointing as I fill our palette with red and then blue.

"This paint is different than what you're used to," I explain. "We have to use some water. It's a little like magic."

I demonstrate, swirling my brush through the paint and then swiping it across my page. Abbie watches in wonder, then picks up her own brush and tries it for herself.

We paint in silence for a while. I don't want to pressure her into talking if she's not ready, but I'm hoping she'll decide to open up. I hate thinking of her keeping her emotions bottled up.

"Daddy said you're the best at painting," she says eventually. She frowns at her paper. "I'm not very good."

"You know what I love about art?" She looks at me, eyes wide in that curious kid way. "You don't have to be great or good or anything at all. You can just *be*. Some people make art as their job, but I like being free to create whatever I want, whenever I want. It helps me process my feelings."

She turns back to her paper, swirling her brush across it in abstract strokes.

"Sometimes it's hard to know what we're feeling," I continue. "Especially when the emotions are new or they feel *really* big. But once I've figured it out, it's a bit easier to talk about them."

I let the quiet settle over us again.

Eventually, she speaks. "Daddy made me mad."

I set my brush down. "Do you know why you felt mad?"

"He got me from school, and he asked why I was sad. And I didn't wanna tell him, but he wanted me to, and that made me mad."

"Did something happen today at school?" She hesitates, so I add, "You don't have to tell me, but you may feel better if you do. How about you practice on me so you can tell your dad after?"

She curls the corner of her page between her thumb and fore-finger. "My teacher got me in trouble for talking when she was talking," she mumbles. Her cheeks pinken at the admission, and she ducks her head.

The pieces begin to click. "Getting in trouble doesn't feel very good, does it?"

When she looks up at me, her eyes are shining. She shakes her head. "No. Everyone looked at me! That made me mad, too. And I didn't want Daddy to know because he doesn't like me being bad at school."

My heart tugs. "Emotions are complicated. Sometimes we think we feel one thing when it's actually something else. Remember how you said that about Gordon? How he might really be sad, not angry? It sounds to me like maybe you weren't actually mad, you were just embarrassed."

"What's that?" she asks.

"What did your body feel like when your classmates were looking at you?"

She presses her hands to her cheeks. "My face felt like it was on *fire*. And I wanted to hide."

"That's what embarrassment can feel like. It also means that sometimes, we don't like talking about the poor decisions we've made because we don't want to disappoint the people who love us," I say. "But let me tell you something. The people who love us? They're not going to love us any less for being wrong. We just have to try to do the right thing the next time."

"I'm not supposed to talk when my teacher's talking," she says.

I nod. "If you go to school on Monday and say sorry, I'm sure she'll forgive you."

"Will Daddy forgive me for slamming my door?" she asks. "I'm not supposed to do that either. That's mean."

This girl. She has the kindest, softest heart.

"Why don't you go talk to him? Tell him what you told me."

She looks unsure, but she slowly agrees. "Will you be there with me?"

"Yeah. I've got your back, babe."

Together, Abbie and I clean up our mess of paints. We leave our papers to dry on the table. Then she takes a fortifying breath and walks with me down the stairs.

We find Gabe in the kitchen, starting on Abbie's dinner. Abbie looks at me for reassurance, then crosses the room to him. I lean against the doorframe, watching them.

Abbie grabs the hem of her shirt with both hands, stretching the fabric slightly. "I'm sorry I was mean, Daddy," she says quietly. "I thought I was mad, but I was really..." She trails off, then looks over her shoulder. "Hallie, what's the word?"

"Embarrassed," I supply.

Gabe's eyes flick to me, then back to his daughter. He lifts her up and sets her on the counter so they're closer to being eye to eye.

"Why were you embarrassed?" he asks. "You can tell me anything, Abbs."

"Because I did a bad thing," she replies. "I talked when my teacher was talking, and she got me in trouble. But I'm not gonna do it anymore, and I'm gonna say sorry when I see her on Monday. Hallie says she'll forgive me."

His gaze flicks to me again. A small smile curves his lips. "Hallie is very smart," he tells her. "It sounds like you've learned your lesson."

"I'm sorry I slammed my door. That wasn't nice."

"Already forgiven." He brushes one of her dark curls out of her face. "I love you, Abbs."

She leans forward, throwing her arms around him as best she can. "Love you, Daddy."

As Gabe hugs her, he looks at me over the top of her head. *Thank you,* he mouths. I simply smile. I'd do anything for her—for both of them. And Gabe is already doing so much for me, helping me with Kevin and his family. If I can do something small like this for him, of course I'm going to.

When Abbie pulls out of his arms, Gabe inspects her face and hands. There's definitely some paint there. "What did you two get up to?" he asks.

I move into the kitchen now, and I meet Abbie's eyes with a wink. "We made a little magic."

Gabe sets Abbie back on the floor. "Maybe wash the magic off before dinner, yeah?"

"You got it, dude," Abbie says, then runs toward the bathroom.

I laugh as I watch her leave. But then I feel Gabe's focus on me, and it feels heavy. That familiar warmth curls around me.

"You're killing me, Foster," he all but groans.

I look at him, worrying my bottom lip. "I'm not trying to."

He steps forward then, into my space. With his thumb, he tugs my lip out from between my teeth. His dark eyes swirl with a mix of pain and longing.

"That's the problem."

TWENTY-TWO
GABE

THE DAY OF THE WEDDING, I drop Abbie off with Larissa, and then Hallie and I board the ferry to the mainland. During the drive, Hallie's knee bounces with nerves, and I catch her chewing on her bottom lip, then scolding herself for messing up her lip gloss.

Caitlyn and Amara's wedding is being held at a golf course about twenty minutes outside of Tobermory. I spot the odd golfer trying to make the most of the snowless ground when we first pull up, but otherwise, the place looks like it's getting ready to shut down for the season.

The ceremony itself is short and to the point, but the main attraction is the reception afterward.

"Whoa," Hallie says as we step inside the room. "It's so beautiful."

The whole place is decked out in fall colours—rusted oranges, golden yellows, rich greens. Different coloured mums dot every table at the centre. Caitlyn wasn't kidding when she said she and Dana went all out with the planning.

The decorations are beautiful, but I find it hard to take my eyes off of Hallie. She's wearing a sage green dress with short sleeves that's fitted at the top, and there's a tie that cinches her waist, accentuating her curves. The skirt flows down to her ankles, and the hem is ruffled. Somehow, it feels exactly like her in dress form.

I set a hand on the small of her back. I can't stop touching her today. "Let's find our seats."

We end up at a table with some of Dana's cousins. Hallie is vague about her connection to the brides when asked. I can hardly blame her. Dana made her feel like a pariah the last time we saw her.

I was worried we'd have a repeat of the food situation and we'd have to dip out early, because like hell was I about to let Hallie pick apart a measly salad in place of a proper dinner for a second time. Thankfully, though, Hallie gets served some fancy-looking eggplant thing that makes her eyes light up in excitement.

As Hallie eats and drinks, my attention snags on her left ring finger. I was a little surprised when she first pulled out the fake diamond for dinner with the Landells, but I quickly found that I didn't mind the way it looked. Tonight, it keeps distracting me.

When the ring flashes at me for the tenth time, I can't help myself. I take her hand, then press a kiss to the spot where the stone rests.

Her blue eyes go wide. They dart around the table before returning to me. "Gabe," she breathes.

I lower our joined hands to my lap, running my thumb over her knuckles. "Yeah, Foster?"

She studies the gentle movement for a moment, then visibly swallows. "Nothing," she whispers.

I wait for her to pull her hand back, but when she doesn't, I keep dragging my thumb back and forth across her soft skin. Her eyelashes fan the tops of her cheekbones as she lets her eyes fall closed for a moment, sinking into the comfort I'm providing.

Eventually, we finish our food, and then the dishes are cleared away. While the dinner portion was served to us, the dessert is buffet-style. I can already tell Hallie is eyeing the cake from across the room, so we'll definitely be stopping by the dessert table before the night is through.

The other people at our table slowly leave as they start to mingle. When it's just Hallie and me, I turn to ask her if she wants to dance, but someone interrupts me.

"Hallie, Gabe, how lovely to see you again."

We both look up to find Dana standing over us. She has a very distinct mother-of-the-bride air about her, and there is zero kindness in her gaze when it rests on Hallie. You would think she'd have more pressing things to focus on, today of all days.

I reach out and place a hand on Hallie's thigh. *I've got you, Foster.*

"Hi, Dana." Hallie pastes on a polite smile. "The wedding was beautiful, and so is the reception. You and Caitlyn did a great job with everything."

"Yes, well, it was all quite expensive," she says. "I wouldn't get your hopes up about having the same kind of assistance with yours."

What the fuck?

Hallie's smile falters. "That's fine. I'm not expecting anything."

Dana nods. "Good. Managing expectations is wise." She waits a beat, then says, "Enjoy the rest of the evening."

When Dana is far enough away, I ask, "Are you alright?"

Hallie nods, but it does little to convince me. "Do you want to dance? We should dance."

She's out of her chair before I can reply, so I simply follow her. She stops at the edge of the dance floor, and suddenly, she looks unsure.

I hold out a hand. "Let me take your mind off things."

Hallie sets her palm in mine, and I pull her close. With my arm around her, my hand resting on her lower back, we begin to sway like the rest of the couples occupying the floor. On the far side, I see Caitlyn and Amara sharing a dance.

"I might step on your toes," Hallie warns.

I grin. "Do your worst, baby. I can take it."

She shakes her head, making the waves of her hair flutter around her shoulders, but her eyes dance with laughter.

From across the room, I can feel Dana's gaze on us. Suddenly, I want nothing more than to sell this thing for Hallie. I want everyone to see how happy we are. How happy I can make her.

"We haven't talked about how far you want to take things," I say quietly, for only Hallie to hear.

"How far?" she asks.

"Yeah." I lick my lips, tilting my head closer. "You're supposed to be my fiancée. We want to make it look real, don't we?" I ask. "So do I have your permission to treat you like you're mine?"

Her fingers tighten on my shoulders, and she inhales an unsteady breath. "What would being yours look like, exactly?"

I tuck a wayward strand of hair behind her ear, delaying as I debate with myself over how to answer that question. With the truth, I decide.

"I wouldn't let you walk home from work. I'd pick you up every time. I'd always let you and Abbie pick the music, even if I can't stand the songs. I'd learn new recipes so you'd always have something you could eat. And I'd watch 10 Things I Hate About You on repeat, just to see you smile."

"That doesn't sound any different than what you do now." Her voice is quiet.

"I would feel lucky as hell to be with you, so I would hold you close every chance I had," I continue, demonstrating by tightening my arm around her waist, pulling her flush to me. She nods, and I continue. "And, most importantly, I would kiss you. All the time."

I might be pushing my luck here, but...*fuck it.*

It's faint, but I swear I hear her breath hitch. I wait for her to protest. She doesn't.

"What do you think, Foster? Can I kiss you to prove that you're mine?"

I'm walking on a tightrope with no safety net below me. All that stands between me and certain death is the beauty in my arms. She can sever that rope with a few sharp words.

Hallie's lips part. "We, um, want it to look real." She nods, resolute. "Treat me like I'm yours, Gabriel."

The room full of people around us ceases to exist. In this world, it's only me and Hallie. With tunnel vision, I cup her cheek, tilt her head, then bring my lips to hers. She feels warm and soft. Her perfume invades my nose, rendering me powerless.

Hallie Foster has left me irrevocably defenseless, and I don't think she even knows it.

So many times, I've thought of kissing her. What she would taste like. If she would gasp in surprise, then lean into it. Nothing prepared me for how it would feel to have her melt in my hold as the tension seeped from her body. How it would feel to have her press herself closer, until her soft curves were all I knew.

Hallie Foster has left me defenseless, but truthfully, I don't give a shit.

I want to take this further. Back her against the wall so I can properly explore her mouth. Map her waist and hips with my hands. I want to feel her long hair threaded between my fingers, wrapped around my fist. I want to watch her come undone, and then do it all over again.

Reluctantly, though, I pull myself away. She blinks dazedly, and I find a small sense of satisfaction in that. In putting that look of sated confusion on her face.

With my thumb, I wipe away a smudge of lip gloss on the corner of her mouth. Then I lick the taste of it off my own lips.

Her gaze dips to my mouth. "I..."

"Mm," I hum. "Strawberry."

She shakes her head, as if to clear it. "You kissed me like you're trying to win something."

You, I want to tell her.

"Come on," I say instead. The song has ended now, and in its place is something more upbeat. "Let's go find some cake."

I take her hand in mine. She still has that slight look of confusion on her face, so it takes her a second, but then she lets me lead her over to the dessert table.

By now, the room has grown relaxed as people have indulged in more drinks and sweets. Both Hallie and I have stuck to water, but she has no qualms about grabbing a generous slice of cake. I do the same.

We retake our seats and start on our dessert. I can't help watching the way Hallie meticulously licks the buttercream frosting off her fork. If I didn't know any better, I'd say she does it on purpose simply to torture me.

We're finishing off our slices when Caitlyn finds us. She sits in the empty chair beside Hallie. "Hi! I'm so glad you could make it."

Hallie beams, and this time, her smile is genuine. I know she's still nervous, but at the core of it, she's happy to be part of her sister's big day.

"Congratulations," Hallie says. "Your dress is stunning. Amara's, too. And this place looks amazing!"

"Thank you. I definitely wasn't one of those girls who always dreamed about what their wedding would look like, but once the theme hit me, I had to make it perfect."

I chuckle. "I'd say you definitely succeeded in that."

She smiles. "Now, not that I don't love chatting with you, but I actually came over here for a reason," Caitlyn says. "You can say no, but I was wondering if you'd come take a picture with us."

Hallie's eyes widen in surprise. "*Me?*"

Caitlyn laughs. "Yeah, you. We got a bunch earlier with Mom, Dad and Bryan, but I'd like some with you, too. If you're alright with it."

Hallie turns to me, and I nod encouragingly. Most of the time, she knows what she wants to do, she just needs a little nudge. A bit of reassurance. I'm glad I can be that for her.

"Sorry to steal your fiancée away, but I promise to return her soon," Caitlyn assures me.

"Good." I grin. "Because I'm quite fond of her."

Hallie stands from her chair, setting her napkin on the table. There's a momentary pause, where it seems like she's making a decision. Then she bends and plants a quick kiss on my lips.

"I'll be back," she murmurs, pulling away before I have time to respond.

I fight the urge to drag her back to the table and ask for a proper kiss. Because I know that soon, we won't be pretending anymore, and I won't have another opportunity to taste her the way I've been craving for years.

TWENTY-THREE

GABE

WE GOT BACK from the wedding two nights ago, and Hallie has made a concerted effort to avoid being alone with me ever since. If Abbie isn't here to act as a buffer, then neither is she. It's like she's still staying out in the guesthouse, trying to keep out of my way, even though she's sleeping down the hall.

I pushed her too far. Pretending to be in a relationship is one thing, but kissing her like that? That was real for me. And my feelings have always been a little too much for Hallie to handle. It somehow feels worse this time, though. Like we took two steps forward and now we've gone ten back.

And now that I know what it's like to live without her, I'm more determined than ever to fix this before it's too late.

I finish pulling the leftovers from the fridge when I hear footsteps behind me. "Hey," I say over my shoulder.

The footsteps slow, then stop altogether. "Hey," Hallie says. Her tone is careful. "Where's Abbie?"

I turn to face her and shrug. "She wanted to spend the night with her mom again."

After I suggested it.

I didn't plan to ambush Hallie, but we do need to talk. I need to know where her head is at. We can't keep living like this, with her tiptoeing again.

"Oh." Hallie chews on her lower lip. "Okay. I'm just gonna grab something to eat and then I'll be out of your hair."

She doesn't make eye contact as she walks around me, toward the pantry. That won't do.

"Hallie."

She pauses. "Yeah?"

"Are we...okay?"

For the first time, I let my worry bleed into my words. I've gotten used to her constant presence, and I've felt unsteady these past forty-eight hours without her. Even when she was here, she wasn't *here*, and I'll be damned if I don't find some way to bring her back. I need her, in whatever way she'll let me have her.

Finally, she looks at me. Her fingers curl into the hem of her shirt, like she's nervous. "What?"

I swallow. "Since the wedding, you've been distant. I want to know if we're okay. If I did something, if I made you uncomfortable..."

If you regret kissing me.

She takes a step forward, catching my hand. She gives it a squeeze. "You've done nothing wrong, Gabriel. I promise."

"But something *is* wrong," I press.

She sighs as she releases my hand. "My brain, it's just...sorting. But we're okay, I swear."

Some of the tension leaves my body. I'm not entirely convinced that's true, but at least she didn't outright lie to me. Hallie has a tendency to compromise her own desires for the sake of others. I don't want her ever doing that with me, if I can help it.

"Do you want to eat dinner together?" I ask.

Hallie offers me a small, genuine smile. "Sure. I just have to figure out what I'm going to make. I swear, I never realized how exhausting it would be to come up with three meals a day for the rest of my life."

I grin, feeling some of that ease coming back to us. "You can have some of this," I tell her, handing her a plate. "Mom wanted to try this vegetarian lasagna recipe she saw in a magazine, and she made me and Dad be her test subjects so she didn't serve you something that tastes awful. I can happily report that it doesn't."

She grips the plate as an expression crosses her face that's hard to read. "She doesn't have to do that."

I set some lasagna on my own plate. "Maybe not, but it's not like it's hard to accommodate you. Besides, you know her. This is how she shows her love."

Before Hallie can protest, our phones chime simultaneously with a text. Opening it, I find that Clara has added Luke, Delilah, Hallie and me to a new group chat. Like always, it has a quirky name that Clara will switch out at will.

Five Peas in a Pod

CLARA

We never properly celebrated our Hallie girl being back in town. Let's go out!

FOSTER

That's really not necessary…

I'm in.

Hallie's phone dings again, and she shoots me a dirty look after she reads my response.

I laugh. "Hey, you never know. It could be fun."

She pouts adorably. "Traitor."

DELILAH

What did you have in mind?

CLARA

There's a karaoke night at a bar in Tobermory?

> **LUKE**
> No.

> **CLARA**
> Don't be a buzzkill, Chief Grumpy! Try to have some fun.

> **LUKE**
> Karaoke is not fun. Staying home is fun.

> Said every grumpy old man ever.

Admittedly, I'm not too fond of our sister's idea either, but I'll take any opportunity to give Luke shit. He has loosened up a little since he's been with Delilah, but overall, he's still as serious as ever.

> **LUKE**
> I'm three years older than you, fucker. Not three decades.

> **FOSTER**
> Being a homebody is perfectly valid.

> **CLARA**
> Hallie! Not you too!

> Delilah, help! Persuade your boyfriend.

> **DELILAH**
> On it. Brb.

"What do you think she's going to do?" Hallie asks. "I can't see Luke giving in."

I shake my head. "I'm not sure we want to know the answer to that."

She blushes, and her lips form a small O as realization hits her.

> **DELILAH**
> I'm sorry, Clara. My hands are tied.

LUKE

Literally.

CLARA

OH MY GOD

MY POOR EYES

DELILAH

Haha. He's messing with you!

CLARA

Promise?

DELILAH

I promise. He isn't even with me right now.

CLARA

I hate you. So much.

LUKE

Love you too, Clarebear.

CLARA

Fine, no karaoke. But can we still go out? Just
to the bar on a regular night.

I look up, gauging Hallie's reaction. "Foster?"

She chews on her lower lip. "I guess it'd be fine."

I arch a brow. "Are you sure? You don't have to say yes just to appease Clara. She can celebrate some other way."

"No," she says. "I want to go. We should go."

I'm a little surprised, but I try not to let it show. "Yeah?"

She nods. "Yeah. I've never been to a bar before. Clara tried to get me to go for my nineteenth birthday, but I was too chicken. So why not?"

The bar in Tobermory isn't the most glamorous of venues, but I don't want to dampen her budding excitement about trying something new, so I hold my tongue.

Hallie and I are in.

DELILAH

Luke and I will be there too!

LUKE

One hour.

CLARA

Yes, we get it. You hate joy.

But yay! I'll coordinate schedules and let you know what day.

DELILAH

That might be tough. My boss is kind of a hard-ass…

Clara sends the middle finger emoji in response. Delilah fires back a GIF of someone blowing a kiss.

I set my phone down, and when I look up, I find Hallie smiling. Her happiness is infectious.

"You like her, huh?"

Hallie looks at me. "Who, Delilah? Yeah. She's a great friend to Clara, and she's good for Luke. She fits with you guys."

Something about the way she says this rubs me the wrong way —as if Delilah fits, but *she* doesn't. That couldn't be further from the truth. Disregarding how I feel about her, Hallie has always been part of our family in my eyes. I know my parents and siblings feel the same.

"You know you fit, too, right?"

Her cheeks turn pink. "Well, sure. But it's different. She's *with* Luke. She'll probably be your sister-in-law one day."

I can't help it. My gaze lands on her bare ring finger. That stupid fake ring is taunting me, even when she's not fucking wearing it.

I meet her eyes again. "You fit," I insist. "Okay?"

After a moment of studying my unmoving expression, she softly says, "Okay."

When our food is warmed up, we take it to the living room and settle on the couch. Despite our more proper setup for Sunday brunch, my family was never big on propriety when it came to meals. Especially when my siblings and I got older, started playing sports or working. We almost never had a schedule that lined up for everyone, so we all ate at separate times and often in our own bedrooms.

I like the idea of eating meals with Hallie. Though it should come as no surprise, considering I like anything that has to do with her.

Turning on the TV, I find a sitcom I know we've both seen a hundred times. And when Hallie takes the first bite of Mom's latest recipe, she practically vibrates with happiness.

"You weren't lying," she says. "This is amazing. I'll have to say thank you next time I see her."

"She'll be glad you like it. I think she's excited to experiment in the kitchen again." One thing Mom has always loved is cooking, especially when it's for the people she cares about. It's part of the reason my parents bought Dockside to begin with. Truthfully, Hallie's vegetarian diet has given her a gift.

We're quiet as we eat. Every once in a while, Hallie will let out a breathy kind of laugh over something that happens on the screen. Each time, my attention gets dragged in her direction, and I can't help watching her for a moment or two.

Eventually, she sets her empty plate beside mine on the coffee table.

"Gabe?"

I turn to her. "Yeah?"

The faint lamplight illuminates her face enough for me to see the indecision in her expression. "I'm sorry I ran from you."

At first, I think she's talking about the past two days. The way she pulled back after the wedding, the kiss. But as I search her face, I realize she's talking about *before*.

I swallow. "Hallie, it's fine. We don't have to—"

"We do." She shifts in her seat, tucking her knees up to her chest. "I know you said it's alright, but I've been thinking about it since my talk with Abbie the other day. It feels like it's just... *hanging there*, and I know that's my fault."

I don't know what to say, so I end up saying nothing. Not the first time she's left me tongue-tied.

"To be completely honest, you scared me." When I rear back, shocked, a little hurt, she hurries to elaborate. "Not in a physical way. Never like that, I promise. But emotionally. When things get real, I get intimidated, and what you said was...*big*."

It was big. I can't deny that. I hadn't so much as admitted to liking her in more than a platonic way, and then I jumped straight to confessing I was in love with her. At the time, I saw no reason to downplay what was on my heart.

She meets my gaze. "I shouldn't have run from you or ignored your texts. Above all else, you were my friend, and you deserved better than that. So I'm sorry. And I'm sorry this apology is ten years late."

I didn't expect her words to hit me as hard as they do, but they slam into me all the same. I thought I didn't need to hear this, but maybe I did. Because for a decade, I've been convinced I did something wrong. That I fucked everything up.

But there's nothing wrong with loving Hallie. There never has been.

"I've thought a lot about that day over the years," I say. "What I should have done differently. It's kept me up some nights, on those days where your mind just won't stop spinning." Hallie grimaces, but I continue. "But to tell you the truth, I'm glad everything happened the way it did."

Her eyes widen, then understanding dawns. "Because of Abbie."

"Yes, but not only that." I can practically hear the blood rushing in my veins, but I don't stop. It's something she should hear. "As much as I couldn't help loving you, I think you needed to be loved by me. To show you it's as effortless as breathing. And I don't regret that for a goddamn second."

Hallie's lips part. My eyes are drawn to them immediately. What I wouldn't give to close the distance between us and take her mouth. Take it all. Time and distance never did manage to dull the pull I feel when I'm in her proximity, and that's only been amplified since our kiss.

I want more. I'll always want more.

"Gabe," Hallie croaks. "I..."

She doesn't finish, but I can see what swims in the depths of her irises. Desire. Maybe I'm not the only one still thinking about the wedding. But mingled with that desire is a small dose of apprehension. She's not ready. So I'll wait.

I lean over, noting the way her breath hitches at my closeness, and press a kiss to her forehead. Then I stand and grab our plates, taking them to the kitchen.

"Do you want some ice cream?" I ask, coming back into the living room. "I think we have cookies and cream."

"Ice cream?" she repeats.

My lips curve into an amused grin. "Yes. Do you want some?"

She stares at me another moment, trying to puzzle me out. Her nose scrunches in that cute, confused way. I pretend not to notice.

"Sure," she finally says. "Thank you."

When I settle back onto the couch with our ice cream in hand, Hallie lets her legs stretch out a bit, until her toes are pressed against my thigh. Again, I pretend not to notice.

She's not ready, but she'll get there. And when she does, I'll be right there to prove to her that we're worth it. She's worth it.

TWENTY-FOUR
GABE

TEN YEARS AGO

MY BEER TASTES LIKE ASH.

Frowning into my bottle, I look for embers that have blown from the fire and into my drink, but it's too dark to see anything. Oh well.

I take another sip as I watch the bonfire crackle in front of me. Shouts rise up from behind me, followed by laughter. Everyone is just tipsy enough to think they're all hilarious.

I'm usually right out there with them, but I can't seem to get myself in the mood tonight. Jealousy that I don't have a right to feel slithers inside my veins. She's just my sister's best friend—she isn't mine to be jealous over. Yet as soon as the thought enters my head, I know it's a lie.

She isn't *just* my sister's best friend. She never has been.

Hallie is in a category entirely her own, and watching Ethan shamelessly flirt with her is quickly driving me mad. There's nothing I can do about it, though. I have no claim over her, and she has every right to do what she wants.

Besides, she doesn't know how I feel. Maybe she suspects it—I *did* almost kiss her a few months ago—but she isn't the type to make the first move. If she even feels the same way I do.

Someone sits down on the log beside me. The slight breeze carries their perfume with it, and I'm instantly enveloped in Hallie's signature scent. I glance sideways at her, noticing the way the firelight illuminates the flush of her cheeks.

She's always blushing, and I'm always trying to think of a hundred more ways to make her.

I knock my knee against hers. "What are you doing over here?"

She shrugs before wrapping her arms around her middle, hugging herself. "You seemed kinda lonely. I thought I'd come keep you company."

"Everyone's here to see you, not me. You should be with the group."

Her nose scrunches in distaste. "Yeah, but they're making me the centre of attention."

I can't help but laugh. "It's your birthday party, Foster. You're supposed to be the centre of attention."

She huffs. "But I don't want to be." She shakes her head as she gives me a shy smile. "Clara was really excited about your parents being away this weekend. This whole thing was her idea. If it was up to me, I wouldn't be spending my birthday like this."

My mouth turns down into a frown at that. "Why didn't you tell her? She wouldn't have invited everyone if she knew how much you didn't want it."

Hallie chews on her bottom lip. "I know. She just got really into the planning and trying to make it fun. I didn't want to seem ungrateful."

I sigh. Now isn't the time to push back against *those* ridiculous thoughts, so I move on.

"What does your ideal birthday look like, then?" I ask. Anything to keep her talking, and to take that vulnerable look off her face.

I didn't think it possible, but her cheeks seem to turn even pinker. "You're gonna think it's lame."

The breeze picks up, sending a strand of Hallie's hair flying into her face. Before I can think better of it, I reach out and tuck it back behind her ear. I have the strongest urge to leave my hand there—to cup her jaw and bring her face close to mine and just fucking *kiss her* already.

I shake my head as I pull my hand back. "I don't think anything you do is lame."

"Well, um—" Her eyes dart away. "I would probably just have dinner with Pops and then watch my favourite rom-com. Nothing big."

"So you'd watch 10 Things I Hate About You for the millionth time." I nod, trying to keep my teasing grin at bay. "Got it."

Hallie shoves at my shoulder, but she laughs. "It's a good movie, okay?"

"I'll take your word for it."

Quiet settles over us, but it's the nice kind. The kind I can only seem to find with Hallie. My friends are great and all, but they aren't her. And when she looks at me, there's no pressure behind her gaze. No questions about what I plan to do with my uncertain future.

Eventually, though, I break the silence. "Are you gonna say yes?" I ask. I can't help myself—it's the whole reason I was over here by myself and not even pretending to be having a good time.

Hallie frowns in confusion. "Yes to what?"

"To Ethan." I look back at the group and find our classmate laughing at something Connor said. "I heard him ask you out earlier."

"*Oh.*"

I pick at the label on my bottle, avoiding her gaze. If I look at her, she'll be able to see the envy in my expression, and that's not fair. Knowing her, she'll feel guilty for how I feel and do everything in her power to make it better. Even if it means saying no to a date she really wants to go on.

"No, I don't think so."

I look at her now, surprised. "Why not?"

"You think I should?"

It's my turn to shrug. "If you like him, you should go for it." Even if seeing them together would fucking gut me.

"I...don't want to go out with Ethan."

"You don't?"

She shakes her head. The words are on the tip of my tongue—the urge to ask her who she *does* want to go out with. If maybe that someone could be me. But, like always, I chicken out.

Still, the relief is overwhelming. I like Ethan well enough, but I'm sure as shit not sorry Hallie doesn't have a thing for him. Maybe that makes me a shitty person, but I don't care.

I drain my bottle, then set it on the ground and push to stand. Holding a hand out for Hallie, I say, "Come with me."

She blinks, her long lashes fanning against her cheeks. *God, she's so fucking pretty.* I have to stop myself from actively staring at her, but I could easily do it all day.

"Where are we going?" she asks.

"Trust me?"

She places her hand in mine and lets me pull her to her feet. "I trust you, Gabe."

Hand in hand, we start across the yard, back toward the house. The party continues behind us, everyone too engrossed in themselves to notice that we're gone. I expect her to pull her palm out of mine, but when she doesn't, I tighten my grip. She squeezes back in reply.

The house is dark when we reach it. Our parents are away, and Luke is who knows where. He took off after unloading the beer our sister convinced him to buy for us, which leaves me and Clara home alone for the night. I'm grateful for their absence, because I know I wouldn't have had this opportunity with Hallie otherwise.

I lead her into the living room and gesture for her to sit on the couch. Then I walk over to the shelf in the corner and pull a DVD case from it.

"What are you doing?" she asks.

"You'll see."

I queue up the DVD and then I join Hallie. She keeps watching me as I grab the remote and turn the TV on. When the opening credits to *10 Things I Hate About You* begin to play, she shakes her head.

"You didn't have to do that," she says quietly.

I'm surprised the disc isn't scratched to hell from the amount of times that Hallie and Clara have watched it, but I'm thankful. Thankful for anything that puts that content expression on her face.

I turn to look at her. "Happy birthday, Foster."

She smiles. "Thank you, Gabriel."

Reaching for the blanket on the back of the couch, I drape it over our laps. Hallie shifts, trying to get comfortable. I hold my arm out, letting her settle against my side. She does, then lets out a little sigh.

Tell her how you feel.

I want to. So many times, I've thought about saying the words. Laying it all out. But there's risk in that. If I tell her, I disrupt the careful balance we've been maintaining for years. Is it worth it?

Yes.

But what if it's not?

I rest my cheek against the top of her head. Her hair smells like bonfire smoke instead of her usual apple scent. But pressed against me, she's soft and warm. She feels like home.

It isn't long before Hallie falls asleep with her head on my chest. I don't dare move. And then I find myself drifting off after her.

TWENTY-FIVE

HALLIE

"TO HALLIE! For finally taking pity on me and coming home."

I laugh as Clara holds her shot glass aloft before tipping her head back and swallowing without a flinch. Delilah takes hers, too, but her face twists as the sting of the alcohol hits her. I grimace in sympathy.

"You sure you don't want one?" Delilah asks.

I shake my head. "I'm good, thanks. Besides, someone has to stay sober here."

"That's Gabe's job tonight," Clara says. "But we won't pressure you, babe."

It isn't like I've never had alcohol before. I went to the liquor store and bought some on my nineteenth birthday like everyone else, but I've never been a fan of the taste. And admittedly, I don't like the idea of getting drunk and feeling out of control. Or using it as a crutch like Amanda has in the past.

"What's it like being the one drinking the drinks tonight instead of pouring them?" I ask, nudging Clara's side.

She grins. "I love Dockside with everything I have, but I won't deny that it's nice to be away from it for the night."

"Cheers to that," Delilah says, raising her empty glass in another toast.

The bar in Tobermory—not the one with the karaoke, much to Luke's delight—is a very different vibe than Dockside. Although Clara conceded on participating in karaoke, she still wanted us to get off the island for a change of scenery.

And this certainly is a change. The music is loud, the voices even louder, and the floor feels a little sticky beneath my boots. Beer signs line the walls, interspersed with old licence plates from all over. It's a bit of an eclectic mix, but I find I don't mind it. In small doses.

"*And*," Clara adds, "I get to hang out with my bestest girls." Her nose wrinkles. "Plus, my brothers."

"They're not so bad!" I defend.

Delilah nods. "Yeah, I happen to be particularly fond of one of them."

Clara waves us off. "Neither of you had to share a bathroom with them growing up. You wouldn't be so *fond* then."

We turn back to the bartender, and they return their shot glasses. Clara and Delilah both order some kind of mixed drink. I stick with my water.

"This is the first time I've been out since I took guardianship of Parker and Sophia," Delilah says. The statement is more factual than sad, but I know it's still hard for her to talk about sometimes.

Clara wraps an arm around her. "All the more reason for us to do this tonight. You deserve a break."

Delilah hugs her back, but then she straightens, her eyes lighting up. "Hey, Luke told me about the movie shoot. I'm so excited!"

"Movie shoot?" I ask.

Clara doesn't answer, so Delilah jumps in. "A production company reached out to Maggie and John a bit ago and offered them a very hefty amount of cash to rent part of their parking lot for a couple weeks."

My eyes widen. "What movie is it?"

It isn't unheard of for bigger Hollywood productions to film some scenes in small-town Canada to save a few bucks, but crews have never come to Kip Island before. At least, not since I've been alive. It is a bit surprising, though. Our little island would make the perfect setting for a cute, cheesy Christmas movie.

"I have to pee," Clara declares, abruptly changing the subject. "I'm going to the bathroom."

I look to Delilah, but she only shrugs. "I'll come with you," she says.

I jerk my thumb over my shoulder. "I'll go find the guys."

My two friends take off, heading toward the back of the building. I turn away from the bar and crane my neck, trying to see which table Gabe and Luke ended up at. They were supposed to be saving us seats, except we got sidetracked when Clara and Delilah decided to do shots.

Before I get very far in my search, a body slides into my line of vision, blocking me in. The man is somewhat attractive. He's slightly taller than me, and he has hair that's blond and shaggy. His smile is nice, if not a little conceited.

I stand there awkwardly as I wait for him to move.

"What are you drinking?" he asks.

It takes me a moment to register that he's speaking to me. "Sorry, what?"

He gestures to my empty glass. "I asked what you were drinking. I'll get your next one."

Oh. *Oh.* Is this flirting?

I feel self-conscious telling him it was just water; that I don't really drink. "Oh, um, that's okay," I say with a tentative smile.

He leans on the bar, pressing into my space. The perusal his eyes make of my body sets my cheeks on fire. "C'mon, let me buy you a drink."

I shake my head. "It's really okay. I'm just trying to find my friends. You don't—"

"I insist. It's not every night I get to talk with a beautiful woman like you."

His eyes seem to bore straight into me, and the pressure mounts. I've always had a hard time saying no, especially in environments I'm not familiar with. If Clara and Delilah weren't in the bathroom, they'd be all over this, telling the guy to get lost. The words are on the tip of my tongue, but I can't quite make myself say them.

"I, um, guess I'll take a strawberry daiquiri." I tuck a strand of hair behind my ear. "Thank you."

Inwardly, I cringe. I don't particularly want the daiquiri, but I can just nurse it for the rest of the night. Or pawn it off on the girls. Clara is always experimenting with drinks at Dockside, so her tastes are vast.

The man flags the bartender down and orders our drinks. Then he turns back to me and flashes a shameless grin. "I'm Deacon."

"Hallie," I reply. I fidget with the zipper on my purse, feeling out of place.

Why didn't you say no? You should've said no. You're such a chicken.

Deacon studies me. "I haven't seen you around here before. You visiting?"

I shake my head. "I'm from Kip Island."

The bartender slides my drink toward me. I swirl the straw around my glass, prolonging having to take a sip.

Deacon lifts his glass of whiskey to his lips. Then he arches a brow when he notices I haven't touched mine. "Is there a problem? Is it your drink?"

I open my mouth, ready to assure him that no, everything is fine and my drink is perfect. But someone else beats me to it.

"Yes," Gabe says. There's a hard edge to his voice that doesn't match his usual disposition. "There's definitely a problem."

I shoot him a look that says, *Don't be rude*. But he doesn't even see it because he's glaring at Deacon.

Deacon glances between me and Gabe, and then he holds his hands up in surrender. "My bad, bud." He plucks his whiskey off the bar and takes a step back. "I didn't realize she was taken." He turns and walks away.

My cheeks blaze. I'm certain I can feel the bartender's eyes on us, drinking in the drama. They most definitely see their fair share, night after night.

I fold my arms across my chest and look up at Gabe. "What did you do that for?"

"What?" he asks. "Get rid of a pest? He was bothering you."

Annoyance swirls, but I'm not entirely sure why. "How do you know I wasn't enjoying myself?"

Gabe takes a step forward, right into my space. I fight the urge to step back. His arms bracket me as he braces against the bar. "Because," he says, those brown eyes piercing, "I know you, Foster."

"Maybe you don't know me as well as you think," I counter, feeling brave. "It's been ten years."

His gaze burns as it travels the planes of my face—maps the slope of my nose, the apples of my cheeks, the ridge of my brow. "It could have been a hundred and I'd still remember the way you touch your hair when you're nervous. The way your eyes dart around, searching for escape. Because *I know you*. Always have and always will."

The conviction in his tone is a promise. And that sends a warning to my brain. Gabe's sincerity scared me back then, and it absolutely terrifies me now. Because all promises end up broken eventually.

"Well, you're wrong." I tip my chin up in defiance. "I was having a really good time getting to know Deacon."

The lie is a little bitter on my tongue, but I'm used to the taste by now.

Gabe's brow raises. He pushes off the bar, releasing me from the cage of his arms. Then he sweeps a hand toward the high top table across the room where Deacon has planted himself. "By all means, don't let me stop you, then."

The look on his face tells me that he thinks I'm bluffing. But I refuse to let him win. I take a sip of my drink, and then I walk away. I can feel Gabe's gaze on me, so I take purposeful strides forward. Let him think I'm way more confident in this half-formed plan than I actually am.

Inside, I feel a little like I'm walking myself to the gallows, but my pride has taken over. Turning around and admitting that I was wrong is not an option. Letting Gabe know just how much I truly haven't changed over the last ten years *is not an option*.

"Um, hey," I say to Deacon. I reach up to tuck my hair behind my ear, but I stop myself. Instead, I flip a strand over my shoulder and hope I don't look like a complete idiot.

Deacon's eyes slide to me. "Hey," he says with a grin. "You ditch your guard dog?"

I shrug. "Something like that." My eyes dart around, looking for something—goddamn it, anything, really—to make conversation about. When they land on the blessedly empty pool table, I have to resist the urge to drop to my knees in prayer. "Do you know how to play pool?"

"I do." He sets his whiskey on the table. "You up for a game?"

"I don't know how to play. Maybe you could teach me?"

Wrong. This feels wrong. Unease settles in my stomach as Deacon drapes an arm over my shoulder and leads me toward the table. As he sets up our cues, I look over my shoulder, and my stomach drops to my feet.

I can finally see the table that the guys managed to claim. Luke is clearly trying to get his brother's attention, but Gabe's gaze is trained across the room. On me. My skin heats, and I know my cheeks are flaming red.

A hand lands on my arm, and I startle. Turning back to

Deacon, I find him studying me. I force myself not to shrug off the contact.

"You ready?" he asks.

I nod. "Yup."

Deacon launches into a demonstration, but I'm hardly paying attention. Because I can still feel Gabe's eyes on me.

And they *burn*.

TWENTY-SIX

GABE

MAYBE YOU DON'T KNOW *me as well as you think.*

Hallie says I don't know her, but that's bullshit. I spent the better part of my life attuned to her every move. A little time and distance won't make me forget. Not a damn thing.

"Gabe? Are you listening?"

Maybe this fake engagement thing has gone to my head. Made me see things that aren't actually there. I thought we had turned a corner. That what I saw in her eyes the other night on the couch was desire. Longing—the same longing I've been struggling with for the past ten years. But maybe that's what I wanted to see. Maybe I was projecting in a desperate hope that it would make it so.

No. I know what I saw.

Only, it apparently doesn't matter. Hallie is determined to push me away, and she's hurting herself in the process.

"Gabe, there's a fire in the backroom."

I finally turn and raise a brow at Delilah. "Really? You couldn't do better than that?"

She shrugs. "Hey, it worked, didn't it?"

I shake my head, and then I reposition in my chair so Hallie is in full view. I regret challenging her. I should've backed off—apologized for inserting myself. Now she's thrown herself headfirst into something she hates just to prove a point to me. It's both infuriating and enticing. Infuriating because I can't stand watching that douchebag hang off her every word, and enticing because of the heat in her eyes when she stood up to me. I've never seen that before.

"If you don't like it, why don't you do something about it?" Luke chimes in.

I'd like to do something about it. Like introduce my fist to that sleazy fucker's face.

I'm not generally a violent person, but I find that watching Hallie with another guy tends to bring out a whole different side of me. If he seemed like a decent enough guy, I could force myself to live with it. But I saw the way he was looking at her. It lacked the respect that Hallie deserves. He sees her as a ticket to getting his dick wet, nothing more. And she is *so much more* than that.

I scrub a hand across my face. "I tried. All that did was push her farther into his arms."

My brother chuckles. "I mean, tell her how you feel. Circling around it isn't helping."

I snort, amused that he, of all people, would be trying to offer me advice. "So you're in a good relationship for all of two seconds and suddenly you're an expert?"

"This is definitely more of a *do as I say, not as I do* type of situation," Delilah says. When she catches Luke's displeased look, she grins and smacks a kiss to his cheek. "Sorry, Chief, but you have to admit that feelings aren't your strong suit."

He smirks. "You weren't saying that when I made you *feel* things last night."

Clara smacks a hand on the table. "Okay, *ew*. I'm all for you two being together, but I do *not* need the mental pictures to go along with it," she admonishes. Then she raises her finger and points it directly at my chest. "And *you*. Quit being a jealous asshole."

"I'm not—" She pins me with a sharp look, daring me to finish lying to her. I slump back in my seat. "How are you okay with this? She's clearly uncomfortable over there."

My sister sighs. "I learned a long time ago that Hallie has to do things her way. She won't believe it unless she figures it out on her own. All you can do is be there when she needs you."

"I wish she would just trust me," I mutter under my breath.

Clara's expression is full of sympathy. I've never outright admitted to having feelings for Hallie, but once Hallie left and my family realized that *something* had happened between the two of us, I think she put the pieces together. I used to wonder how she'd feel about it, but Clara hasn't made it seem like an issue.

"It's not about trusting you, Gabe," she says. "She trusts you. But her mom really fucked with her head. You know what Amanda is like."

I do, somewhat. I've heard stories, and I know Hallie doesn't really talk to her anymore. She never mentions her, anyway.

"I'm sure she'll come around," Delilah says. "Sometimes you have to go through some shit to realize what you really want."

Luke's hand tightens on the back of her chair at her words. He's probably thinking about how he almost screwed things up for good at the end of the summer.

"It's not even that," I say. As much as I'd like to be with her, that isn't the point right now. "I hate that she's putting herself in an uncomfortable position because of me."

Yet again, she's *running* because of me.

My brother, sister and Delilah offer me identical pitying looks.

I cross my arms and slump in my chair, turning back to the pool tables across the bar. I'm beginning to regret agreeing to this night. Luke was definitely on to something about staying home.

Clara changes the subject, asking Delilah if she's given any more thought to starting her own photography business. I think

Delilah says yes, but then I tune them out. I'm too busy watching the way *Deacon's* hand hovers on Hallie's lower back, entirely too close to her ass.

He comes up behind her, then his hand slides to her hip. She sidesteps out of his hold. But he just latches on like the leech he is, tighter this time. I've had about enough. I don't care if it makes me an asshole—I have to put an end to this.

Clara must see the same thing I do because her expression hardens. "Okay, if you don't go over there, *I* will."

I'm out of my seat before my sister even finishes talking.

I stalk across the bar. I'm not sure if the other patrons can feel the ire radiating off me or what, but they move for me all the same. I'm thankful, because I wouldn't have hesitated to shove someone aside if they got in my way.

"Deacon, can you give me some space?" Hallie asks, her voice timid.

Her tone alone should be enough to give him pause, but the guy doesn't listen. He continues to box her in against the pool table, uncaring that she's leaning away from him. There's a flash of panic in her expression.

"C'mon, sweetheart," he croons. "Let's get out of here. Go somewhere more private."

Her spine snaps straight. "No, thanks. I think I'm done playing now. I need to get back to my friends."

Deacon leans toward her, but before he can say something else, I speak through gritted teeth. "I believe she asked for some space."

When *Deacon* looks at me, he rolls his eyes. "Oh, you again. Didn't you get the hint before?"

I step closer, angling between him and Hallie. Hand on his chest, I shove him back a step. "You want to talk about hints, let's talk about hints. How about we start with the fact that she is *clearly* uncomfortable with you touching her? Yet you don't seem to give a fuck. How's *that* for a hint?"

"Gabe," Hallie says. She clutches the back of my shirt, trying to pull me away. "I'm fine."

"See?" Deacon's expression is smug as hell. "She's *fine*. Wouldn't want to cause a scene for nothing."

I step forward, crowding his space the same way he did Hallie's. "I wouldn't consider giving you a well-earned lesson on respecting women to be nothing."

"Hey, *she* came to me. I was doing what she wanted."

"Until she changed her mind, and you conveniently stopped caring about what she wanted."

His lip curls. "Whatever, bud. She's not worth all this shit." He shrugs. "She's not even that hot."

People have said many stupid things in my presence, but this takes the goddamn cake. Though it's not hard to believe he'd be the type of man whose ego is so fragile, he has to mask the sting of rejection by insulting the very woman he was just trying to sleep with. Not only that, but it's not even *true*. Hallie Foster is beautiful in a way that commands acknowledgment.

"Say it again," I dare him. Anything to give me the justification to give him a bloody nose.

"Gabriel."

I don't take my eyes off Deacon. Vaguely, I sense that some of the chatter around us has died down, which means a good chunk of the bar is looking our way. This establishment isn't a stranger to bar fights, and they're probably all wondering if they're about to get a front row seat to the next one.

God, do I want to. My parents would be disappointed as hell, and I'm not sure I could look my daughter in the eye if I got arrested for hitting someone, but wiping that look off Deacon's face would feel phenomenal.

"*Gabriel*," Hallie says again, louder. She fists my shirt and tugs on it hard. "Let's just go. I want to go home."

I finally look at her. The satisfaction I would normally feel from her calling my place *home* is drowned out by the overwhelming feeling of dread. The expression on her face is one I haven't seen often, if ever.

She's *angry*. At me.

I take a step back from Deacon, and he scoffs, walking away. After a moment, the people around us return to their own drinks and conversations, disappointed the altercation didn't turn into an all-out brawl.

Placing my hand on the small of Hallie's back, I lead her away. She goes stiff at the contact, but she stays close, letting me part the crowd. At least she isn't retreating from me completely.

We meet up with Luke halfway back to the table. He was probably on his way to intervene, to pull me back before I did something I would regret. Because that's what he does. *Big brother to the rescue.*

"You good?" he asks quietly.

I shake my head. I'm not good. Not until I talk to Hallie.

Our group is quick to slip their jackets on and finish off their drinks. Then we all file out to the parking lot. No one utters a word about the tension radiating between me and Hallie. In fact, no one speaks at all, even when Clara and Delilah take turns wrapping their arms around Hallie, who is shaking like a leaf.

She won't look at me.

The drive home is eerily silent.

Luke and Delilah get out of the truck first. My brother loops an arm around Delilah's waist when she stumbles, and then I watch them climb the porch to her front door. Once they're inside, I head for Clara's apartment on the main street. She lives above The Dusty Rose, the café and bakery most locals frequent almost daily.

When I roll to a stop outside her building, my sister unhooks her seatbelt and then leans forward between the front seats.

"Thanks for the drive," she says. She kisses my cheek and then pats Hallie on the head. "Goodnight, kids. And good luck."

"Night," I mutter.

Once Clara is safely inside, I pull away. Hallie still refuses to look in my direction. I glance at her every couple minutes, trying to catch her gaze, but she keeps staring out the window. I clench my jaw and tighten my hands on the steering wheel.

When I park in the driveway, Hallie is quick to slip out of the passenger seat and head for the front door. She tries the handle, but it's locked. I watch her huff as she starts to dig inside her purse for her set of keys.

Wordlessly, I come up behind her and unlock the door.

She spins on me, not making a move to head inside. "I can't believe you did that. Do you have any idea how *embarrassing* that was?" Hallie doesn't wait for me to respond. "*Extremely*. The whole bar was looking at us, Gabe!"

I pause, taken aback. "You're yelling at me."

She crosses her arms defensively. "Yeah, so? I'm mad at you."

"You never yell."

Hallie opens her mouth to argue, then closes it again. Because she can't deny it.

"I know you. You never yell," I say again. "Because you're scared you'll push people away if you're not so damn agreeable all the time. But you just yelled at me. Why?"

She swallows visibly, taking an involuntary step backwards, into the house. "I don't know, Gabe. I just did."

I follow her, not letting her retreat. Not letting her run. "You do know, and I do, too. You yelled at me because you're comfortable with me. You feel safe with me." Like Abbie feels safe to express her emotions.

"That...may be true."

I close the front door behind us, and then I hook an arm around Hallie's waist. Spinning us, I pin her back to the door, one of my hands braced beside her head.

"Gabriel," she breathes. She fists the front of my jacket.

This need I have for her has been building for too fucking long, and once I give in, I fear I won't ever be the same. Shit, I *know* I won't be. I don't want to be.

"You know what this proves, Hallie?" She shakes her head. "This proves you want to stay with me. You want to fight."

Her blue eyes are shining, but she doesn't try to refute me.

"So let me fight with you, Foster."

TWENTY-SEVEN

HALLIE

ALL THE OXYGEN in my lungs is sucked out with Gabe's words.

"You want to argue? I'll bite," he says. "Let's start with how I fucking *hated* seeing you with Deacon."

Gabe wears his anger well. He doesn't often let it get the best of him. Now, though, his expression is wild. Unrestrained. I can see *everything* in his eyes—he isn't holding anything back.

My heart throbs. It's all too much, yet... Yet it's not enough. I'm terrified of what I'll say if I open my mouth, so I don't.

"If I thought for one *single* second that he was a decent guy, I would have kept my mouth shut," he continues. "I would've watched him touch you. Would've forced myself to be alright with him taking you home. But a man like that doesn't deserve to breathe the same air as you, let alone have you in his bed. And you don't deserve to be treated the way he treated you."

"I think I know what I deserve," I say weakly.

In my head, I'm chanting, *You were right, you were right. I was so wrong, and you were right.*

From the moment he walked up to me, Deacon gave me this slippery kind of feeling. I didn't realize I was in too deep until he was winding his body around me, constricting like a boa. But Gabe knew, and I shouldn't have been so stubborn.

Gabe shakes his head. "If you did, you'd see what's right in front of you." His arm tightens around my waist, and when he speaks, his voice is low. "If you want someone to buy you a drink, let it be me. Someone to flirt with? I can do that, too. And, baby, if you want someone to fuck you..." His eyes blaze. "All you have to do is ask."

His words stun me for half a second. I swallow, clearing my throat before speaking. "You're...jealous?"

He almost laughs, but it lacks any kind of humour. "Of course I am, Foster. Some asshole had his hands all over my fiancée tonight."

My fiancée.

It isn't the first time Gabe has let that slip. Mostly, he makes a joke of it. But this is the first time that he's called me his fiancée where it feels like it means something. Something more than just playing a part.

My teeth snag my bottom lip. Gabe's attention is instantly drawn there.

Words lodge in my throat. Being honest means being vulnerable, and I'm not very good at that. But Gabe was right about everything. I don't yell, I don't fight. Except with him... With him, it feels like something worth fighting for.

"When he touched me," I say, watching as his eyes darken, "I wished it was your hands on me instead."

He groans. "Killing me, Foster."

My lips twitch with a slight smile. "Sorry."

Gabe takes his hand off the door beside my head. It trembles slightly as it curves along my jaw, slipping through strands of golden hair before cupping the back of my head. He looks pained, like holding himself back truly is akin to the greatest torture, but still, he takes his time. Like he's savouring this. Us. *Me.*

"Tell me you want me, Hallie, because I want you so fucking bad, I can hardly think. Tell me you want this, too."

The plea in his voice—the pure *yearning*—breaks me and then stitches me back together. It's a lifetime of stop and go, push and pull, all culminating in this beautiful moment.

"Yes," I breathe. "I want you."

I've never stopped.

He searches my eyes. "You want me?"

I nod. "This is me asking, Gabe."

His hand on my hip squeezes, drawing me closer. His eyes trace my face slowly, memorizing it, before landing on my lips again. They part involuntarily, and he takes this as his invitation. As his face lowers to mine, I push up onto the tips of my toes, meeting him halfway.

I always thought my first kiss would belong to Gabe. I hoped for it—dreamt of it. Life, it turned out, had other plans, but I wouldn't change things. Not when this moment right here is so perfect, I could cry.

The kiss is gentle at first. Tentative, like when he kissed me at the wedding. It's everything I both wanted and needed, and my body sings in pleasure. His mouth moves against mine in a practiced rhythm, as if we've been doing this all our lives. As if this is where we were destined to end up. Maybe it is.

Quickly, though, everything shifts. We aren't at the wedding anymore—there are no prying eyes, and we're over pretending. So when Gabe deepens the kiss, when his tongue slides against mine, I let him take it all.

My heart has always belonged to him, so he might as well have my body, too.

Clinging to him, I'm desperate to be closer. I *need* to be closer. All the layers between us are too much. But I don't know how to verbalize what I want, what I think I might die without.

Woman up, Hallie. Tell him.

Before I can properly begin to spiral, Gabe pulls back slightly.

"*Hallie*," he groans against my mouth. "Baby. Can I take you upstairs now?"

Upstairs. To his bedroom. To his *bed*. This time, for a lot more than sleep.

I nod, not caring if I seem overeager. "Please, yes. Please."

He nips at my lower lip. "I'll be so good to you, baby. Show you exactly what you deserve."

I don't even have time to swoon or melt into a puddle because then he's tugging me toward the stairs. He gestures for me to go up first, but when I'm too slow, he slaps me playfully on the ass. I let out a sound of surprise, looking at him over my shoulder. He only grins, and *God*, it's a pretty sight.

I stomp on the nervous butterflies that try to take flight as I walk toward Gabe's room. I can feel his body heat, confirming he's not far behind me.

We're really doing this. I'm really about to have sex with my best friend's brother.

As soon as the thought hits, I curse myself. Like the butterflies, I shove Clara firmly out of my mind. Now is definitely *not* the time for me to be picturing her face.

With the bedroom door shut, Gabe tugs his jacket off. I follow suit, tossing mine onto the chair in the corner. When I face Gabe again, he slips his fingers through my belt loops and guides me closer. Against my stomach, through the denim of his pants, I can feel that he's turned on. A dull throb settles between my legs.

His hands slide over my hips, then to my ass, cupping me there. "These jeans. *Fuck*, Hallie, these jeans," he groans. "They've been testing me since the minute you walked into my house for the first time."

"Sorry," I say with a sheepish smile.

He shakes his head. "Don't be sorry, baby. I've loved every minute. But now you need to take them off."

"Off?" I squeak.

Logically, I knew this would require me to take off my clothes.

But standing here in front of him, having him tell me to do it, makes it seem so *real*.

Gabriel Bowman wants me to take my pants off. Oh my God.

"Strip, Hallie," he commands.

And I am powerless to resist.

I unbutton my pants and slowly peel them off my legs. Removing skinny jeans seems like the least sexy thing one could do, especially when they get caught on my ankles and turn inside out, but Gabe's eyes flash as he watches me. The next thing to go is my top. And then I'm standing there in nothing but my bra and underwear.

I can feel my face heating—my entire body, really. I'm not used to being observed like this. It's been a while since I last had sex, and we left the lights off. But in the warm lamplight, Gabe's eyes are roving over me like I'm painted in vivid colour.

The urge to cover myself up is hard to resist, but something tells me Gabe would take issue with that. Still, I wring my hands together in front of my stomach.

"You are a fucking masterpiece, Hallie Foster," he says. "A masterpiece made just for me."

His words twist around my heart, giving it a painful squeeze.

"Can you—? Would you—?" I inhale a deep breath. "Take your shirt off?" I finish quietly.

He obliges, then draws me back into his arms. "I can tell you're nervous, but you have the control here. We won't do anything you're not comfortable with. And if you want something, you can ask for it. Chances are, I'll want it, too."

I peer shyly up at him. "I don't really...want control." For once, I'd love nothing more than to shut my brain *off*.

His eyes sweep over my face. "Trust me?"

"I trust you, Gabe."

He starts with kissing me on the mouth. Then he nips at my jaw, trails his lips over my neck. Soon, he's sucking on the swell of one breast, and I wonder briefly if it'll leave a mark. I hope it does.

Slowly, I melt against him. My bra comes off, then my underwear. The air should feel cool against my naked skin, but all I feel is heat. Mind blissfully empty, I let Gabe guide me onto my back, let my head sink into the mattress.

The weight of him above me feels amazing, but when he rocks his hips against mine, I feel like I'm in heaven. His lower half is still clothed, and that won't do. I reach out, fumbling with the button on his jeans.

He grabs my hands, holding them above my head. "We don't have to rush, baby. We've got forever, and I intend to use every second."

A kind of content sigh escapes me, followed quickly by a moan when he rocks his hips again. My back arches, pressing my breasts against his bare chest. My nipples tighten as they brush the hard planes.

Can't he just put it inside me already?

He doesn't. Instead, he releases my hands, then works his way steadily down my body. When he settles himself between my thighs, face extremely close to my aching core, I let out a gasp.

"Gabe," I whine. My voice doesn't even sound like my own. "Please."

"I have been waiting for this day since I was eighteen fucking years old, Hallie. Let me admire the art before I devour it."

"*Oh.* You don't have to—" I try to sit up, close my legs, but Gabe pins me with a look that makes me freeze. "I've never... No one has ever...done that to me before."

Surprise etches itself in his expression, but it quickly gives way to satisfaction. That almost makes him...happy?

"Say the word and I won't, but if you'll let me, I want to make you feel good, baby. Show you what all those other guys have been stupid enough to miss."

I have the urge to laugh at that. *All* is generous. I've slept with two men in my entire adult life.

"And if you don't like it," Gabe continues, "then I keep exploring until I find something you do like."

Cheeks flaming, hands fisting the sheets beneath me, I nod. "Okay. You can...proceed."

I can't look at him, so I stare at the ceiling. I feel his hair brushing the insides of my thighs, and I squirm as it tickles. But I soon stop moving altogether as he spreads me open and traces a path up my slit with his tongue.

"Relax, baby," Gabe says. "Let me make this good for you."

I try to do as he says. Try to force my muscles to unclench. But it isn't until he does another pass with his tongue that my hips buck involuntarily, and I let out a surprised gasp, fisting the sheets once again.

Holy shit.

He laps and sucks, and I fall victim to the intensity of my building orgasm. Although it's getting closer, it still feels out of reach.

"Gabe," I whisper.

"Yeah, baby?"

"I... I need something, um, more?"

Voicing my needs like this is new, but I feel safe doing that with Gabe. He makes me feel safe.

With his thumb, he circles my clit. "Better?"

"Mhm." I pinch my eyes closed. "Just a little more."

He slips two fingers inside me, and I bite my lip at the stretch. I try to shift, my instinct being to squirm, but he has me pinned down, which only excites me more.

"How's that?" he asks.

I nod. "Yes. Good," I croak. *So good.*

With his fingers now pumping into me, when he returns his mouth to my clit, my hips buck again. My cheeks flame, but Gabe doesn't seem to mind. In fact, he seems to be enjoying himself.

"Oh, God, Gabe. I can't— I—"

I squeeze my eyes shut as my orgasm slams into me, covering

me in pleasure from head to toe. My thighs tremble, and my hips protest at being held open at this angle, but I don't care. Because that felt *otherworldly*.

Or maybe it's not even the fact that he went down on me. Maybe it's just that after so many years of thinking I won't ever get to experience this, sex with Gabe is actually *happening*, so my body is overwhelmed with pleasure and a giddy kind of euphoria.

Gabe sits up, licking his lips. Licking *me* from his lips. My knees knock together as I close my legs and push up onto my elbows. I almost ask, *What now?* But my question is already answered when Gabe slides from the bed and starts removing his pants. Then his underwear.

And then, *oh my God*, I'm seeing my best friend's brother naked.

I've fantasized about this moment far more than I care to admit, but nothing could have prepared me for the way I would feel when I saw Gabriel Bowman's cock for the first time.

My thighs press closer together, and the nerves suddenly hit me full-force. This is something we can't come back from. I mean, he's seen me. *All* of me. More than that, though, I think I'm scared by how much I want this. And I want it *a lot*.

"Hey." Gabe's voice is gentle, and my worried gaze meets his. "We can stop, Hallie. If this is too much, we won't do anything else."

Moving forward is scary, but... My eyes trail down his body, admiring the muscles he maintains for work, and land on his hard cock. That ache in me grows, and I know that as much as I'm nervous about going all the way, stopping right now would be an absolute *crime*.

"I don't want to stop," I tell him. "I need you."

In more ways than one. It isn't simply my body that aches for him, it's my soul. My whole being. For now, though, I focus on the way an anticipatory shiver runs down my spine as he collects a condom from his bedside drawer.

Gabe places a hand on my bent knee. "Then let me in, baby."

I scoot up the bed, resting against the pillows, and let my legs fall open again. He wastes no time donning the condom and settling himself over me. Then he kisses me.

With his mouth against mine and our bare skin pressed together, I feel alive. More alive than I've ever been before. Maybe it's the thrill of finally having something you've wanted for so long.

"This mouth," Gabe murmurs. "So soft."

I wiggle beneath him. "Gabe, *please*."

He answers my plea. Lining his cock up with my entrance, he circles it, gathering my arousal. Then he slowly begins to push inside.

"Fuck, Hallie," he groans. "You're tight."

I have a feeling he isn't just talking about my pussy. My whole body feels coiled with tension, and those pesky worries threaten to creep back in and ruin this. *Stop thinking. Enjoy this while you have it.*

"Hallie, baby, look at me."

My eyes snap open, meeting Gabe's familiar brown irises. He holds my gaze as he continues to ease inside, and my lips part on a silent moan.

He rolls his hips, filling me, and I gasp.

"Let go, Foster. Show me how well you can take me."

He thrusts again, and I grab the back of his neck, holding him to me. And when he starts to fuck me, I lose what little poise I still had, yielding to my body's desires.

Bit by bit, my limbs loosen, and I let myself go. I meet his thrusts. I press kisses to his throat when he's buried deep inside me.

As my release crashes through me, I claw at his back, no doubt leaving marks. Through the shockwaves, I feel Gabe's pace picking up. He chases his own release, and then he's coming with a guttural groan that has satisfaction zipping through me.

Slowly, we come down from the high, and he slips out of me. Gabe nuzzles his face against my neck.

"I'll be right back," he says. With a quick kiss to my forehead, he heads to the en suite.

I want nothing more than to stay where I am, but if I don't force myself to the bathroom to clean up and get ready for bed right now, it's not happening at all. My legs feel a little wobbly when my feet hit the ground, but I scoop Gabe's t-shirt up from the floor and slide it over my head.

Even though Abbie isn't here tonight, I still find myself creeping down the hall and quietly shutting the bathroom door behind me. I cringe at my reflection in the mirror. My hair is a disaster, and my makeup is smudged. *Great.*

I should probably shower, but I'm beyond tired at this point, so I quickly use the bathroom, brush my teeth and wash my face. After I run my brush through my hair to untangle the knots, I head back to Gabe's bedroom.

When I get back, Gabe is pacing in the middle of the room. He's wearing his boxers again, but otherwise, his tattoos are on full display. I almost say something about them, tell him how much I like them, but then he turns to face me. My words dry up.

He runs a hand through his hair, which is almost as messy as mine. He looks wrecked, devastated, so similar to that day on the beach. My knees almost buckle at the realization.

"I thought you left."

My heart cracks wide open. I shake my head. "I'm right here."

Gabe gathers me against his chest, and with my head resting over his heart, I can hear how fast it's beating. "Please don't go."

Not again.

"I won't," I promise.

Not until he leaves me first.

TWENTY-EIGHT

GABE

WHEN I OPEN MY EYES, I'm half convinced that last night was a dream. That I'm going to roll over and discover that I'm alone because Hallie, in my arms, in my bed, was just a figment of my imagination. It wouldn't be the first time I've woken up aching for her.

But when I turn on my side and reach out, I find her there. Her bare skin is warm against mine as I tug her closer. With her back to my chest, I wrap my arm around her waist, securing her there. The content sigh she lets out makes me smile.

She stayed.

I place a kiss on the top of her head. "Morning, beautiful."

Hallie groans, pressing her face into the pillow. "Is it already morning?"

I chuckle as my arm tightens around her. "Afraid so. How did you sleep?"

She turns to face me. "The best I have in a while. Since the night of the storm when you made me stay with you."

I didn't think I'd get to experience that again—falling asleep with her. The night of the storm, and the morning after, when I asked her to move into the main house, feel like a lifetime ago. So much has changed between us.

Flashes of last night play across my mind. For a split second when we got home, I worried I had shown my hand without any guarantee. But something about what happened with Deacon shifted things for Hallie. Whatever it is, I'm damn grateful.

I roll onto my back, taking Hallie with me. She squeals as I position her over me, straddling my waist.

I hum. "I think I like this position."

Hallie rolls her eyes as she crosses her arms, covering her breasts. Her cheeks are already stained in a pretty pink blush. "I'm sure you do."

I reach up and take her hands, pulling her arms away from her chest. "You don't have to be shy with me, Foster. I love every fucking inch of your body."

I thought I showed her as much when I ripped my shirt over her head after she came back into the bedroom after cleaning herself up. I was trying not to let that initial panic of finding my bed empty get to me, so I focused on Hallie and her pleasure instead.

Now, for emphasis, I let my eyes roam. My cock is already hard, and when Hallie shifts under my gaze, she rubs against it. When she bites her lower lip, I groan.

"Your parents will be dropping Abbie off soon," she says. "We probably shouldn't be naked when they get here."

Reluctantly, I let her slide off of me. She grabs my shirt from last night and slips it on again, then starts collecting her clothes. I get the strangest urge to have her leave them on the floor, just to prove she was here. That last night was real.

"I'm going to shower," she declares.

"Want some company?" I ask with a grin.

She smiles, but it doesn't sit right—doesn't fully reach her eyes. "You know very well that shower wouldn't be productive. I'll meet you downstairs after I'm done."

And then she's gone.

I run a hand through my hair as frustration washes over me. *Did I push her too hard? Again?* After last night, I thought we were on the same page. I thought everything was falling into place, the way it should have when we were eighteen. I can't regret those years we spent apart because they gave me Abbie, and I wouldn't trade her for anything. But having this second chance—this chance to do things *right* with Hallie... I won't mess that up.

With a sigh, I stand from the bed, then head to my en suite to take my own shower. Now that the lust has been cleared from my brain, I know Hallie was right. Showering with her likely wouldn't have been productive, and I would rather not scar my daughter by being found in a compromising position when she gets home. So I shower and dress, and then I make my way downstairs to get started on breakfast.

Just as I finish cooking the scrambled eggs, soft footsteps pad across the floor, and Hallie appears in the doorway. She's wearing yoga pants and a t-shirt—*my* t-shirt—but fuck, she looks beautiful. She always looks beautiful. Her hair is still damp from her shower, but I know she prefers to let it air dry.

"Hey," she says, almost shy.

"Hey, yourself."

"So, um." She glances away and then back up, meeting my eyes. "We should probably...talk about last night. I know things maybe got said in the heat of the moment and—"

"Last night," I say, cutting her off as I cross to her in two quick strides, "I meant every fucking word I said."

Her blue eyes widen. "Gabe, I..."

I cup her face, and my right thumb smooths over her cheekbone. "I adore you, Hallie Foster, and I meant it when I said I want you. I've *been* wanting you, for as long as I care to remember."

Her fingers curl into my shirt, grappling for something to hold on to. "You want me...for sex?"

I frown in confusion. "No, baby, I want *you*. For so much

more than just sex. I want it all." She shakes her head, disbelieving, so I continue. "I dreamed about this when we were younger. Getting to hold you like this."

She closes her eyes, leaning into my touch. "You did?" Her words are a mere whisper.

"I did. But you, the real you, is more than I could've ever hoped for."

Her eyes open with startling clarity. "I dreamed about you, too."

Then why did you run?

She explained some when she apologized the other day, but I still don't understand where those impulses came from. Why my feelings scared her so much. I don't let myself ask, though. This thing between us is fragile, and I fear that bringing up the past will put our future in jeopardy. So for now, I swallow my curiosity.

"What do you say?" My eyes trace her face, drinking her in. "Will you give us a shot? A real shot."

Hallie smiles softly. "I think I can manage that."

I grin. My hand slides into her hair, and the other settles on her waist, pulling her closer. I haven't even had breakfast yet and this is already the second best day of my life, following close behind Abbie's birth.

Some small part of me warns to be cautious. She already left me once before. I brush it off. I'm not going to let that fear take root. Not when I have Hallie here, in my house, in my arms, wanting to be with me. This is how I wanted that day on the beach to turn out.

Hallie peers up at me. "Can we...maybe not tell anyone?" she asks. My heart sinks, and my smile falls. "Not for long! I just... This is a lot, Gabe, and everything feels so complicated right now. You know I love your family like they're my own, but..."

I swallow back my disappointment. "They can be a bit invasive."

Her eyes plead with me to understand. "I know it's not fair to ask, and I'm sorry. I just need a little time."

A little time. I would find a way to give Hallie the whole world if she wanted it, so a little time is pretty tame in comparison. I can do that. If it was solely up to me, I wouldn't want to keep this from anyone, but Hallie has her reasons.

"I'll give you time," I say. "To get used to this. Used to *us*. But if you think I'm going anywhere, you're mistaken."

Her hands tighten in my shirt again. "Promise?"

"Cross my heart."

The first touch of her lips is gentle. Then she pushes onto her tiptoes, wrapping her arms around my neck, and leans in. I let her take the lead this time. Even in this, she's a little shy, but she'll get used to it.

I turn her around and start walking her backwards. When her back meets the island, my hands find the backs of her thighs, and then I hoist her up onto the countertop. Situating myself between her legs, I return my mouth to hers.

If only eighteen-year-old Gabe could see me now... All I wanted back then was for Hallie to give me a chance. Finally getting to kiss her—to fuck her—is better than my wildest dreams. I want to soak her in and let her flood my veins.

Hallie pulls back, but then she presses a kiss to my jaw and runs her fingers along the waistband of my sweatpants. I grab her hand, bringing it away from my groin, and interlace our fingers.

I raise a brow. "That is a dangerous game, Hallie. One we don't have time for. Though I will gladly show you how I would have won later."

She laughs, shaking her head. "You're rather cocky this morning, Bowman."

"Happy," I correct. "The word you're looking for is happy."

Hallie's expression softens, and her usual blush spreads across her cheeks. "I'm happy, too."

I press another kiss to her lips. "Good."

"I'll be even happier if you show me what you made me for breakfast, though."

I chuckle, helping her down from the island. The eggs and veggie bacon, which I have come to appreciate, are a little cold once we get to them, but we don't care. We eat quickly, stealing glances at one another. Hallie's blush seems to be permanent at this point. I love it.

The pink in her cheeks only deepens when there's a knock at the front door, followed by voices and three pairs of footsteps. As we're setting our plates in the dishwasher, Abbie and my parents come into the room.

"Good morning, Daddy!"

My daughter makes a beeline for me. This part never gets old. I know one day, her greetings will get less enthusiastic, so I cherish each one I get. I wrap my arms around Abbie, lifting her off her feet as I hug her. "Hi, Princess. I missed you."

"Good morning," Dad says to Hallie.

"Morning," she squeaks, then takes a long sip of her orange juice.

I cough to hide my laugh. For someone who doesn't want my family to know we're together, she isn't very good at acting inconspicuous.

"How was your night?" Dad asks. "Get up to anything exciting?"

Hallie chokes on her juice. Mom pats her back, then looks between the two of us suspiciously. She assesses Hallie. "Are you alright, sweetheart?"

"Oh, me?" Hallie waves her off. "I'm fine! And last night was good. Great. Really great."

When she meets my gaze, I wink. She blushes harder.

Thankfully, Abbie steals everyone's attention away. "Can I paint today?" she asks, pulling out of my arms. "I have my paints from Mommy's house. Please, please, *please*. I promise I won't make a mess."

I openly laugh at that. There's no way we're getting out of this scot free. "You can."

She turns to Hallie, clasping her hands together. "Will you paint with me again?"

Hallie smiles warmly. "Of course I will."

"I'm gonna go get my paints! And my brushes!" Abbie tears out of the kitchen and up the stairs.

"Thanks for taking her last night," I say to my parents. I itch to move closer to Hallie, but I refrain.

Mom shakes her head. "You know it's no trouble, sweetie. We love spending time with our granddaughter." Her eyes ping-pong between me and Hallie again. "We'll babysit anytime."

When Abbie comes back downstairs with her paint supplies and starts setting them up at the kitchen table, my parents see themselves out.

Before Hallie goes to help, I grab her hand. "Hey," I say.

She smiles. "Hi."

My eyes flick to my daughter, but she's engrossed with her art, so they settle back on Hallie. "I just want to tell you that I really like you, Foster."

She squeezes my palm. "I really like you, too."

TWENTY-NINE

HALLIE

I THOUGHT LIVING with Gabe was temptation before, but now that we're sleeping together, it's a million times worse. Even more so because we have to hide our affection from Abbie, which has led to secret touches and me sneaking down the hall to Gabe's bedroom once we're sure she's asleep for the night.

It feels scandalous and dangerous, and fun. But I also know that not being open about our relationship with his family eats at Gabe every time we run into his parents or one of his siblings.

Just a little longer, I keep promising him. But time keeps stretching, and the longer we wait, the bigger the omission feels. I know this, but I still can't make myself agree. It feels safer here, existing in our bubble of two. I'm well aware that it could pop any day, but I cling to the illusion that it will protect me.

As I finish adding the chocolate-covered strawberries to the plate, a familiar pair of tattooed arms bracket me against the counter on either side.

"What's all this for?" Gabe asks, looking over my shoulder at the spread of food on the island. Along with the strawberries, I bought some fancy cheese and crackers from Sunnyside.

"Clara and Delilah are coming over," I reply. Then I freeze. "I'm sorry, I should have asked if that was alright."

He presses a kiss to my shoulder, where my shirt has slipped down to reveal bare skin. I suppress a shiver.

"You don't need my permission," he says. "Besides, one of the people you invited is my sister. I can hardly complain about that."

"It's your house," I argue.

"It's yours, too." He steps closer, pressing his chest to my back. "So invite whoever you like."

"In that case...you have to leave."

He chuckles. "You're kicking me out?"

I set the strawberry container down and turn, leaning back against the counter. And I come face to face with Gabe's bare chest. The ink on his skin taunts me, begging for me to trace it with my fingers. And, if I'm feeling brave one night, maybe my tongue.

Cheeks blazing, I meet his amused gaze. "Temporarily. It's girls' night, and I know you. You wouldn't know how to behave if your life depended on it."

Gabe grins. He lets go of the counter and sets his hands on my hips, squeezing. "I can keep my hands to myself. I think it's *you* who would have trouble. You can't resist me, Foster."

He's not entirely wrong...

I playfully push at his chest. He just tugs me closer, trapping my palm against his bare skin. His dark hair is still damp from his shower, and I truly can't stop my free hand from reaching up and brushing a fallen strand off his forehead.

"See?" he says. "That was entirely unprovoked touching."

My jaw drops. "You're the one who won't let me go."

He leans closer, his lips still tilted up in amusement. "Maybe we should just agree that we both lack self-control in this relationship."

Relationship. My heart skips a beat or two. I still can't let myself fully believe it.

I tip my head up toward him. "Maybe that's why we fit so well together."

Gabe hums. "Told you that you were made for me, baby."

My breath stutters in my chest. His eyes lock on mine, and then the distance between us is getting smaller. Just as our lips brush, a loud knock sounds on the front door.

I jump at the sound. Then my eyes widen when I hear Clara's voice as she pushes into the house without waiting for someone to answer.

"Go put a shirt on!" I hiss at Gabe, shooing him away.

His hands fall from my sides, leaving me feeling cold. "Relax," he says quietly. "They aren't going to suspect anything."

I cross my arms. "Have you met your sister?"

He throws his hands up in surrender as he heads toward the hallway. "I'm going, I'm going."

I spin around, busying myself with the rest of the food preparation as I attempt to pretend nothing weird is going on. I have to fan my face to try to tame the redness I can feel spreading.

"Hi, Gabe," Delilah says. She and Clara are in the kitchen now. They pass Gabe on their way over to me.

Clara wrinkles her nose. "Don't you own a shirt?"

"Don't you have some manners?" he counters. "What's the point of knocking if you're just gonna barge in anyway?"

She waves him off. "Twin privileges. Besides, you're hogging my best friend."

I go completely still. *Does she know?* But she can't. We haven't let anything slip at Sunday brunch. We act exactly like we always have, except our longing glances across the table have a touch more sexual tension than they used to.

Gabe grins. "That's because she likes me better than you."

Clara flips him the bird as he saunters out of the room. I try not to, but I can't help watching him walk away. The tattoo on his right shoulder blade isn't a bad sight either.

Stop drooling, Hallie. That's a surefire way to blow your cover.

Delilah holds up a bottle of rosé. "I brought the good stuff."

I smile. When Clara suggested we have a do-over of the other night, at home instead of the bar, I readily agreed. I'll take any opportunity to spend time with Clara, and I really want to get to know Delilah better.

I grab three wine glasses from the cupboard and set them on the island. Delilah uncorks the bottle and begins to pour. And pour. The wine is almost to the top when Clara sets a hand on her wrist.

"You doing alright there, Dee?" Clara asks.

"Huh? Oh." Delilah shakes her head and sets the bottle down. "Sorry, I'm a little out of it today."

"Late night?" I tease.

Clara grimaces. "I flew too close to the sun with you," she says to Delilah. "I don't think I like you talking about banging my brother."

Delilah laughs, shaking her head. "*Yes*, it was a late night, but not like that. I was helping Parker with his project for his science class and we lost track of time. We would've kept going, too, if Luke hadn't woken up for work and made us go to bed."

Clara picks up the bottle and finishes doling out the rosé. "It sounds like things are getting better between you two."

She nods. "We're getting there. Therapy has really been helping."

I wasn't here to witness it, but Delilah and her brother went through a rough patch after they first moved to the island. I'm sure it's not easy to navigate the kind of loss they experienced, so I'm glad they're doing better.

I take my glass of wine just as Gabe strolls back into the kitchen, looking entirely too good. Who am I kidding? He *always* looks good. I take a healthy sip of my drink.

"Seeing as I'm unwanted here, I'm going to hang out with Luke," he says. "I'll be home later. You ladies have fun."

The urge to kiss him goodbye is strong. He must feel it, too, because his hand brushes against the small of my back on his way out of the room.

"What's new with you?" I ask Clara, forcing myself to forget about Gabe for the time being. "How's the movie shoot going?"

Clara purses her lips. "Fine," she grumbles.

Usually, my best friend would be all over something like this. She'd be the first to tell us all the details she's learned from being in such close proximity to the production and its crew. The fact that she isn't leaves me suspicious.

"You didn't tell us what movie it was. Does it star anyone good?"

"Debatable," she replies.

"Clara," I say, "we're going to need a little more than that."

She sighs. "It's Cooper's movie, okay?"

I gasp. "*Cooper*? As in, *that* Cooper?"

"Wait," Delilah interjects, "I'm missing something. What's wrong with Cooper?"

"A great many things." Clara tops up her glass of wine, then takes a generous sip. "I want to poke his eyeballs out with a tiny fork."

I pause, my own drink suspended halfway to my mouth.

"*Pardon*?" Delilah sputters.

Neither one of us are used to our friend, the bubbly woman that she is, being so hostile. She takes most everything in stride. Except this, apparently.

"I want to poke his eyeballs out with a tiny fork," she repeats.

Delilah and I share a worried look. When we both turn to Clara, I'm the first to speak. "We heard you. We're just...surprised."

"Though you *have* been kind of violent lately," Delilah adds. "Are you okay?"

She huffs. "Cooper deserves it. He's an arrogant, self-centered prick who insulted my restaurant, and he broke my teenage heart."

I grimace. Clara, who rarely leaves Kip Island as a general rule, drove all the way down to Toronto the day she and Cooper broke up for good. She stayed in my room in my university residence hall for three days. They had always been on and off when they dated during high school, but that breakup was different. Permanent.

Delilah's eyebrows shoot up in surprise. "This guy is your ex?"

I nod in confirmation. "He grew up with us, but he left the island behind when he started gaining popularity for his acting. He doesn't even go by Cooper anymore. Now he's Hudson LeFort."

"You dated *Hudson LeFort*?" Delilah shrieks.

Clara groans, dropping her upper body onto the island, covering her face with her hands. "Not you, too."

"No, wait." Delilah reaches out, grabbing Clara's hands and coaxing them away from her face. "I'm sorry. We hate him. We hate him!"

"We *do* hate him." She looks at Delilah sternly. "No matter how pretty he is, do not fall for it. He left this place behind the second he could, and he stepped on anyone he needed to in order to make it happen. He used his own brother's notoriety as an NHL player to get a leg up, and they don't even talk. Everything that comes out of his mouth is bullshit."

"Fuck him," Delilah says.

"*Fuck* him," Clara agrees.

We all clink our glasses together, and then Delilah artfully switches the subject. With a little assistance from the rosé, it doesn't take long for our friend to forget all about her stupid ex. With any luck, his movie will wrap and he'll be back on a plane to California before we know it.

———

GABRIEL

What are the chances girls' night wraps up soon so we can pick up where we left off earlier?

I told you that you don't know how to behave!

> This is why you had to leave. If Clara saw you touching me, she would know.

GABRIEL

> Funny. Touching you is exactly what I'm thinking about right now.

My teeth ensnare my bottom lip as I glance up from my phone to make sure Clara and Delilah are both still occupied by the movie. Thankfully, they're very engrossed in our screening of *10 Things I Hate About You*. I could recite the dialogue in my sleep, I've watched it so many times, so I don't mind missing a couple scenes.

> Gabriel.

GABRIEL

> Foster.

> You're incorrigible.

GABRIEL

> I'll be whatever you want me to be, as long as I get to be buried inside you at the end of the day.

I can feel the flush on my cheeks. Another quick peek at my friends reveals they're still preoccupied. I slide down lower in my corner of the couch, hiding my phone from them.

This feels *wrong* on so many levels. But then again, every sinful thing about Gabriel Bowman has this preternatural rightness to it I can't explain.

> Flirt.

> What happened to hanging out with Luke?

GABRIEL

> He's watching Soph tonight. He's putting her to bed. Pretty sure he's conked out on the floor based on how long he's been gone though.

I have to stifle my giggle at the thought of Luke amidst all the pink and frills in Sophia's bedroom, fast asleep.

> So I'm the cure to your boredom.

GABRIEL

No, baby. My mind's been on you all night.
Kitchen, remember?

I remember. Of course I do. If Clara and Delilah hadn't walked in when they did, I'm sure they would have found more than just Gabe without a shirt.

I chew on my lip as I think about what to say. I've never done... *this* before. But something about it sends heat through my veins. I don't know if I'll be any good at it, but I want to try.

> If you were here right now, how would you touch me?

I can picture his smirk. The upward curve of his lips is a sight I know well, particularly after the past few weeks.

Waiting with bated breath, I watch as he types a response. My heart stutters, and an ache blooms between my thighs when the message rolls through.

GABRIEL

First I'd have you strip bare while I watched.
Then I'd have you touch yourself like you do when you're alone, show me exactly what you like.

> That was quick. It seems you've given some thought to this.

GABRIEL

You have no idea.

> So in this scenario, I would be at your mercy.
> What else would you do?

GABRIEL

Why don't I come home and show you?

Yes, please.

My mind runs away with itself as I reread his texts. Soon, I'm imagining what he'll do when he gets me into bed. The anticipation is almost too much.

"Hallie?"

My head snaps up as I press my phone against my chest, hiding my screen. My stomach feels like it's in my throat.

Clara laughs as she stands to stretch. "The movie's over." Her head tilts to the side. "Are you okay? You look a little flushed."

Thank your brother.

Shoving that thought down, I nod. "I'm alright. Must be the wine."

"I'm feeling it, too," Delilah says, followed by a yawn. "We should get going. Since *someone's* making me help with the deliveries in the morning."

Clara whacks her arm with a throw pillow. "You love me and you know it."

As they both help me bring our dirty glasses to the kitchen, I hear the familiar sound of a door slamming outside. When the three of us make it to the front hallway, Gabe is toeing off his boots.

"Perfect timing," he says, his eyes landing on me. Then his gaze slides to Delilah. "There's a very tired fire chief asleep on your sister's bedroom floor."

She laughs. "Thanks. I'll take care of him."

Clara and Delilah both shrug on their jackets, and then Clara kisses her brother's cheek before they slip out to Delilah's car. Gabe has one hand on the door. As soon as her Audi starts backing out of the driveway, he presses it closed.

Then his gaze settles on me, and I know I'm in big trouble.

THIRTY

GABE

HALLIE IMMEDIATELY STARTS BACKING AWAY from me. I'm not about to let her get far, though. Not after the way she's been teasing me tonight.

"Where are you going, Foster?"

Her cheeks are flushed. They have been since I walked in the door and set eyes on her. Clearly, I'm not the only one affected by our texts.

"Just, um—" She swallows nervously, but there's also something else in her expression. A heady kind of anticipation. "Going to bed."

I flip the lock on the front door and then take a step toward her. She takes another back, inching closer to the staircase.

"Did you have fun tonight?" I ask.

"Mhm," she hums. "Lots."

"Good," I say. I slip out of my coat and hang it on a hook on the wall. "I'm glad." And I am. She deserves everything good in life, and having friends like Delilah and my sister is part of that.

Hallie glances over her shoulder, gauging the distance to the stairs, then back at me. "Did you have fun tonight?"

I nod. "Oh, you have no idea."

Luke falling asleep while putting Sophia to bed gave me plenty of time to let my imagination wander. Fuelled by Hallie's messages, I couldn't stop myself from thinking about everything I planned to do to her when I got home.

Another step forward. Another step back.

"What's the matter, baby? Scared I'm going to make good on my promises?"

She shakes her head. "Not scared. I'm counting on it, actually."

Then she spins around and makes a beeline for the stairs. I'm faster, though, and just as her foot makes contact with the first step, my arm snakes around her middle. She lets out a sound of surprise, but her body melts in my hold.

Pulling her back flush against my chest, I lean down by her ear and say, "You should know better than to run by now. You're mine, Foster, and I have no intention of letting you go."

A shiver travels down her spine.

I press a kiss to her pulse, and then I spin her around. Backing her against the nearest wall, I relish the small gasp that leaves her. The way lust clouds her irises as my thigh wedges hers apart.

Grabbing her left hand, I bring it up to my lips and place a kiss on her fourth finger. The exact place she wears that fake ring. She doesn't have it on tonight—no need to pretend in front of Clara and Delilah.

But *fuck*, how I wish it was real.

Hallie's pupils dilate as she watches me. I kiss her knuckle a second time, then guide her hand to the back of my neck. Instantly, she threads her fingers through the hair at my nape.

With one hand braced on the wall beside her head, the other takes her chin, tilting it. And then I close the distance between us, claiming her lips. She sighs at the contact, opening for me without hesitation. My tongue sweeps inside her mouth, and I savour her taste. A hint of sweet wine and something uniquely her.

I've kissed her countless times since the wedding. I have her in my bed every night. But each time, my first instinct is to hold on as tight as I can, because I never quite know when she's going to decide to leave again.

"Is this the part where you show me?" she asks when my lips hit her neck.

I pinch her side lightly. "You are trouble."

She only smiles.

We make it to the second level in record time. Soon, I'm shutting my bedroom door behind us. Not that it matters—we have the house completely to ourselves tonight.

I draw her into my arms again, stealing another kiss. Her lips are soft, but they match mine in intensity. Further proof that Hallie Foster was created for me in every way imaginable.

Hallie starts working on my belt. She unhooks the buckle, then slides it from my belt loops. It lands on the floor audibly. I let her unfasten the button of my pants and tug down my fly before stepping out of her hold.

"Where are you going?" she asks.

I sit back on the end of the bed, and the confused pout that appears on her lips makes me want to kiss her all over again.

"Take your clothes off for me, baby."

She must have wanted to be comfortable for girls' night because she's wearing yoga pants and a t-shirt. Only, now I realize it isn't her shirt—it's mine. I'm not sure how I missed the Kip Island Fire Department logo on her chest earlier, but I can't now.

Hooking her thumbs into her waistband, Hallie drags her pants down her legs, baring her skin. She tosses them aside and grabs the hem of the shirt.

"You like wearing my shirt, Foster?" I ask. She gives a sheepish nod. "You look damn good in it."

"Still want me to take it off?" She blinks innocently, but there's a mischievous edge to her words.

"Yeah, baby. I need to see you."

The shirt comes off, and she stands before me in her bra and underwear.

She takes a step toward me, but I shake my head. With a frustrated huff, she unclasps her bra, letting her breasts free. They're the perfect handful. Everything about Hallie was made to fit my hands. The soft give at her hips, the curve of her stomach. She looks like one of those old paintings you would see in a museum.

I have to stop myself from reaching for her as I conveniently forget why I'm torturing both of us in the first place.

Hallie dips two fingers inside her underwear, rubbing herself. My fists clench on top of my knees.

"Off, baby. I want them off."

"Gabriel," she says, breathless, "please touch me."

I shake my head. "Not yet."

"*Why?*"

"I haven't made good on my promises yet." I stand from the bed. "I want you bare, and then I want you on your back."

Her irises flare at my words. In a blink, her underwear is pulled down her thighs and discarded. This woman... I still can't quite believe I get to have her like this.

For now, a quiet voice in the back of my mind hisses. *Until she disappears again.*

I shake off the uncertainty, focusing on Hallie. She's still here, and she's all mine.

She climbs onto my bed and lies back, her hair fanning out around her. With her feet propped up on the mattress and her thighs parted, I have the perfect view of her hand sliding down her stomach to reach her clit.

Hallie's fingers circle her clit, and then two dip inside her entrance, gathering her wetness. Those same fingers rub her clit again before plunging back inside. Her thighs widen, and her hips lift off the bed. She's mesmerizing as she works herself over.

Keeping my eyes trained on her movements, I remove my

clothes. Then I kneel at the foot of the bed, stroking myself. My cock has been fully hard since Hallie started taking her clothes off, and now the tip is leaking.

"*Gabe*," she pleads. "I want...more. I want you."

My restraint is on the verge of snapping. After the buildup earlier and watching her touch herself, I'm beyond ready to bury myself inside her. But still, I wait.

With the hand that isn't between her legs, Hallie rolls one nipple between her thumb and forefinger. It further stiffens at her touch. She quickens the pace on her clit, chasing release, but I can see the frustration building when she can't quite get there.

"Make me come, Gabe."

The demand in her voice rips my restraint to shreds. Hands on her knees, I widen her thighs, then take hold of her wrist, pulling her hand away from her pussy. Her fingers are slick.

I guide her hand to her mouth. She gazes up at me in confusion, those baby blues big and wide.

"Suck."

Understanding flashes, and I watch as she cleans her own arousal from her fingers. The sight makes me impossibly harder.

"You're doing so good, baby, doing everything I tell you," I say. "Now I'll give you what you want."

Hallie sits up, grabbing the condom I tossed on the mattress beside her. She shoves me until I land back on my ass, and then she's climbing into my lap.

"Greedy girl," I murmur against her ear.

"I want you," she says.

"You have me." *Forever, if you want it.*

I can't hold back any longer. As soon as she rolls the condom onto my length, I'm finding her entrance and pushing inside. Her fingers dig into my shoulders, and her lips part with a cry as I fill her.

Hallie's knees dig into the mattress on either side of my hips, and she grinds against me as she lets herself drop down. My hands find her lush hips, fitting themselves there.

Now that we're joined, there isn't any hurry to our movements. Hallie wraps her arms around the back of my neck, bringing her bare chest flush to mine as she rocks against me. Despite the torture now, the slow build will be worth it.

"Will it always feel like this?" she asks, her words loose, followed by a gasp when my cock hits a certain spot inside her.

"I fucking hope so, baby," I murmur.

Hallie tips her head back, exposing the column of her throat, and her hair brushes my fingers where they sit at the top of her ass.

"Gabe. More, please."

I don't waste a second reaching between us to thumb her clit. Her thighs tighten around my hips at the pressure, and the next time she grinds her pelvis against mine, she seems to take me impossibly deeper.

"Fuck, Hallie," I grit out. "You feel so good."

"I want to come now. Make me come."

Gripping her waist, I lift her off my cock, despite her protests. Then I lay her on her back. She's reaching for me, a question on her lips, when I take hold of a pillow.

"Lift your hips for me, baby."

She complies immediately, and I slide the pillow beneath her. Then I grip her thighs, helping her spread them, before plunging inside her again. Her pussy flutters around me.

"Don't stop," she demands.

With each thrust, I watch her breasts bounce.

Soon, I can't stop my orgasm from barrelling through me. With the way Hallie clenches around me, she's in the same boat.

We're both breathing heavily, trying to come down from the high. I slide out of her, and she sits up, wrapping her arms around me and pressing soft kisses to my lips.

We take turns in the bathroom, getting ready for bed.

After that first night, she moved her toiletries to my en suite. I didn't ask her to, but she saw the look on my face when I found her missing from my bed. She knew it would make me feel better having her stuff here, and it does.

Now every time she gets up and starts her night routine, I have no doubt she'll be finding her way back to me.

Until she decides she needs to run again.

THIRTY-ONE

GABE

AS THE WEEKS GO BY, Hallie and I settle into a routine. Being with her is everything I thought it would be and more. So much more. I'm a little surprised with how okay she's been about us living together as more than roommates. I thought for sure she'd spook by now, worry we're moving too fast.

But with each passing day, when nothing happens, I start to believe that she really will stay this time.

Except we still haven't told anyone.

Hallie goes to see her grandfather at least twice a week. I keep waiting for her to say that she told him about us, but she never does. The only people who know we're together are the Landells, and even they don't know the full truth about us.

Glancing in the rearview mirror of my truck, I find Abbie engrossed in some game with her dolls. She insisted on bringing an armful to Haven House for brunch, even though she has a stockpile at my parents' place. They range in size from Barbies to baby dolls, and whatever she's cooking up in her imagination has her concentrating so hard, a line has formed between her brows.

I smile, returning my eyes to the road. Then I reach out and place a hand on Hallie's thigh. She startles, and I chuckle.

"You alright?" I ask.

She's nodding when I glance over. "Yeah. I just didn't expect you to do that here."

"She can't see anything," I say quietly. Even if she wasn't distracted, the centre console blocks Abbie's view of my hand. "But...we could just tell them. All of them."

I know I said I'd give Hallie time, and I have, but I also can't deny the way the secrecy is eating at me. Even lying to Kevin and his family about our engagement felt more genuine than this. At least then I wasn't forbidden from touching her when we weren't alone.

It doesn't help that I feel like I'm keeping my own secrets from them. Ethan's offer has been in the back of my mind for over a month. I spoke to him again the other day, asked some questions. The job is similar to my current one in some ways, but there's still some things I'd need to do to make the cut. It's tempting, but then I think about having to hand in my resignation to Luke.

It's my life, sure, but I value my family's opinions. They're important to me. I don't want to hide from them.

I almost miss it, but I swear Hallie flinches.

"Foster..."

She turns to look out her window, and my stomach sinks. I pull my hand from her thigh and return it to the steering wheel, tightening my grip. My jaw clenches.

The rest of the ride to Haven House is silent, save for Abbie's chatter in the back seat. The awkwardness I thought Hallie and I left behind is back again, and I hate it with every fibre of my being.

What I don't get is why Hallie is so against my family knowing about us. I understood her initial hesitation—agreeing to a relationship with me was already a big step, after denying ourselves for so long, without my family being involved. But I figured by now, she would have felt comfortable letting them know. That leaves me wondering if I've done something and she's just too nervous to tell me.

When we get to the house, I help Abbie out of the back. Hallie slips from the passenger seat, but she hangs around, waiting for me. Her shoulders are curved inward, and her gaze is trained on her feet.

Abbie skips up the steps, then looks back at me. I haven't moved from beside the truck. "Daddy?"

"Go on inside, Abbs," I say. "We'll be right behind you."

When the front door shuts, I turn to face Hallie. She clutches the strap of her purse, like it will offer her the strength she needs to face this conversation.

"Fight with me, Foster," I plead. *Fight* for *me. For us.*

She shakes her head. "I don't want to fight. Not today."

"You have reservations, I know. But you're not letting me in," I say, taking a step closer. "So I'm just left wondering what it is I'm doing wrong, with no way to fix it."

Her blue eyes turn sad. "It's not you, Gabe. It's..."

I laugh without humour. "*It's not you, it's me.* Seriously?"

Hallie frowns. "Well, it's the truth. You're amazing, damn near perfect. You've done nothing wrong. It's me who is messed up."

It's not the first time I've heard words like that from Hallie, but they don't make sense. "You keep saying that, but that's not how I see you. Who put these fucking ridiculous ideas in your head?"

She looks downright miserable. "Please, Gabe," she whispers. "I'm sorry."

I shake my head. "I can't keep doing this."

Hallie inhales a shuddering breath, and I can see her eyes turning glassy. She steps into me, setting a hand on my chest. It rests over my heart, and I wonder if she can feel how hard it beats for her. Always her, even when it hurts.

"This won't be a secret forever," she says. Promises. "Soon. We'll tell everyone soon. I just need a little more time."

The front door creaks open, and Hallie jumps back, dropping her hand. The guilty look on her face guts me.

"You guys coming inside?" Clara asks, sticking her head out. "Or are you just gonna stand in the cold all day?"

Hallie and I stay silent.

"I don't care one way or the other," my sister continues, either totally oblivious to the tension or doing her damnedest to pretend. "But Mom won't let us eat until I get an answer, and I'm *hungry*."

"We're coming," I reply. My voice doesn't sound entirely like my own, thick with strain.

With one final, suspicious glance, Clara shuts the door.

I look at Hallie again. "A little while longer."

Without another word, I start up the porch steps. After a moment, she follows behind me. When I enter the kitchen, Abbie is already situated in her own chair. She doesn't like to sit with me anymore. Instead, she chooses to sit next to Sophia. It usually works out alright because then I can sit next to Hallie.

Today, though, I head for the open chair between Delilah and Dad. Hallie freezes in the doorway, but I don't look at her. I can't. It's petty, I know, but I need a minute to work through my shit. Sitting beside Hallie, catching whiffs of her apple shampoo, would only be torture.

I can feel Delilah's eyes on the side of my face. I turn to her. "What?" I ask, a little rougher than intended.

Luke's arm tightens across her shoulders as he leans around her. "I don't know what crawled up your ass today, but watch your tone when you speak to her," he warns.

Delilah pats his thigh. "It's alright, Luke." Then she lowers her voice. "I was going to ask if you're okay."

I sigh, forcing my shoulders to relax. "I'm fine. Just... I'm fine. I shouldn't have snapped at you, though. I'm sorry."

She smiles. "You're forgiven."

One look at my brother and I'm not so sure about that, but I nod gratefully.

"Looks like it's you and me, babycakes," Clara says, patting the remaining seat for Hallie. Then she sends me a confused glare. "Seeing as someone stole my spot."

I shrug. "Sucks to suck. You were too slow."

"Clary doesn't suck!" Abbie chimes in. "That's mean, Daddy."

"You tell him," my sister says.

Abbie crosses her arms. "You have to say sorry."

Clara grins, and I roll my eyes. "Sorry, Clara." Unlike my apology to Delilah, this one is lacking in sincerity.

"I'd give that a two out of ten, but I'll let it slide." She grabs a croissant and drops it on her plate. "Let's eat."

Hallie finally slides into her chair. We make eye contact for a brief second before she looks away. It kills me, being at odds with her, but I also can't deny how shitty I feel when she won't open up to me fully. Clara says it's not about a lack of trust, but it certainly feels that way.

Does she think I can't handle whatever it is she's gone through? Does she doubt my ability to love her through it? Because I know without a shadow of a doubt that whatever she tells me won't make my feelings go away.

Abbie sits up on her knees, trying to cut her pancake, to no avail. It would help if she held the plastic knife the right way up, but she got mad at me the last time I pointed that out. My little girl is independent to a fault.

She lets her fork and knife clatter to her plate. "Hallie," she says with a frustrated huff, "can you help me?"

"Of course," Hallie says immediately. "These pancakes are tricky, aren't they?"

What guts me even more is how good Hallie is with my daughter. She doesn't see it, but I do. Abbie will always have me and Larissa, but the connection she shares with Hallie is different. Special. I don't want her to lose that.

As everyone eats, conversation springs up around the table. Luke and I inevitably start talking about work, and Dad chimes in on occasion. The urge to tell them both about Ethan's offer presses on me, but I hold back. Breaking the news in the middle of brunch is not how I would want to go about it, especially after the not-a-fight Hallie and I had beforehand.

When the food is almost gone, and the girls have gone off to play, there's a lull in conversation. Dad shares a look with Mom across the table, and then he clears his throat. "Your mom and I have something we'd like to tell you."

Clara's head jerks up. "What's wrong? Are you sick?" She turns to Mom. "Are *you* sick?"

"Jesus Christ, Clara," I curse. It isn't uncommon for her to jump to conclusions, but damn.

"No one's sick," Mom is quick to reply. "It's nothing like that, sweetheart. Nothing bad. It's just something we've been mulling over."

"What is it?" Luke asks. Even though Mom said it wasn't bad, he's still wearing that uber serious expression of his. The one he uses to brace for unfavourable news.

"We were thinking of taking a trip," Dad says. "Friends of ours have a place down in Mexico. They invited us to spend the winter there."

"A trip? Out of the country?" Clara's eyes have almost bugged out of her head. "You don't even have passports. And *all* winter? What about Christmas? What about Haven House? I mean, have you really thought about—"

"I think it's a great idea," I interrupt, before my twin lets her imagination run wild. "The bed-and-breakfast will be closed for the season soon. As for Christmas, we don't do much anyway."

The holiday is always a low-key affair. Even when we were kids, besides opening presents, it was a calm day at home. It's no different now that we're adults, only Abbie and Sophia will be the ones waiting for Santa.

I'd been looking forward to spending the day with my girls. Last year, I had to work, and my daughter spent the holiday with

Larissa. This year was supposed to be different. Only, now I'm not sure where Hallie and I will stand by the end of next month.

"It's still tradition," Clara argues. "You're with me, right, Luke?"

Our brother scratches the back of his neck awkwardly. "Traditions change, Clarebear…"

Realization dawns on her. He wants to spend the holiday with Delilah and her siblings.

Clara crosses her arms. "I see."

"Clara," Mom says gently. "We don't have to go, if you really don't want us to. It was just a thought."

As stubborn as Clara is, she also has the biggest heart. So when she sighs, I know she's giving in. She may be disappointed, but she'd never stand in our parents' way.

"No," my sister says. "If you want to go, you should go. You've worked hard for a lot of years. You deserve a vacation."

Dad smiles. "We'll send you a postcard."

She points a finger at him. "You two better call me all the time. I don't care how much it costs!"

I fight back a laugh. Clara has often lamented Luke being overprotective, but she can be no better. I think that's just what we do in this family—we care, sometimes too much.

"Will you watch the house for us while we're gone?" Mom asks her. "I'm worried the pipes might freeze, but I also don't want to keep the heat on blast if no one will be here."

Clara nods. "I can just stay here instead. My apartment will be fine." With it being above the bakery, the heat is always on inside the building, and I'm sure the warmth from the ovens travels up to her place, too.

Dad throws his arm over Clara's shoulders, hugging her to his side. "What would we do without you?"

"Well, you wouldn't have a favourite child," she replies.

Luke flicks a sliced strawberry across the table at her, and she gasps, pulling out of Dad's arms. "Delilah! Do you see what kind of uncivilized man-child you're in a relationship with?"

Delilah can't hide her giggles. "I'm incredibly sorry, Clara, but I'm kinda in love with him."

"Kinda?" Luke presses.

She rolls her eyes, though she grins. "Hopelessly, deeply, madly," she amends.

"That's what I thought," he says, then takes her by the chin and kisses her.

Mom looks on with delight, and Clara starts making fake gagging noises. Through the chaos, I find Hallie. She has a slight grin on her face as she watches Luke and Delilah together, but when her gaze lands on mine, her smile turns sad.

I still have her, but it feels like I'm watching her slip right through my fingers, and there's not a goddamn thing I can do to stop it.

THIRTY-TWO

HALLIE

TEN YEARS AGO

PACKING up my whole life was easier than I thought it would be. I've never been one to hold on to belongings. Mostly because I hate taking up more space than absolutely necessary. But I didn't truly realize how plain my life has been until this moment.

It's better this way, though. Now I can reinvent myself in the city without my past dragging me down. The only things I'll really miss about this island are Pops and Clara.

And Gabe.

Not being able to see Clara regularly will take some getting used to, but so will missing him. He's been a constant in my life since kindergarten. We'll talk, I'm sure, but it won't be the same.

My phone burns a hole in my pocket, a reminder of the texts we exchanged earlier. He wants to tell me something. My stupid heart has been racing since, getting carried away with all sorts of fanciful ideas. Like maybe he feels the same way about me as I do him. Like maybe he likes me. Loves me, even.

He almost kissed you at the fair last year.

But he hasn't tried since. What if he realized it was a mistake? That he didn't actually want to?

My brain is a hard place to be when it's playing tug of war with itself. It's a game I can never win. The only hope I have of pulling myself from the toxic cycle is distracting my mind until there's no room left for arguing.

I fold another shirt and shove it into my suitcase. Running my fingers over the material, I smile softly. Gabe let me borrow it once when we went swimming and I forgot a coverup. I never intended to keep it, but...

Raised voices travel up the stairs, instantly turning my mood sour. I open my bedroom door and head out into the hallway. Leaning over the banister, I peer down toward the foyer. Pops stands in front of the stairs, talking to my mother.

I haven't seen her in months. The last time she blew through town, she took me out to dinner, and then she stole all the money in my wallet. I didn't find out until she was already long gone. At least she had the decency to cover the bill before she left.

"Mandy, please don't do this," Pops pleads. "Don't ruin this for her."

Mom sneers. "I'm not ruining anything, Dad. I'm here to see my baby before she heads off to her fancy new school and decides she's too good for us small-town folk."

"Amanda—"

"Mom?" I come down the stairs, letting them both know I'm there. I hate being talked about like I'm not.

My mother smiles, but there's something off about it. Her smiles never seem sincere. Maybe because she's never truly been happy as long as I've been alive. "Hallie, there you are. Your grandfather said you were out."

When I look at Pops, his expression is full of apology. *It's okay,* I tell him silently. He does what he can to shield me from her, but she's my mom. I can't cut her out entirely.

"I was at Clara's," I lie. I've been home all day. "I guess he didn't hear me come back. How long are you in town for?"

"Not long." She raises a brow. "Well, aren't you gonna come give your mama a hug?"

I descend the stairs, then let her pull me against her. Like always, she smells of cigarettes and vanilla body spray. Sometimes liquor, if she's dating a heavy drinker at the time.

"Do you want some lunch?" I ask. "I was just about to make some."

"Now that you mention it, I could use something to eat," she says.

We all head into the kitchen, and my mom plunks herself down at the table. Pops tries to help me, but I shoo him away to sit down. I need a minute to myself, to prepare to spend a whole meal with her. At least my wallet is upstairs this time.

I make us some sandwiches, and when I set them down, Mom wastes no time digging in. Conversation is stilted. There are so many topics I avoid talking about with her because I know from experience they'll only cause a fight. My leaving for school, for example.

Another thing I avoid is my art. That's mine and mine alone. I don't even share it with Pops.

After lunch, Pops and I wash the dishes. We have a dishwasher, but we like the routine of washing and drying by hand when we both have the time. I'm going to miss our routines when I'm gone.

Once the dishes are clean, I head to the bathroom. But when I get back to the kitchen, I stop short. Mom has her face buried in my phone. She must have guessed my password.

"What are you doing?"

She flashes the screen at me, showing me the text thread I have with Gabe. "What's this?"

GABRIEL

Meet me at the tree tonight? I wanna tell you something.

Can't you just tell me now?

GABRIEL

Later. It's better in person.

Okay. I'll see you later, then.

I try to pull my phone out of her hand, but she brings her arm back, just out of reach.

"Give it back!" My cheeks flame. "That's private."

She holds my phone up. "Does your little friend know you're sneaking around with her brother?"

Guilt sinks to the bottom of my stomach like an anchor. I cross my arms, my shoulders curving. "We're not sneaking! We're not doing anything."

Even to my own ears, I don't sound convincing, but it's the truth. Gabe and I *haven't* done anything. We may have come close to kissing once, but that's it.

Mom shakes her head. "It's not worth it, Hallie. He'll just turn around and cut you loose when he gets what he wants. When he decides you're not worth the trouble."

A tear slips down my cheek. "Gabe's not like that. He's sweet."

She snorts. "Listen, I'm just trying to save you some heartache. Because *you* are exactly like your mama, and men don't stay with women like us."

I blink, almost in slow motion, as her words hit me. When I was younger, I heard some of her boyfriends call her *damaged* and *toxic*. They wouldn't hang around much longer after that.

And people are always saying how alike we are. I used to think it a compliment because that meant I looked like Pops, too, but maybe that's not what they meant. Maybe I resemble her as a person.

"Amanda, that's *enough*," Pops snaps, coming back into the room. He almost never gets angry, but he must have caught the tail end of our conversation.

I force myself to take a deep breath, to shove down the hurt. Pops doesn't need the stress. "It's fine."

It's not.

He ignores me. "I think it's best you go," he tells her. "Say your goodbyes."

Mom rolls her eyes, throwing her arm up in exasperation. "Whatever." She shoves my phone into my chest. "Good luck with that."

Pops and I trail behind her as she stalks to the front door and throws it open. As she barrels onto the porch, she narrowly misses shoulder-checking Gabe, who watches her stomp down the walkway and to her beat-up car.

My cheeks flame with embarrassment. "I'm sorry," I say quietly.

I can't be certain, but I think *sorry* was probably my first word. I've been apologizing for my mother for as long as I can remember.

Gabe shakes his head. "Don't be. That's on her, not you." He shoves his hands into his pockets, then rocks back on his heels. "Any chance I can steal you away from your packing? I decided I didn't want to wait until tonight to see you."

"Oh, I..." My cheeks remain red for an entirely different reason.

Pops nudges me. "Go, Junebug. You've been at it all morning."

I agree, following Gabe out to his truck. Those butterflies I've become familiar with over the years take flight. Only, I don't realize it will be their last until it's too late.

With the windows rolled down, I savour the sounds and smells of the island as Gabe's truck ambles through traffic. Well, what little traffic Kip Island has to offer. It's busier in the summer, sure, but it's not exactly known for its gridlock.

I keep sneaking glances over at Gabe. His right hand is on the wheel, but his left arm is resting on the open window. The sun illuminates the tattoo he got for his eighteenth birthday, the start of what I know he's planning to be a sleeve. He looks, to be entirely honest, *hot*.

Does your little friend know you're sneaking around with her brother?

I shove my mother's voice down deep, where it can't hurt me. I'll worry her words to death later, in the solitude of my bedroom. For now, I won't let myself think about how Clara would feel if she knew.

Gabe parks in the lot for Anchor's Bay Beach and hops out of the truck faster than I can blink. Before I've unbuckled my seatbelt, he's opening my door for me.

When I jump down, we head for the sand. We don't talk, instead walking in silence. I want to say something, but my nerves leave me tongue-tied.

The far section of the beach sees little to no tourists, given it's so rocky, so local kids tend to go there to hang out. Or cause trouble. Today, it's empty.

"What are we doing out here?" I ask.

Gabe takes a seat on one of the crates that stands in as a chair around the fire pit. I sit beside him, breathing in the nostalgia. I know for a fact Luke is the one who stole the crates from Dockside a few years ago.

Can I really give this all up?

Yes. I have to. Besides the fact that there's no university close by, there's no life for me here. Not in the town that raised my mother and became witness to her misdeeds. Her destructive behaviour.

I have to go.

"I wanted to see you," Gabe says. "Alone."

The intense expression he wears sends a shiver down my spine. One full of both apprehension and a smidge of excitement.

"Yeah?"

A breeze floats through the air, cooling my heated skin. The summer temperatures have come back with a vengeance, especially when the sun is out.

"Hallie, I love you," he blurts.

My heart stops. "What?"

Blood rushes in my ears, threatening to drown out anything else Gabe says. And the heart that stopped beating suddenly kicks into overdrive, thumping against my ribcage like it's trying to break free. Trying to jump right into his hands.

"I love you." *Oh, God. I did hear him right.* "I'm in love with you."

The earnest expression he wears makes me want to cry.

This is everything I've ever wanted. The moment I've been dreaming of for years. All I have to do is say four little words. *I love you, too.* But the words don't come.

Instead, this yawning abyss opens up inside me, and all of the fears and insecurities I've collected over my eighteen years come tumbling out. They trip me up, jam my mouth so full, I can't speak. And Gabe looks at me, hopeful, and I know all I'm capable of is ruining him.

He doesn't know. He doesn't see me, truly, deeply. I'm a mess. I've been one all my life. Like mother, like daughter. He may think he loves me, but he doesn't. Or he wouldn't—not if he *knew*. So it's better this way, breaking his heart now, instead of down the line when he's grown even more attached.

"I, um—" My throat feels thick, like I could throw up at any moment. I stand from the crate, stumbling backwards. "I'm sorry. I can't... I can't do this right now."

For as long as I live, I don't think I'll ever be able to forget the look on his face. The pain. The *regret*.

"Hallie, wait." He stands, reaching for me. "Don't—"

"I'm sorry," I whisper.
And then, like the coward I am, I run.

THIRTY-THREE

HALLIE

EVER SINCE I chickened out of telling his family on Sunday, Gabe has been slightly withdrawn. He agreed to give it more time, but I can tell it still hurts him. That *I* hurt him. Again.

To make matters worse, Kevin has invited us to some kind of outing, and I don't know what to say. My web of lies has spun so far out of control, I can't find my way out.

I want to stop. I don't want to lie anymore, to anyone. But I don't know how to come clean without everything around me crumbling to ruin. If it does, I know it's what I deserve. I brought this mess on myself.

Men don't stay with women like us.

As much as I try not to let them, my mother's words are always close by to remind me of where I come from. And right now, they feel pretty truthful. If something doesn't give, I'm going to lose Gabe, and I won't be able to come crawling back in another ten years.

No, once I leave again, he's going to find someone else. He's going to find someone he can marry and have a whole brood of kids with. He deserves that. He deserves to have a wife who isn't a coward. He doesn't deserve—

Stop.

Blinking back the tears that have sprung up from my spiralling dread, I focus on the plate I'm scrubbing within an inch of its life. Gabe doesn't understand why I don't always use the dishwasher, but the routine grounds me, and it reminds me of Pops.

I set the plate out to dry, then wipe my hands on a towel. The kitchen is spotless now, and I'm on the fourth episode of a random podcast I started listening to. For a while, the strangers' voices were enough to trick my brain into thinking it was too busy to catastrophize, but evidently, that didn't last forever.

Leaning back against the counter, I rub my eyes. I need to stop acting like our breakup is a foregone conclusion. I still have time. Not much, but a little.

When the front door opens, I brace. I want to earn back Gabe's smile. Now more than ever, I'm determined to, because I don't want another woman coming in here and claiming what's mine.

Gabe pokes his head into the kitchen, letting me know he's back from work. The days when he's on shift seem long, especially when I don't have my own job to keep me preoccupied. I spend a lot of time out in the guesthouse on those days.

"Hi," I say. I smile tentatively. "I made dinner. Pasta. It's a new recipe, but hopefully it's alright. The reviews online were pretty good, so…"

Stop talking, Hallie.

"It smells great. I'm just gonna take a quick shower first," he says, then beelines for the stairs.

I frown as he leaves. He didn't completely brush me off, but things are still weird. He didn't even kiss me, and he *always* kisses me when he comes home.

My timer goes off, so I take the pasta out of the oven and set it on the stove. A few more minutes pass, and then I can't take it anymore. I march out of the kitchen and up the stairs. Gabe's bedroom door is open, but the one to his en suite is closed. My hand rests on the door handle.

Just do it. Be brave.

But what if he turns me down?

You can't be a coward forever. Tiptoeing gets tiring after a while.

I step into the bathroom. The warm air hits me instantly, thick and cloying.

Gabe swipes a hand across the shower glass, clearing some of the steam. "Hallie?"

I grip the hem of my shirt and tug it over my head, dropping it to the floor. "I hope you weren't expecting some other woman to join you in the shower," I say. I aim for a teasing tone, but even I can hear my words are wracked with nerves.

I'm not *sexy*. I can't do this. Except...maybe I can, if the darkening of Gabe's eyes is anything to go by.

When he speaks, his voice is clear. "You know it's only ever been you."

It goes against everything my mother taught me to believe about myself, but when he says things like this, I want to listen. I want to be that woman for him. The one he can't seem to live without.

I want to be Gabe's one and only.

Once the rest of my clothes are on the floor, I step through the glass door Gabe is holding open for me. The mist from the shower head hits me instantly, water droplets sliding down my skin.

I reach toward him, brushing a strand of hair off his forehead. "I'm sorry for the other day, with your family. I'm trying *so* hard to be what you need. To be ready for you. Us. But I need you to know that, for me, it has *always* been you."

A rush of emotions hit me, just as Gabe's mouth descends on mine. I meet his kiss with fervour, threading my fingers through the wet strands of his hair. Our slick bodies come together, strong muscle meeting soft curves and divots. His cock begins to harden between us.

When I eventually manage to separate our lips, I slide to my knees. The tiles bite into my skin, but I pay them no mind. Instead, I drag my gaze up to meet a pair of intense brown eyes.

"What are you doing?" Gabe asks, tone ragged.

"Showing you that I want you," I reply. "And I do. So much that it *aches*."

Try as I may to deny myself, Gabe has been and always will be a part of me. From the moment I met him, he stole my heart, and all these years, he's kept it safe. Even when I was hours away, out of reach.

"Show me."

With his permission granted, I wrap my hand around his cock. Admittedly, this is one part of sex I'll admit I'm not half bad at. Maybe because the focus isn't on me. I'm much more comfortable on the sidelines, helping someone else get off.

But Gabe also makes me feel bold. More confident. He makes me feel like no matter what I do, he'll come undone at my hands.

I keep my grip firm, like I know Gabe prefers. And then I spit on his cock.

"Hallie, *holy shit*."

I blink up at him, feigning innocence. "Something wrong?"

Gabe swallows, his Adam's apple bobbing. "Just surprised me, is all."

I work my hand up and down his shaft. And then I wrap my lips around his tip, swirling my tongue.

Gabe gathers my hair in his fist, holding it like a ponytail. "You like having your mouth on my cock, baby?"

In answer, I take him deeper, hollowing my cheeks. Gabe tightens his grip on my hair, letting out a groan. I take another inch.

"So good, baby," Gabe murmurs. "So *fucking* good."

That spurs me on. I want it to be good for him. So good, he can't think straight. I want him to come down my throat.

Before I can go any further, Gabe grabs me by the elbows,

hauling me to my feet. I barely have time to catch my breath before he's slamming his lips against mine, kissing me.

"Need to be inside you," he murmurs.

"*Yes.*"

Gabe hikes my left leg over his hip, opening me to him. My lips part as I feel the tip of his cock nudging my entrance. If he tipped his hips forward just a little...

A shock of cold water hits me then, making me gasp. Gabe grapples for the temperature dial, shutting the shower off completely.

"Crap," I say. "I was doing a bunch of laundry and dishes earlier. I must've used too much hot water." Me and my damn brain. What a day to go on a cleaning spree.

With a chuckle, Gabe drops his forehead to mine. I press a quick kiss to his lips, then tug on his hand, pulling him out of the shower. We were having such a good moment. I'll be damned if a little cold water gets in our way.

When I'm standing in front of the double sinks, Gabe at my back, I swipe a hand over the fogged mirror. Then I meet his gaze in the reflection.

"Touch me."

First, he sets his hands on my hips. Kneads the flesh there. My head rolls back, resting against his shoulder, but I keep my eyes open, watching. Slowly, one of his hands leaves my hip, caressing my waist, then slides over my stomach. I don't have abs by any stretch of the imagination; my lower stomach is soft and curves outward. But Gabe doesn't balk. In fact, he holds me tighter.

"You are so fucking beautiful," he says into my ear, sending a shiver skittering down my spine. "And all mine."

"All yours," I echo.

His hand travels up my abdomen, to my chest, until he's cupping one of my breasts. I can feel his erection pressing against my back, and I have truly never felt more desired. Gabe takes my nipple between his thumb and forefinger, rolling the bud until it's hard. I watch it all in the mirror.

"Tell me what you want, baby."

I lean back, giving him some of my weight. "You," I whimper. "Always you. Please, Gabe."

"Where do you want me?" he asks. "Here?"

With one of his hands still working on my breast, the other dips between my legs, circling my clit. My knees tremble.

"Yes. Oh, God, *yes*."

"You're inflating my ego, Foster. Who knew my touch could turn a woman religious."

I want to roll my eyes at his ridiculousness, but instead I cry out in indignation when his hands abandon me. Until I'm spun around and promptly hoisted onto the bathroom counter, between the double sinks.

My thighs seem to part themselves, my body taking control. And it wants this ache between my legs soothed. Frankly, I do, too.

Gabe steps closer, and my legs wrap around him. I search for something to hold on to and wind up grasping the faucet on my right.

His hands smooth up my thighs, then rest on my hips. He tugs a little, until my ass is on the edge of the counter. Then he slips his cock inside me, burying himself deep. It feels incredible. And it's like—

I gasp. "Condom?"

Gabe freezes. "Fuck," he grits out. "I'm sorry. I wasn't thinking."

"I wasn't either. I, um... I've been getting back into the habit of taking my birth control. We should be okay."

"Okay, like you want to keep going?"

I bite my lip, then nod. "If you want. I've been good about taking the pills, but I don't want you to worry about...you know. So only if you want."

He pulls his cock part of the way out, then flexes his hips forward. My head tips back, hitting the mirror.

"If you think I'm worried about that..." Gabe drawls, "you." Thrust. "Haven't." Thrust. "Been." Thrust. "Listening."

My back arches. "*Gabe.*"

"I'll pull out," he promises, "to be cautious. But make no mistake, Hallie, I'm not afraid of more with you."

This is very much *not* the time to be having this conversation, but my heart flutters all the same. My pussy, too, which earns me a groan.

And then Gabe lets go. He buries himself to the hilt, his cock hitting someplace inside of me that makes me see stars. I cry out.

One of his hands leaves my hip, and he starts circling my clit again. This time, he's relentless. Between his cock driving into me and the pressure on that bundle of nerves, I know I won't last much longer.

"Gabriel," I plead. "Don't stop."

He doesn't. Not until I fall apart, mouth open, no words escaping. All I can feel is bliss.

He pulls out, and I slump back against the mirror for support. Then with one final tug on his cock, he comes. His release hits my stomach.

"Holy shit," he breathes. One hand is braced beside my head as his chest heaves.

"That was..." *Mindblowing.*

"Yeah." He looks down at me, looks down at the mess he made on my skin, and groans. "*Fuck*, Hallie."

He swipes a finger through his release, drags it up my sternum, then swirls it around my nipple, painting it in cum. I whimper.

"What do you think the chances are that there's some hot water now?" he asks.

I shake my head. After that, I have no concept of time. I feel boneless.

Gabe turns the shower on and checks the temperature. Once

he deems it safe, he pulls me back in with him. We make quick work of washing off, no funny business this time, because neither of us is interested in being blasted with cold water again.

After we dry off and get dressed, we head downstairs. The pasta I cooked is lukewarm at this point, but we dish it up and sit down on the couch. I throw my legs over Gabe's lap, and he turns the TV on, and all is right in the world again.

Except for this nagging thought in the back of my mind.

As much as Gabe says he isn't afraid of more with me, everything about this situation we're in is messy enough. And if I'm honest, the idea of him wanting that with me scares me as much as it comforts me.

You are exactly like your mama, and men don't stay with women like us.

THIRTY-FOUR

GABE

IT ISN'T uncommon for me to come home to an empty house these days. Even with Abbie at her mom's house half the time, I figured I'd at least have Hallie here, but generally, if she isn't at work, she's out in the guesthouse.

Today is no exception. After an initial sweep, I find the kitchen and living room empty. Same with the guest room where Hallie still keeps her clothes.

I take a quick shower to rinse off the workday, then set out in search of Hallie. When I come down the stairs, I find her phone sitting on the kitchen island. It's ringing, and just when it seems to stop, it starts up again.

The caller ID says Amanda. Hallie's mom.

The latest call goes to voicemail, and that's when I notice all the notifications littering Hallie's lock screen. Her mom has been texting her, too.

AMANDA

You're really going to ignore your own mother?

I know I wasn't perfect but I wasn't that bad.
You're fine. You survived.

You've always been ungrateful. Even after everything I went through for you.

I force myself to stop reading. Those texts aren't for me, for one thing, but they also make me feel sick. I can't imagine my mom sending texts like those, even if we were having some kind of disagreement. Knowing that this is what Hallie has been dealing with for years—for most of her life, really—makes me all the more determined to show her she belongs with us. My mom is more than willing to claim her.

The walk through the backyard is a chilly one. November has set in fully now, and with it, the cold. Hallie's phone rings again in my hand, but I quickly put it on silent.

"Hey, baby," I say, letting myself into the guesthouse.

Hallie turns from her easel, smiling at me. "Hey, handsome."

"What are you working on?"

The guesthouse itself is kind of in limbo. Although it's clean and has a new coat of paint, and Hallie finished the accent wall, the plumbing still doesn't work. After Hallie moved inside, I didn't think it mattered much. But since she's been using it as a studio lately, I know I need to call someone to get it fixed.

"Carole's friends needed a painting done," she explains. "Their mom's house from when she was a kid." She gestures to the reference photo tacked up beside the canvas. "What do you think?"

The photo is in black and white, showcasing an old farmhouse not unlike my own childhood home. The building looks worn, lived in. There's even a cat sleeping on the front porch.

When I look at Hallie's painting, I freeze. It looks identical, like the photo has come to life. Even the orange tabby on the steps.

"You're incredible," I tell her, voice full of awe and pride. Now I know how Luke must feel when he talks about Delilah's photography.

"Do you think they'll like it?" she asks.

"Baby, they'll love it." A vibration against my hand catches my attention, and I look at Hallie's phone again. "This has been ringing off the hook since I got home."

Her smile slips, and she reaches out, taking the device. Her shoulders slump. "Sorry. I would've put it on silent before, but I figured she'd stop after I didn't call her back yesterday. I...need to block her."

She doesn't seem surprised by this behaviour, and that doesn't sit right with me. I know her relationship with her mom has always been complicated, but this seems extreme.

"Is your mom usually this...insistent?"

"Worse, actually. She'll go months without saying a word, then suddenly, she'll get the urge to see me." She huffs a laugh, though it lacks humour. "Foolishly, I used to look forward to those moments."

I shake my head. "I don't think that's foolish, to want a relationship with your parent. Either one of them."

When Hallie looks up at me, her eyes are glassy. "It is when every time you try, you end up getting hurt. It's always the same. She misses me, we agree to meet up, she either convinces me to loan her cash or flat out steals it, and then she's gone. And while she is here, every conversation leads back to her and how hard done by she is."

Amanda Foster is certainly not known for being the greatest mother, but *stealing* from your kid? That's low.

"She's the reason I'm scared during storms. It's not because of the thunder or lightning, or the rain like Delilah. It's the *wind*." I take Hallie's hand, giving her something to hold on to as she opens up to me. "An old tree fell on our house when I was a kid, back when it was just me and Amanda. It broke my window, and the glass scratched up my arms and some of my face. I was terrified. She wasn't even *home*."

"How old were you?" I ask. My voice has a hard edge.

"Seven," she whispers.

I don't think I've ever hated someone more than I hate

Amanda. Hallie was only a year older than Abbie is now. I can't imagine leaving my daughter home alone like that. *Anything* can happen when kids are left to their own devices. I know that better than anyone.

"Come here."

I pull Hallie toward me, and when I sit on the edge of the bed, I pull her into my lap. She comes willingly, wrapping herself around me. I'd hold her here forever if that would take all her pain away.

"Amanda lost her mom when she was pretty young," Hallie says. "It was really sudden. A ruptured brain aneurysm. And I think, after that, she never felt whole. She blamed Pops for a lot, for only raising her halfway. That's why she couldn't be a good mom to me, she'd say. But if I had to guess, I'd say it hurt too much for her to try. She didn't want that relationship with me because she never got to experience it fully herself."

"That's why you wanted a relationship with Kevin," I say, putting the pieces together.

"On days when Amanda made me really mad, I'd sit in my room and blame it all on her. *She* was the reason my dad didn't want me. *She* made him move out of town. *She* was the reason he never tried to reach out. But if I thought about it hard enough, wished on all the stars, maybe he'd hear me and come anyway. Take me away."

"Hallie," I say, pained.

She swipes at a lone tear. "Of course, it's not all her fault. She knew he was married, and I'm sure she wasn't rainbows and sunshines to deal with when they broke things off, but he could've fought for me if he wanted."

"He's trying now."

"Yeah," she agrees. "He's trying now."

For a few minutes, we sit in silence. It's grown even darker outside, bathing the backyard in night. My gaze roams the guesthouse, taking in the changes Hallie has made. It's a far cry from what it used to look like. Now it looks like someone could actually comfortably stay out here—once I get the plumbing fixed.

"Do you think people can change?" she asks quietly.

I think for a moment. "I think, as a general rule, people are complicated. Nothing is purely black and white, good and bad. So yeah, Foster, I think people can change. If they want it bad enough."

"Am I making a mistake?"

I run my fingers through her hair. "With what?"

"Trying to make things work with Kevin. I mean, it's been twenty-eight years. Is it too late?"

When Hallie meets my gaze, I can see the uncertainty in her blue eyes. The worry that she's setting herself up for more heartbreak, the kind her mother has been inflicting on her for years. I'd do anything to make it better for her. To take all her worries away.

"I'll admit, I was a bit skeptical at first, but after meeting him, it seems to me like Kevin truly does want this. That doesn't erase the lifetime you spent without him, though. So if you think it's too late, if you don't want to give him this chance after all, that's valid. But if you *do*, I don't think it's a mistake to try."

Knowing what I know about Amanda now, I can understand Hallie's initial motivations better. She wants to try, even if it may not turn out the way she hopes it will.

"Thank you for being here," she says.

I wrap my arm tighter around her. "Thank you for telling me."

Hallie runs her fingers over the tattoos on my right arm. "I don't think I've mentioned it, but these are one of my favourite things about you."

I chuckle. "I'm happy you like them."

She shifts so she's straddling my lap now. "They make you, like, ten times hotter. And you were already *very* hot."

Threading my fingers through her hair, I tip her head up so she's looking at me. "Hallie Foster, do you have a crush on me?"

Her cheeks are tinged pink. She pinches her fingers together in front of her face. "Maybe a small one."

"*Liar.*"

"Fine." Her lips stretch into a grin. "A big one."

"Good," I say, leaning close. "Because I've got a huge crush on you."

Her nose bumps mine. "Prove it."

So I do. I take her mouth slowly, wanting to savour every moment I have with her. Every touch of her lips, every inch of her body pressed against mine, still feels surreal. Like I'm having an out-of-body experience, watching another version of myself have what I've wanted for ten *long* years.

Hallie melts in my embrace. In this, she surrenders herself completely to me. She *trusts* me, and I don't take that for granted.

Pulling back from her mouth, I press a kiss to her neck, where her pulse thunders beneath her skin. She whimpers, and then she grabs my shirt and tugs on it. Hallie pulls the tee over my head. It falls to the floor somewhere by my feet.

She leans back, running her hands over my chest, tracing the tattoos there. When they land on one in particular, her fingers still.

"*Wait.*"

I watch her face carefully, looking for the smallest clues as to what she's thinking. I'm surprised it's taken her this long to spot it. I thought for sure I would've been busted long before now.

Her eyes meet mine. "Gabe," she whispers.

I tuck a lock of hair behind her ear. "Foster."

She looks down again, staring at my chest as she gently traces the tattoo. "I drew this."

I nod. "During math in grade eleven." A smile tugs at my lips. "Mrs. Feinberg confiscated it because we were passing notes instead of paying attention."

Hallie pokes me. "*You* were distracting me, actually."

"Semantics." She rolls her eyes, and I pinch her hip. "I had to plead my case to her after class that day. Convince her I needed that paper back."

She shakes her head. "I can't believe you kept it. And you got it *tattooed*. When?"

I purse my lips. "Just before you left."

Her touch falls away. "Oh."

I take her hand and place it back on my chest, over her tattoo. It isn't far from where I have Abbie's name inked on my skin, because she and Hallie are the two most important people in my life. When Hallie drew it, it was a simple sketch of one of the autumn crocus flowers that grows along the front of Haven House in the fall.

Now it reminds me of her.

"Do you know why I got it?" I ask.

"Why?"

"Because even though it was likely just a doodle to you, it made me feel special. I know how close you keep your art. Seeing it made me feel like I'd earned the privilege."

Hallie leans in and places a kiss on my lips. "You are special. You always have been."

"Hallie, I..."

I love you.

I want to say the words, but they get stuck in my throat. Flashbacks of that day on the beach cross my mind. The look on Hallie's face is burned into my memory. I couldn't survive that a second time.

"Yeah?"

"I'm glad you came home," I say instead.

Her expression warms. "I'm glad I came home, too."

It isn't a profession of love, but it's enough for now. It has to be enough.

THIRTY-FIVE

HALLIE

WALKING INTO THE RETIREMENT HOME, I'm greeted with a blast of warm air. I quickly unzip my coat and pull it off, draping it over my arm. Pops isn't in the lobby like usual, so I take the elevator up to his floor. I find him in the lounge.

Pops smiles when he sees me. "There's my Junebug."

I shake my head at the nickname, but a smile still stretches my lips. "Hi, Pops."

He adjusts his glasses, then scrutinizes me with his assessing stare. "You seem sad."

Taking a seat across from him, I try to school my expression. "I'm not sad. I've been helping Carole a bit more lately. Maybe I just look tired."

His lips flatten into an unimpressed line. "You don't have to share if you're not ready, but don't play me for a fool, young lady."

I sigh, giving in. "Amanda has been calling me."

"Ah." Understanding washes over his features. "I take it you haven't answered?"

My grandfather has his own complicated relationship with his daughter. Despite all she's done to break it, I don't think Pops could ever sever their connection, no matter how much it hurts to hang on to. Still, he has never judged me for how I choose to deal with her, just like I never hold his choices against him. Family ties are prone to tangle, and they're hard to remove.

I chew on my lip. "No. I told myself I wouldn't after last time. I'm done. But I just…"

Pops waits patiently as I collect my scattered thoughts.

"I guess I'm just grieving what could have been."

I've come to terms with who my mother is, which is why I've finally made the decision to go fully no-contact. I officially blocked her number last night after I sent her a long message reminding her why we don't talk. But that doesn't mean I don't still mourn the version of us that exists in my imagination. The version of us that's happy and unburdened by everything that tries to weigh us down.

He gives me a sad smile. "I am, too."

I don't say anything else, and neither does he. There isn't anything *to* say. But simply sitting here with Pops, who understands Amanda like I do, makes me feel better.

Soon, some of the residents on Pops's floor start heading downstairs for the day's activity. My grandfather plays a lot of bingo, and he wins a lot, too. Today's activity, I quickly learn, is painting.

Pops smooth-talks the activities director into letting me join in on the fun. She has an extra easel and canvas, so she agrees on the condition I help her clean up afterward. I readily accept.

As I begin setting brush to canvas, the tension in my shoulders slowly lessens. It doesn't disappear entirely, but it's a start. Pops definitely knew what he was doing by convincing me to stay. Art has always been therapeutic for me. He was the one to give me that tool, back when I was a quiet little girl with the weight of the world on her shoulders.

"Do you have anything else on your mind?" Pops asks gently. "Or was it only your mother?"

I thought I could get away without crying, but my eyes fill with tears at his question. I take a deep, fortifying breath. "I have to tell you something, and you're probably going to be disappointed in me when you hear it."

Pops places a hand over mine. "I may not always agree with your actions, Hallie, but I will never be disappointed in *you*. You've made me the proudest a grandpa possibly could be, I reckon."

His words cut me somewhere deep, and I feel even worse for what I'm about to reveal. I should have never lied. Never asked Gabe to help me.

"I'm sorry I didn't tell you, but...my father reached out a couple months ago. I decided to meet him. When we were at Dockside, there was this whole thing about me being engaged to Gabe. It was a rumour, of course, but I...let my father believe it. I've been pretending Gabe is my fiancé."

Pops sets his paintbrush down, his attention fully on me. "Why did you do that?" His tone holds no judgment, only simple curiosity.

I shrug, looking down at my hands. There are tiny flecks of blue paint on my skin. "Because I'm twenty-eight years old and I don't know what I'm doing with my life. But the prospect of being engaged to Gabe made me feel like I had at least something figured out."

"You wanted to impress him," he says.

My cheeks heat in embarrassment. "Looking back, it was incredibly stupid. But things have changed and now I'm stuck, and the only way out is to tell the truth."

"What was your original plan?" he asks.

I grimace. "I was going to fake a breakup with Gabe and pretend we decided we'd be better off as friends. Except now I can't do that because..."

"Because?"

"Because I accidentally fell in love with him. Again."

Gabe has always had my heart, but, like I knew he would, this version of him won me over all the same.

My grandfather's laugh is hearty, filling the room. "Junebug, that just means you did it right."

I cover my face with my hands, no doubt getting paint in my hair. "I didn't stand a chance."

"I always thought that boy took a special liking to you."

I look up at Pops again. "He told me he loved me when we were eighteen. I didn't take it well. That's why I left for school earlier than planned. Then moving to his guesthouse, then into the main house, it was impossible to stop my old feelings from surfacing again."

"So are you together, then?" Pops asks. Again, without any judgment, even though he really should be judging me for keeping all of this to myself for so long.

"We are, but..." I frown. "I asked him to keep us a secret from his family. It's hurting him—I know it is—but I can't seem to let go of what's holding me back. I want to, but...I'm scared."

"What are you afraid of?"

"That his family is going to think I'm not good enough for him. That I'll do something to mess it up and he'll hate me. That I'll hurt him beyond repair. The list goes on."

Pops is quiet for a moment, thinking over his words. "You just said that keeping your relationship from his family is hurting him. Do you think that, perhaps, your present reality should be more important than your fears regarding hypothetical future situations that may not even come true?"

The world seems to tilt on its axis. When he puts it like that...I *know* Pops is right.

"I get so caught up in my head sometimes, I forget about what's right in front of me," I admit.

He pats my hand. "Nothing in life is perfect, Hallie. If you are in this with Gabe, *truly* in this, there are going to be moments where you disagree. Where you stumble. Yes, that might hurt a little. That's the nature of loving someone. But if you prioritize the care you have for one another, I believe there is nothing that can't be overcome."

His words put me at ease. Pops has always been a steady presence in my life, and he has never once lied to me. If he thinks I can do this, then...I can. *I will.*

"How do we even go about telling people?" I ask. "Just thinking about it makes my stomach tie itself into knots."

"Our minds are powerful, and this secret has been built up in your brain to feel bigger than it is. That's bound to be scary."

I chew on my lower lip. "It is."

I've always been like this. My worries start small, but before long, they've snowballed into something of epic proportions. It takes me twice as long to talk myself down as it did to work myself up.

"Why don't you start by telling one person?" Pops suggests. "I'm sure you'll find it less intimidating after that."

I swallow. "I guess I'll try. Gabe deserves at least that much."

He nods. "That's all you can do."

Feeling significantly lighter, I spend the rest of the time letting my paintbrush do the talking. After a while, I start to draw attention, and I spend an hour fielding questions from octogenarians. Pops snickers beside me every time one of his fellow residents starts to fawn over my painting, which depicts a simple vase of flowers the activities director set out.

After I help clean up the paints and brushes, I walk Pops back to his apartment. My canvas hangs from my hand, the paint still tacky.

"Hey," I say, when we're just outside his door, "how come you never told me about Gabe coming to visit you?" I've mentioned it before, but I never asked why.

Pops side-eyes me. "I wasn't aware I had to tell you everything."

I huff a laugh. "You don't. I just figured it's something you would've mentioned."

He turns to look at me fully. "If I had, would it have made you feel less guilty for not being here?"

No. It would have made me feel worse. It *did*, when Gabe dropped the news. I think that's a sign I need to stop underestimating my grandfather.

"Fair point."

"You have a big heart," he says. "Fill it with all the good things life has to offer."

As I make my way back to Kip Island, back home, I take my grandfather's words with me. Gabe is a good thing—the *best* thing—in my life, and I want everyone to know it.

THIRTY-SIX

GABE

AFTER WORK, instead of driving home, I find myself taking the long road out to Haven House. If I can't tell my family about me and Hallie yet, I need to unload one thing off my chest. I need to tell them about Ethan's job offer.

When I park in the driveway behind my dad's truck, I pull out my phone and navigate to my texts with Hallie. I pause when I see her new contact name. Maybe it was a ridiculous thing to do, but *technically*, it's true. Sort of. Clara would probably call it mani-festation.

> I'll be home late. Just stopping to see my parents for a bit.

As I slip out of the truck and head for the front door, my phone buzzes with Hallie's response.

FIANCÉE

> Larissa had to drop Abbie off a bit ago. Hospital was short staffed. We'll be here waiting for you.

That stops me in my tracks. After what happened with Luke's

ex, Larissa and I have been more selective of who watches Abbie. We don't hire babysitters. If she's not with one of us, she's with Larissa's parents or mine. Always family. The fact that Larissa clearly trusts Hallie enough to leave our daughter with her means a hell of a lot.

> I can come home now if you want.

FIANCÉE

> Stay and see your parents. I promise we're fine!

Her text is followed up with a selfie of the two of them. My girls. They're eating pizza, and it looks like they've turned the living room into some kind of fort. I'm already itching to get home to them, but first, I need to talk to my dad.

Pocketing my phone, I head inside. It felt weird being here when they first turned part of the house into a bed-and-breakfast, but now that I'm used to it, it still feels like coming home.

"Hey, anybody here?" I call out as I slip off my boots.

"Living room!" Mom calls back.

I walk down the hall lined with photos of me and my siblings as kids. There are quite a few of Abbie, too, ranging from when she was a newborn to just last year. My eyes catch on a particular picture at the end of the hallway. She didn't have the purple hair back then, but Hallie still stands out to me. She always has.

Rounding the corner into the living room, I find Mom sitting on the couch. A fire is roaring in the fireplace, and a throw blanket is thrown across her lap.

"Hi, sweetie," she says when she looks up from her book. "What are you doing here?"

I bend to place a kiss on her cheek. "Can't I come visit my favourite woman without an ulterior motive?"

She arches a brow. "You and I both know your *favourite woman* is on the other side of the island right now, in your house."

I cross my arms. "You know?"

Mom laughs. She places her bookmark in between the pages and shuts her book. "Gabriel, of course I know. We *all* know. Why do you think we suddenly came down with a case of termites?"

I shake my head. "I knew you all were up to no good."

She shrugs. "We simply provided a little forced proximity to get things moving. I'm not getting any younger, you know. I want more grandchildren before I'm too old to enjoy them."

The laugh comes out before I can stop it. "Well, *anyway*, I actually came by to see Dad. Is he around?"

Mom flicks a hand toward the guest side of the house. "He's fixing something or other in one of the bedrooms."

Now that it's winter, Haven House is closed to guests. While the tourist season is well and truly over, so there's no point in staying open, it also gives my parents a break. After being constantly on the go for a good chunk of the year, it's much needed.

I leave Mom to her book and head in search of my dad. Once I hit the second level, I can hear some banging and familiar cursing.

"Dad?"

"In here!"

I step into the bedroom, taking in the mess of tools on the floor. The door is off its hinges, leaning against the bed. "Need any help?"

"You know what, that'd be great," he says. Then he narrows his eyes at me. Assessing. "I didn't know you were coming by tonight."

"It wasn't planned. I, uh, was hoping to talk to you about something."

Suddenly, the nerves hit me full-force. I haven't been this nervous to share something with my dad since I had to tell him I'd gotten Larissa pregnant at twenty-one after a one-night stand. But I'm twenty-eight now, a full-blown adult. A father. Something like this shouldn't rattle me, but deep down, I'm still that kid who seeks approval from his parents.

He leans back against the dresser. "Is this about Hallie?"

My brows furrow. "Hallie? No. Why would this be about her?"

He chuckles. "Oh, maybe because you've been mooning after her since you were a kid, and now she's living in your house. Excuse me for assuming. What's on your mind?"

I shake my head. "It's about work."

This gets all of his attention. "What about it?"

He's been retired for a while now, but Dad took his job as seriously as Luke does. They both knew from a young age that they wanted to work for the department, and they both worked hard when they got there.

"I think I want to quit."

Dad's brows draw together. He's quiet for a moment. Then he simply says, "Okay."

"*Okay*? That's all you have to say?" I shake my head. "You're not going to ask how I plan to pay my bills? Keep supporting Abbie?"

"You've been out on your own for quite some time now, Gabe, and you've never given me any reason to doubt your capabilities. So no, I'm not going to ask because I'm sure you have a plan. Or if you don't, you'll make one."

Admittedly, I'm a little taken aback. It's not like Dad has ever been on my case about figuring shit out, even back in high school. This is a pressure I've put on myself.

Self-inflicted pressure is almost worse than that of others. Because at the end of the day, you have to be able to live with yourself, and that's a hell of a lot easier when you like who you are.

"You're not disappointed?"

He straightens. "Of course not. All I want for you and your siblings is happiness. There's about a million paths to fulfillment, son. I don't care which you pick or if you change your mind along the way."

At least half of the weight sitting on my shoulders falls away.

Though between him and Luke, I knew Dad would be the easiest to tell. Still, I feel relieved.

"An old classmate works for the coast guard out of Tobermory," I say. "I'm thinking about reaching out, seeing what I'd need to do to get on his search and rescue team."

He nods. "I think you should. They'd be lucky to have you."

"Thanks, Dad."

He smiles. "Anytime. Now can you hand me the Phillipshead?"

———

I open the front door to the sound of giggling. It instantly puts me at ease, and I quickly shuck my jacket and boots so I can join in on the fun.

When I turn the corner, I find Hallie sitting on the couch alone. My daughter is nowhere in sight, and the remnants of their fort litter the floor.

"Hey," she says. "How are your parents?"

"They're good. I helped my dad fix one of the guest bedroom doors," I reply. "Where's Abbs?"

Hallie shrugs. "I'm not sure..." Her smile is a bit mischievous, and I get the hint. "I swear she was just here a second ago."

"Hmm. I guess I'll have to find her..." I lift the cushion on the armchair and pretend to look under it. Another giggle rings out. "Did you hear that?"

Hallie shakes her head. She rolls her lips inward as she tries not to smile. "Hear what?"

I walk around the back of the couch, but I catch movement across the room. The curtains are swaying, and a small pair of feet are sticking out the bottom. *Busted.*

"Maybe she's over here." I round the couch again, crossing the room. Another peal of laughter sounds, which is music to my fucking ears.

"She has to be close by," Hallie says.

I shrug. "I give up. I think she's gone."

After hearing my fake dejected tone, Abbie pops out from behind the curtain. "Look! I'm right here, Daddy!"

I feign shock, and then I scoop her into my arms. She shrieks her laughter, growing louder as I begin to tickle her sides.

"Hallie!" she gasps. "Hallie, help me!"

I shake my head. "She can't save you. She was in on your plan to trick me."

Hallie stands from the couch, looking contemplative. "What if we negotiate?"

"What's...that?" Abbie asks between gasping breaths. I let up on the tickling a little.

"Making a deal. Like if we tell your dad he can have our left-over pizza, but *only* if he lets you go."

"Yes!" Abbie yells. "Let's 'gotiate!"

"I do love pizza..."

"Daddy, please! My tummy hurts from laughing!"

I stop my assault, and Abbie goes limp in my arms. "You drive a hard bargain, dude, but I accept."

"Put me down!" I set her on her feet, and she runs for the kitchen. "I'll get the pizza."

While we have a minute, I reach out and grab Hallie's hand, tugging her closer. I wrap an arm around her waist. "Thanks for staying with her."

She smiles, then glances over her shoulder. Abbie is still banging around in the kitchen, so she turns back to me. "Of course. You know I love hanging out with her. Even more than I love spending time with her dad."

My brows raise. "Oh, really? I suppose you won't be sneaking into my bed tonight, then."

"Well, I wouldn't go *that* far," she amends.

"Hmm. I thought so." Hallie pushes up on tiptoe, leaning in to kiss me. I draw back. "Abbs will be back any second."

She shocks the hell out of me by saying, "I know. I'm done hiding, Gabe."

So I kiss her. I can't help myself. After the talk with my dad, and coming home to my girls, I'm feeling pretty damn invincible.

"*Ew!*"

Hallie and I break apart, and my wide eyes meet hers. *Shit*. I lower my arm from Hallie's waist, and we both turn to find Abbie, nose scrunched, looking up at us. A plate of pizza—six or seven slices, way more than I can eat—is balancing precariously in her hand.

I hook my pinkie around Hallie's, grabbing her attention. *Sorry*, I mouth.

She tightens her pinkie, then lets go. "It's okay," she says. "It's time."

My heart kicks into overdrive as I watch Hallie take the plate from Abbie and ask her to sit on the couch. Then Hallie looks at me. "Can I?"

I'm not entirely sure what I'm supposed to say in this situation, so I nod. Maybe she'll have better luck than me.

Hallie sits beside my daughter. "Abbie, can I tell you something?" she asks. "It's a bit of a secret, because I've been scared to tell a lot of people, but it's important to me that you know."

"But grown ups don't get scared," Abbie protests.

"Sure we do," Hallie replies. "There's different types of scared. Sometimes, you get scared of the shadows in your room, and you have to turn on the light to prove there are no monsters. And sometimes, it's scary being vulnerable—sharing your feelings. But that's what friends are for, and you and I are friends, right?"

"Yes! You can tell me."

Hallie leans in close. "I really, *really* like your dad."

My daughter gasps, then lets out a giggle that she covers with her hand. "You *like like* him? Like Sophia's sister likes Lukey?"

"Yes, exactly like that. And I think—" Hallie's eyes drift to me. "No, I *know* he likes me, too."

Abbie nods. "Yes! Daddy's always happy to see you, and you're really pretty."

Hallie's cheeks pinken at the compliment. "Thank you. You're really pretty, too. But, Abbs, do you think you'd be okay if me and your dad were together?"

She cocks her head. "Like boyfriend and girlfriend?"

"Yeah, Princess," I say, finally finding my voice. "Do you think that would be okay with you?"

Abbie seems to think on it for a moment. Slowly, she begins to nod. "Yeah. But...can I get a cat, Daddy?"

I arch a brow. "Are you trying to negotiate with me?"

She shrugs, but a grin tugs at her lips. Hallie, on the other hand, can't contain her laughter.

I point to her. "This is your fault."

Hallie blinks innocently up at me. "I'm not sure what you mean. But that is an excellent question, Abbs. What do you say, Daddy? Can she get a cat?"

The look I give her is full of promise. *Later*. Her eyes sparkle in challenge.

"Let's work our way up to a cat when you're older. We can start with a fish, though. Do we have a deal?"

Abbie holds out her hand. "Deal."

I grab her hand, pretending to shake it, but then I take the opportunity to tickle under her arm. With a giggle, she pulls away immediately, then jumps on the couch and crawls behind Hallie, hiding.

And for a second, time seems to stop. Wishful thinking, maybe. But if I could freeze this moment right here and live in it forever, I'd do it in a heartbeat.

THIRTY-SEVEN
GABE

UNLIKE THE LAST Sunday brunch we attended, I feel lighter than I ever have before. Because by the afternoon, my family will know everything.

Abbie runs into the house ahead of us, not bothering to wait. As we ascend the porch steps, I grab Hallie's hand and interlace our fingers. Her head snaps in my direction.

"We're telling them today, right?" I confirm. It's our last brunch before Clara drives our parents down to Toronto to catch their flight to Mexico.

Hallie nods, though her eyes are wide with worry. "Yes, but I thought maybe we would, you know, ease them in."

I press a kiss to her bare ring finger. "You should know by now that I like to cannonball into the deep end, baby."

Her irises flare, just like they always do when I call her that. She pushes onto the tips of her toes, leaning into me. I meet her halfway, and our lips meld together. If anyone were to look out the window now, there would be no denying what they saw.

When we break apart, Hallie sighs. "I guess we'd better tell them before Abbs beats us to it."

I chuckle at that. "When you decided to tell her first, you definitely chose the least likely person in this family to keep a secret."

She tries to look annoyed, but her smile breaks through. "Yeah, but she's also the most important. If she wasn't happy, then nothing else would have really mattered."

Hallie lets out a noise of surprise when I bend and claim her lips again. That four-letter word is on the tip of my tongue, but I shove it down. One thing at a time. So instead, I let myself savour her.

"What was that for?" she asks, slightly breathless.

I cup her cheek. "Thank you. For never once thinking that Abbie shouldn't come first."

Hallie's brows furrow. "Of course she should. Nothing else ever crossed my mind."

"I know, and that's why I lo—" I cut myself off. "Why I'm lucky as hell to call you mine."

Thankfully, she doesn't seem to catch on to my near slip. We decide to head into the house before Clara can come looking for us again.

My parents and siblings, along with Delilah and Parker, are already in the kitchen. Abbie is in the other room with Sophia, playing until the food is ready. When Hallie and I enter, conversation grinds to a halt.

Six pairs of eyes lock onto our joined hands, and then they search our faces. Hallie's grip tightens; I give her a squeeze back in reassurance.

"Oh. My. *God*!" Clara finally exclaims.

Hallie pales beside me, guilt threaded through her expression. "Clara, listen. I—"

"Do you have any idea how *long* I have been waiting for this day?" my sister shrieks, her body practically vibrating with excitement. "Over a fucking *decade*, Hallie Foster!"

She explodes out of her seat and makes a beeline for Hallie, gathering her in a tight hug. It might be ridiculous, but I refuse to let go of her hand. As Hallie hugs Clara back with her free arm, I can practically see the relief wash over her.

When they pull apart, Clara is still smiling. I didn't necessarily think my twin would make a huge deal about us being together, but I also didn't think she would be this excited either.

"When did this happen?" she asks, circling her finger to indicate our interlocked fingers.

Hallie grimaces, and I say, "Officially? The night we went to the bar."

Clara spins around to look at Delilah. "I *told* you!" Then she turns back to us. "I had a feeling things changed after that. That drive home was awkward as hell for the rest of us, by the way."

"You aren't mad I kept this from you?" Hallie asks tentatively.

"Babe," she says flatly, "you were wearing his shirt on girls' night. We knew. We *all* knew."

Hallie blushes bright red, and I release her hand so I can pull her against my side. She tucks herself in close, not caring that everyone's eyes are still on us, and my heart soars. Fucking finally, we're not a secret anymore, and I don't have to pretend to not want my hands on her.

"Besides," Delilah adds, "you two can barely keep your eyes off each other. It was only a matter of time."

I like to think that's true. That Hallie and I were so inevitable, nothing could keep us apart. Not forever.

Clara nods. "We've just been waiting for you to catch up."

Hallie inhales deeply. "Gabe wanted to tell you—all of you—from the start, but I was scared. I was scared it would jeopardize our friendship or that you wouldn't think I was right for him. It's silly, really, but I let my worries win." She looks at my parents. "I'm sorry."

"Oh, sweetheart," Mom says. She drops her oven mitt and rushes over, cupping Hallie's face. "*I'm* sorry you felt like you had to hide from us, but I can't tell you how excited I am."

"Really?"

Mom smiles. "You've always been part of this family, Hallie, and you make my son happy. What more could I want?"

Mom returns to the food she was going to pull out of the oven, and Clara retakes her seat at the table. I start to follow, but Hallie stays rooted to her spot. When I look at her, she has a determined expression on her face.

"There's something else," Hallie says. "In the interest of being completely honest."

I didn't think we needed to tell my family about our fake engagement, but Hallie decided she would rather lay it all out in the open. Start fresh.

Clara gasps, perking up. "Are you pregnant?"

Hallie's cheeks flame. "What? That's not— I— *What?*"

I chuckle at how flustered she is, and at my sister's overactive imagination. "Hallie isn't pregnant."

Yet. But that's a conversation for another time.

"Then what is it?" Dad asks. He and Mom are standing by the island, plating something that looks like home fries.

"Gabe and I have been pretending to be engaged in front of my father and his family," she blurts, so fast her words all jumble together.

For a moment, everyone is silent.

Then Parker says, "That's some serious rom-com type of shit."

Delilah cuts him a look, likely for swearing when Abbie and Sophia could be in earshot, but he isn't fazed.

"He's not wrong," Clara says. "And I definitely didn't see *that* coming. After Carole spilled the beans, I figured you would have told Kevin it was just a rumour."

"I should have, but it's for some of the same reasons I wouldn't let Gabe tell you about us." Hallie looks down at her hands, then back up. "I was worried about what people would think of me. Of what I had to show for myself. I'm done with all that now. I don't want to be anyone but exactly who I am."

"Good," Mom says. "Because we happen to love her very much."

Hallie's expression lightens as all of her previous worries melt away.

I lean closer, speaking only for her. "That wasn't so bad, was it?"

She shakes her head. "I should have known your family would be amazing, as always."

Hallie goes to join Clara and Delilah at the table, and they start whispering together. It looks like Clara and Delilah are both interrogating her.

Someone claps me on the back, and I turn to find my brother sporting a smug grin. "I was beginning to think I'd never see the day you finally decided to make a real move," Luke says.

I shake my head. "Again, you're a hypocrite."

He ignores my jab, and his grin turns sincere. He tips his head in an approving nod. "Happy for you, Gabe."

"Thanks." He goes to move away, but I stop him. "Hey, Luke? Can I talk to you for a minute?"

Now that Hallie has confessed, I feel like I need to do the same. Dad said he wouldn't say anything until I did, but I'm sure Mom knows by now. Those two tell each other everything.

Luke gestures to the door. After receiving a reassuring smile from Hallie, I follow him out to the front porch.

"Mind making this quick?" he asks, leaning back against the wooden railing. "It's fucking freezing out here."

It is, but outside is the only place we're guaranteed a lick of privacy. Everyone else will find out eventually, so maybe it's a moot point to talk to Luke alone, but I figured I owe him that much. As my boss, but also as my brother.

I grit my teeth, gathering my nerve. "I just wanted to give you a heads up that I'll be quitting sometime in the near future."

Luke rears back, looking like I slapped him. "Quitting? You planning to move or something?"

I shake my head. "No, I'm staying on the island. But I've been thinking, reevaluating what I want my life to look like. And I've come to the conclusion that being a firefighter isn't what I want. It never really was."

I don't think I've ever seen Luke look so shocked. "What? You were so proud to join the crew."

"No, *you and Dad* were proud. I was just following in your shadow."

"You mean my footsteps?"

My smile is more of a cringe. "All my life, I've looked up to you. I mean, of course I have. You're my older brother. But I've never really been allowed to be *me* the way you and Clara have. In school, I was always *Luke's brother*, never just Gabe. Always measured against you. And when it came down to it, I chose the path that everyone else thought I should take because I didn't want to be known as the family fuck-up."

"What the hell are you talking about?"

"You and Clara, you've always been so sure of yourselves. Knew exactly what you wanted to be. I had no fucking clue, but I knew I couldn't do nothing, so I joined the department." I blow out a breath before admitting something even Hallie doesn't know. "I almost quit once before, years ago. Had my resignation signed and sealed, ready to go."

Luke stares at me. His expression is unreadable. "What stopped you?"

"Larissa told me she was pregnant. I couldn't quit then. Not when I needed a steady job to take care of my daughter. Not when I was already the irresponsible kid who got a girl pregnant who I wasn't even dating."

My brother shakes his head. "You know we never gave a shit about that, Gabe. We never judged you."

"Maybe you didn't, but when all anyone else has ever done is compare me to my perfect, dependable older brother, I'm going to fall short every damn time." And after a while, it starts getting to you, until you start to believe there's truth in it.

Luke runs a hand through his hair. "Shit, Gabe," he says. "I had no idea you felt that way."

I shrug, then cross my arms against the chill. It really is fucking cold out here. "Because I didn't tell you. I didn't tell anyone."

Except Hallie. While she doesn't know that I had been on the verge of resigning before, she knows how everything else has affected me.

"Still, I'm sorry. I'll admit, I've been wrapped up in my own shit these past few years. I should've paid better attention to you, though. I'm sorry I dropped the ball."

Shaking my head, I say, "You've gotta cut that shit out, too. I'm not telling you all this because I want you to manage my problems for me. In fact, I'd rather you didn't."

"I don't—"

"You *do.*" I raise my brows. "You let me get away with being late all the time, and that's just one example. I know why you do it, but I don't want to be treated differently. I can't prove I'm capable if you don't give me the space to do it."

He frowns. "You don't have to prove yourself to us. To me."

"I want to prove it to myself."

For years, I've been carrying these feelings around. Finally voicing them feels better than I thought it would.

"So if you're quitting, what are you going to do next?" he asks. And I'm pleasantly surprised to find there's no anger there, only genuine curiosity.

"Ethan was in town a while ago, and we ran into him at Sunnyside. He works with the coast guard now. He offered me an in, if I wanted it."

Luke's expression is serious, jaw set, as he considers this. Slowly, he nods. "Sounds perfect for you. Mom's gonna hate it, though."

I laugh as a ton of weight falls off my shoulders. "Hallie's not too jazzed either. She's happy for me, but I know a small part of her wishes I could work a desk job."

"Yeah," he says, swinging an arm around my shoulder and tucking me in tight so he can give me a noogie, like the good ol' days. "But where's the fun in that?"

I break out of his hold, flip him the bird, and then we both chuckle as we head back inside to our family.

THIRTY-EIGHT

HALLIE

GUILT HAS BEEN SLOWLY EATING me alive. Telling Gabe's family the truth about our relationship made it even more apparent I need to do the same with mine. Despite all my fears, I can't truly have a clean slate with Kevin if our foundation is muddled with lies.

Thankfully, Clara is very generous with her car. I could've asked Gabe to drive me to the mainland, but this is something I need to do on my own.

My phone buzzes in my purse, and I pull it out to check it. My heart thumps in my chest. I half expect it to be Kevin, telling me now actually isn't a good time to come over. I'm a little disappointed when it isn't, if only for my own self-preservation.

GABRIEL

Hey, you headed back? I thought you finished work at three today.

Just running some errands on the mainland. I'll be home in a bit.

Home.

I put up a valiant fight, but somewhere along the way, I lost the battle. For the longest time, the only home I had ever known was with Pops. Living with Gabe—letting him back into my life— has made me realize just how safe he makes me feel. Cared for. *Loved*.

GABRIEL

Abbs is spending the night with my parents.

You better get your fine ass back here soon, Foster. I have plans for you.

A thrill travels down my spine at the promise. Not only do I feel loved by Gabe—I feel wanted. Craved. It's a feeling I've never experienced before, and one I wasn't sure existed.

I tuck my phone away and look toward the house I've parked in front of. I recognize Caitlyn's and Bryan's vehicles in the drive-way. *I guess now is as good of a time as any.* Might as well rip the Band-Aid off for the whole family.

Walking up to the door and knocking feels a hundred times more nerve-wracking than it did that first time. Part of that is because I don't have Gabe here to hold my hand, but I also know it's the dread of finally coming clean. Telling the truth.

The door opens before I'm ready.

"Hallie," Kevin says with a smile, "come in."

"I know you said it was fine, but I'm sorry for coming on such short notice," I say, stepping over the threshold.

"That's alright. You're welcome here anytime."

Not for long. Not once you know what I've done.

I toe off my boots, then follow Kevin into the kitchen. Caitlyn and Bryan are sitting at the island, squabbling over something. A smile tugs at my mouth—they remind me so much of the Bowmans.

When my gaze lands on Dana, my smile slowly falls. I swallow the lump in my throat. "Hi," I say.

"Hello," she says coolly.

"Hey, Hallie," Bryan says with a smile. "Good to see you."

Caitlyn hops off her stool and digs through her bag. "I got you something from Fiji," she says. She and Amara just got back from their honeymoon there. "It's nothing fancy, but it made me think of you."

She holds a bracelet out to me. It's made from different shades of purple beads, threaded into a repeating pattern. It's beautiful.

And that does it. I break under the pressure of all the lies I've told, and the truth begins to force its way out.

"Thank you, but I..." I blink to hold back tears as I set the bracelet on the counter. "I can't."

Caitlyn's expression falls. "You don't like it."

My gut churns. "No! I love it, I swear. But I don't deserve it."

Kevin and Dana have stopped their conversation now. Four pairs of eyes settle on me.

"What are you talking about?" Bryan asks. "It's just a bracelet."

But it's *not* just a bracelet. Not really. Caitlyn went on her honeymoon, and she thought of *me*. The half sister she just met. My siblings have welcomed me with open arms, and all I've done is lie.

I take a deep breath. "I want to start by saying that I'm truly sorry. My intention was never to hurt anyone, but that doesn't excuse anything. I've been lying to you all, and I can't do it anymore." I offer Kevin a sad smile. "Gabe and I...we aren't really engaged. His daughter got confused when I moved into their house because I needed a place to stay, and she accidentally started the rumour. That day I met you at Dockside? That was the first I had heard of it."

"I...don't understand," Kevin says. "Why didn't you tell me?"

Why? Because I'm a coward. That's what all of this comes down to, at the end of the day.

"When you heard I was engaged, you looked so happy. And I felt, at the time, that I didn't have much to show for myself. I wanted you to like me. To...want me. So I figured it wouldn't hurt to pretend a little. Only, now it's become a whole mess and I never meant for things to get this far, and I'm sorry."

"So you and Gabe *aren't* together?" Caitlyn clarifies.

I debate how to answer this. "We are now. It's...complicated. He and I have been orbiting each other for years, and we finally gave in. But engaged? No."

My fingers twist together in front of me as I wait with bated breath for someone to say something. I've shocked them, but I know the anger is coming. I brace for the impact.

Finally, Dana scoffs. "We should have known better. You know what her mother is like."

"*Mom*," Bryan chastises.

"Well, it's true, Bryan. She seduced your father, and now look what's happening."

I'm not sure why, but it's this comment, above all the others, that breaks my resolve. For *years*, I've held my tongue when people have made snide comments about Amanda. About me. But I'm done feeling small.

"Forgive him or don't. That's your business," I say to Dana. All four of them look a little stunned at the force of my words. "But I will not be made to feel less than for choices I had no hand in making. What I did was wrong, I won't deny that, but I've been treated no better by you."

Dana rears back like I've slapped her.

"I can appreciate that this situation is hard for you. It's hard for me, too. But I didn't ask for any of this. So if you can't accept me based on some moral failing you think I have, simply based on who birthed me, then that's fine. I won't bother you anymore."

My monologue has rendered everyone speechless. I wait a beat, to see if Kevin or my half siblings are going to say anything. When they don't, I turn on my heel and slip out of the house.

No one stops me.

I don't look back.

————

The familiar numbness sets in on my drive home. Every disappointment, every failed visit from my mother has prepared me well for this. The only way to get over these feelings is to ice them out. So that's what I do.

Or what I try to do anyway.

Confidence is a finicky thing. I used every ounce of it back at that house, and now that it's gone, there's room for self-doubt to come trickling in. My mother's voice isn't far behind.

Amanda Foster hasn't come out of life unscathed. But instead of owning her issues, confronting them, she blames them all on Pops. On the men she's been with. On me. And after years of internalizing that, it's hard to separate her opinions from the truth.

In a daze, I pull into the driveway behind Gabe's truck. Thankfully, Clara will be swinging by later to pick her car up. If I had to see her right now, she would definitely know something is wrong, and I don't have the energy to convince her I'm alright. It's bad enough I'll have to face Gabe so soon after that epic showdown.

I shut the front door quietly behind me, hoping Gabe doesn't hear. I need another moment to compose myself. But when I hear his footsteps coming down the hall, I silently curse.

"Hi, beautiful," he says, and even that hurts.

Everything hurts.

"Hi," I reply. Despite how much I try to mask it, that one syllable is fraught with despair.

As it turns out, telling the truth isn't enough to wash away the guilt. The shame. I feel dirty for letting him pull me into his arms, like I'm still using him.

He starts kissing me, and I try—I try so hard to kiss him back. But I feel hollow, like my soul has been sucked from my body. Every movement feels robotic.

Men don't stay with women like us.

Gabe draws back, his brows furrowed. Concern mars his handsome face. "What's wrong?"

I shake my head, trying to pull his mouth back to mine. "Nothing," I lie. All I do is *lie*.

He doesn't let me get far. "Hallie, I can tell you're not with me right now. What's going on?"

Tears spring to my eyes. "Sorry. I'm sorry. I know you had plans for us and—"

"Hey." He cups my cheek, brushing away a tear that manages to fall. "I don't want you to *ever* feel like you need to have sex with me if you're not up for it. I love spending time with you, Foster. It doesn't matter what we do."

Doubt still swirls in my mind. "Are you sure? I'm sorry. I can—"

"Hallie, baby, no more apologies. There's nothing you need to be sorry for." Gabe's arm drops from my waist, and he grabs my hand. "Come with me."

"Where are we going?"

"We're going to sit on the couch and watch a movie. And later, if you feel like it, you can tell me what has you thinking so hard over there."

I think my feet carry me to the living room, but it feels like I'm floating the whole time. Gabe nudges me to sit in my usual spot on the sectional, and then he drapes a blanket over my lap. My fingers curl into the plush material as I watch him turn the TV on and queue up our movie. When *10 Things I Hate About You* starts playing, my eyes burn.

The last time we watched this together was the night of my eighteenth birthday party. I had never been happier to ditch Clara and our classmates in favour of curling up against Gabe's side.

Now as he settles beside me, I feel terrible for the comfort he brings me. For the plans I ruined. Gabe already doesn't get to spend as much time with his daughter as he'd like. She's staying with her grandparents tonight because he wanted to be alone with me, and now he can't even do what he wanted.

"I'm sorry," I whisper.

He places a kiss on the crown of my head. "I'm not. I'm living eighteen-year-old Gabe's dream right now. Couldn't be happier if I tried."

I look up at him, skeptical. "Your dream was to watch movies with me?"

"No, Foster. My dream was to call you mine."

Mine.

I cast my eyes downward as I rest my head against him. And I let myself have this. Indulge in it. Because I can already picture it slipping from my grasp, just like my mother warned me.

THIRTY-NINE

GABE

AS THE NIGHT WEARS ON, Hallie grows more distant, even in sleep.

The moment she stepped through the front door earlier, I felt it. Something was *off*. But it wasn't until I started kissing her that I realized she wasn't in it. Something happened, I just didn't know what.

Was it a mistake to keep those three words from her? Should I have told her again that I love her? Hallie has faced her own fears, but I haven't faced mine.

My sleep is anything but restful. I have horrible dreams that feel sickeningly like some kind of bad omen, warning me I'm on the verge of losing everything I hold close. I haven't felt fear like that since the night Abbie was in that fire.

Hours later, I wake with a start. *Abbie's safe. She's with my parents. Hallie's safe. She's right beside me.* I repeat the words in my head until my heart rate has slowed.

But when I turn over, I find her side of the bed empty. It's still dark out, and when I check the time, I see that it's three in the morning. My stomach drops.

Immediately, I'm out of bed. I check my en suite, the guest

279

room, the hallway bathroom. I even check Abbie's room. When I don't find her, I fly down the stairs. She isn't on the main level either. But when I look out the window in the kitchen, I notice the light is on out in the guesthouse.

I grab a hoodie off the hook by the back door and shrug it on, and then I head outside. We haven't gotten any snow yet, but the temperatures have dipped low enough for frost to coat almost everything. The grass crunches beneath my shoes as I walk across the backyard.

The door swings open silently, and I peer inside, not wanting to startle her. Hallie is standing in the middle of the room, her hands on her hips. She's still wearing the pajamas she went to sleep in, but she's also wearing her coat. The heat hasn't quite kicked in yet, which means she hasn't been out here long.

"Hallie," I say gently as I step inside, "what are you doing out here?"

Her shoulders slump. "I've decided I don't like this paint colour after all."

"That's fine, baby. We can change it." I step closer, taking the dry paintbrush from her hand and setting it on the counter. I wrap an arm around her, and she curls into me, her face pressed into my chest. "But is there a reason this couldn't wait until the sun came up?"

Her hands fist the sides of my hoodie. "Couldn't sleep," she mumbles, face still hidden.

"Does this have anything to do with the reason you came home upset?" I ask. When she came back from her errands looking like she had seen a ghost, she hadn't been ready to talk. Maybe she would be now.

She pulls back a bit and looks up at me. "I told Kevin and everyone the truth today," she admits. Her voice is quiet, bordering on a whisper.

A lock of hair falls across Hallie's cheek, and I reach out to tuck it behind her ear. "How did that go?"

Her face crumples. "Not well."

"What happened?"

Hallie swipes at her cheek, where tears are beginning to make their way down her face. "I said I was sorry for lying and told them that we aren't actually engaged. Then Dana started making comments about how they should've known better, considering who my mom is, and I just...snapped."

I pull her tighter to me. "Dana had no right to speak to you like that."

She shrugs. "Maybe she's right."

My body goes rigid at her words. Her defeated tone. "She's not," I declare.

"Amanda blows through town, leaving wreckage in her wake. Isn't that *exactly* what I've done? I inserted myself into Kevin's family, foolishly thinking I could belong. But I *never* have."

"Hallie, no. None of that is true. Kevin reached out to you. He wants you there. Now that you've cleared the air, I'm sure this will all blow over. I'll apologize to them, too. You weren't the only person who lied."

I'm grasping at straws, trying to get her to see. Trying to stop her from leaving me again. Because I can feel it happening, the crack that's beginning to form. How many times can you patch over something before the effort won't matter anymore?

Hallie takes a deep breath and then a step back, pulling out of my embrace, like she's preparing herself for something.

"Gabe, I've been thinking," she says. "And...I think we should stop."

My heart splinters. "Stop *what*?"

She crosses her arms over her chest defensively. "Stop kidding ourselves. Stop. Just...*stop*."

"Are you trying to break up with me right now?"

She opens her mouth, but the words seem to get caught. So she nods instead, then ducks to hide her face.

"No."

Her head snaps up, her gaze meeting mine. "No?"

"*No.*" I take a step closer, eating up that distance she tried to create. "I'm not letting you run away this time. Because you're right where you belong. You were made for me, Hallie, and I was made for you. I've never been more sure of anything in my life."

The fear in her eyes damn near kills me. Even after all this time, she's afraid of me. Of us.

"How do you know?" She shakes her head. "Because I've been trying to fight the voice inside my head that keeps telling me this is too good to be true. That you're too good to be true."

I cup her jaw and tip her chin up, forcing her eyes back to me. "Let me be a good thing."

Another tear slips down her cheek. "I don't want you to be a good thing because all the good things go away eventually."

I shake my head. "Not me. Not this."

"Gabe, *please.* I can't."

My jaw clenches as the hurt settles in. "Do you still not trust me?"

"It's not you I don't trust!" she cries, pulling away from me again. "Don't you get it? It's *me.*" She jabs a finger against her chest. "I don't trust myself because I've spent my whole life *terrified* of turning into her. Of hurting the people I love."

"That will never be you, baby. *Never.* You want to know why?" More tears trail down Hallie's cheeks, and the sight kills me inside. I wipe them away with my thumbs. "Because the fact that you're scared right now proves to me that you care. Your mom isn't concerned with any of that. She couldn't care less about the damage she does to her daughter. You aren't her, Foster, and you *never* will be."

I tuck her against my chest, holding her as she sobs. I wish that I had known the extent of her issues with her mom back when we were in high school. When we were kids. Hallie has spent so long dealing with all this on her own, and none of it is fair.

Eventually, her crying lessens. "I'm sorry," she croaks.

I swallow thickly. "If you really don't want to be with me—if you got caught up in the fake engagement—then I'll understand. But if you're doing this to try and spare me some kind of pain you think you'll inflict on me, then I don't accept."

She chokes on a laugh. "Just like that?"

"Just like that. I'm prepared to keep you, Hallie Foster, for however long you'll let me."

"And if I said you could have me forever?"

My forehead drops to hers. "I'd tell you that's nowhere near long enough, but I'll take it."

Hallie closes her eyes for a moment, but when she opens them again, there's clarity there. "I want to fight with you. Will you fight with me, baby? Because I love you, Gabriel Bowman. *I love you*, and I want this kind of forever."

Hearing those words pass her lips is the sweetest fucking sound I've ever heard. I dip my head, crushing my mouth to hers. Her lips are salty with her tears.

When we draw apart, my breathing feels ragged. "I'll fight with you. Until they put me in the ground. Because there is nothing in this world that could stop me from loving you."

A relieved cry passes her lips, and then I'm on her again.

Hallie unzips her coat and lets it slip from her shoulders. The heater has filled the guesthouse with a haze of warm air, but goosebumps still rise on her arms. I tug the hoodie over my head, tossing it to the floor.

Hand on her waist, I guide her back toward the bed. She lands on the mattress, then pulls me down after her. Our clothes come off, one piece after the other.

I love you, I love you, I love you—a chorus of whispers against lips, against skin.

I want you, I need you—stolen words between kisses.

Hallie's breath catches when I slip inside her. Her legs wrap around me, holding me there. And when I eventually begin to move, I relish the slow slide of our bodies coming together, over and over again.

After we're both spent, we lie there, tangled together. We'll have to move eventually, but not now. Not yet.

"I love you," she says, unburdened.

"I love you. Forever."

A little of Hallie is better than none of her. But *all* of her? That's everything.

FORTY

HALLIE

"A LITTLE MORE TO THE LEFT."

He moves to the right. "This good?"

I sigh. "No, Gabriel, your *other* left. It's not centered at all."

He looks over his shoulder at me, still holding the painting against the wall. "Baby, I don't even know which way is up anymore, we've been doing this so long."

I roll my eyes, crossing my arms from where I stand on the couch, facing the wall behind it. "Don't be so dramatic. What good are those muscles of yours if we can't put them to good use?"

Gabe grins. "Man, you're bossy today."

"And you said you knew what you were doing!" I counter. "Do I need to text your dad?"

His grin falters, turning into a frown. "No."

I suppress my laugh as he turns back to the wall. Thankfully, when he shifts the painting slightly to the left, it's perfect. I tell him so, and he carefully removes his hands.

Gabe spins to face me. "Damn, my girl knows how to paint."

I shake my head. "It's not my best work. I'm still a little rusty."

"If this is rusty, then you'll be hanging in some fancy European museum before long."

This elicits a loud laugh from me. "I'm hardly Louvre material, but I appreciate the confidence."

His eyes bore into me, and once upon a time, the intensity would have sent me running. Not now. "You've always had faith in me," he says. "Let me have faith in you."

Warmth spreads over me, from my head to my toes. "I love you." The novelty of saying it still hasn't worn off, and I hope it never does.

"Love you, too."

He crosses the distance between us, wrapping his arms around the backs of my thighs and throwing me over his shoulder. I shriek as I'm lifted off the couch, my head swimming as the blood rushes there.

"Gabriel!"

He smacks a hand to my ass. "I upheld my end of the bargain. Now I want my reward."

We both know he would have put the painting up for me regardless. In fact, he's the one who wanted me to start making art for the house. *Our* house, he says. Part of me wonders if we're moving too fast, but the bigger part of me has been waiting too damn long for this to tap on the brakes now.

As soon as his foot hits the bottom step, the doorbell rings. We both freeze. The chime sounds again, and Gabe pivots and deposits me back on the floor. I blink as I reorient myself.

Gabe heads for the door, peeking out the side panel. "It's Kevin," he says to me.

If the mood wasn't dead before, it certainly is now.

I haven't heard from any of the Landells since I stormed out of their house. That was two weeks ago now. I've been trying to move on, to forget about them, but that has proven to be more difficult than I thought. I evidently have issues with letting things go.

My palms grow clammy as I walk toward him. Gabe waits until I nod before he opens the door.

Sure enough, my father stands on the porch, hands tucked into the pockets of his wool coat. He gives us a sheepish smile.

I stare at him like a fool.

"Hi," he says. "Sorry to drop in unannounced. Do you have a minute, Hallie? I'd like to talk, if that's alright."

Gabe looks down at me. He sets a hand on my back, and I lean into him. "Foster?"

The unspoken question hangs in the air. He wouldn't hesitate to shut the door in Kevin's face if that's what I needed. What I wanted. But...I find myself nodding.

"I'll be upstairs if you need me," he says.

Gabe drops a kiss to my forehead and then walks away, and I'm left alone with my father.

I clear my throat. "Come in," I say. "We can sit in the living room."

My limbs feel stiff, like a wooden toy soldier's, as I lead him from the front hallway. Part of me wishes Gabe would have stayed, if only so I had something steady to lean on. But the other part of me knows I need to do this on my own.

These demons—the scars my parents, inadvertently or not, left behind—are mine to vanquish alone.

I turn to offer Kevin a seat on the couch, but I find him looking at the freshly hung painting. It's a rendering of the guesthouse, with its green siding and all the fallen leaves around it. Gabe told me to fill this house with my art—I figured something that represents the newest chapter of our story was a good place to start.

He gestures to it, walking closer. "That's beautiful."

I blush, looking down at my feet. "Thank you. I... I painted it."

He smiles warmly. "You have remarkable talent, Hallie. Though I suppose you should take what I say with a grain of salt, given I'm just a layman when it comes to fine art." He laughs softly at that, and I manage a smile. "I mean it. You're incredible."

Though I've made progress, I still don't know how to properly receive compliments. So I awkwardly clear my throat, shuffling toward the chair perpendicular to the couch. Kevin takes the hint and rounds the couch, settling onto the cushions.

For a moment, we simply look at one another. I wonder if he's thinking the same things as me. If he's replaying our last encounter on a loop, trying to pick apart all the ways he went wrong.

He sighs. "About the other day—"

"I'm sorry," I blurt, then cringe. "And I'm sorry I interrupted you. Before you go any further, though, I just want to say that I know I shouldn't have lashed out at Dana like I did. I—"

"You were right." The words stun me enough to dry up my voice. Kevin gives me a sad smile. "Everything you said was right, and I'm glad you were able to stand up for yourself...when I didn't."

I shift in my seat, even more uncomfortable now. When I imagined speaking with Kevin again, I wasn't expecting the conversation to go like...this.

"When I set out to get to know you, to have you in my life, I never meant for anyone to get hurt," he says. "Perhaps it was naïve of me, but I figured all our lives would be better for it. Now I can't help feeling as if I've made yours worse in the process."

I shake my head. "This was never going to be easy," I say. "But...I'm glad you reached out. I needed to know. To know you. Please know I am grateful for that."

Kevin sets his hands on his knees. "I shouldn't have pushed so hard, so fast. Dana and I... We haven't ever properly sorted through what my affair did to our relationship. That hurt has been ignored for far too long, by us both, and you bore the consequences of that. For that, *I* am sorry. I put you in an impossible situation."

I can see the sincerity shining in his eyes. Gabe said he had been skeptical of Kevin's intentions in the beginning, and I can't blame him, but it's clear to see that Kevin means what he says now.

"To be honest, I'm not really sure where we go from here," I admit.

"It's long overdue, but Dana and I are going to counselling. Regardless of the outcome of my marriage, though, I want to have a relationship with you. If you're willing." He inhales shakily. "I'm not the best man, I know, but I want to do better. To do right by those I love. I don't want to live any longer with regrets, and my biggest is letting you down."

I swallow down the wave of emotion threatening to sweep me away. "I want that, too," I admit. For the longest time, it was all that I had wanted. "But I think maybe we should start slow." I offer him a smile. "You weren't the only one who got carried away."

I was so excited about the prospect of being wanted, I didn't stop to think about how diving in headfirst might end poorly. There are so many feelings involved here, and not only mine.

"For what it's worth, there isn't some kind of standard I expect you to meet," Kevin says. "I want to know you simply because you exist. That's enough for me. Hearing about all the wonderful facets of your life is an added bonus."

Something inside me shifts then. It's slight, but it's like some small fissure in the deepest part of me is being mended.

Tears line my lashes, and I nod. "Thank you. I... Thank you."

Kevin pushes to his feet, and I stand, too. "I should get going. I don't want to take up too much of your time," he says. "Maybe we could meet at Dockside for lunch next week? Just you and me."

"I'd like that."

"Oh." He slips a hand into his pocket. "I almost forgot."

When he extends his palm toward me, the purple bracelet Caitlyn got me is sitting there. I take it, smoothing my thumb over the beads.

"She wanted me to make sure you got it," he explains. "And when you're ready, she'd like to spend some time with you. Bryan, too."

"They don't hate me?"

Kevin shakes his head. "Not at all. They understand why you did what you did, and they regret how things went with their mother."

I walk my father to the exit, and then I wave when he stops beside his car. Only once he's backing down the driveway do I shut the door.

Pulling my phone from my pocket, I send a quick text.

> Kevin gave me the bracelet. Thank you again. I think I need a little time, but I'd like to get to know you and Bryan too.

I barely make it halfway up the stairs when a reply comes through.

CAITLYN

> Take all the time you need! We're not going anywhere.

> And I'm glad you like the bracelet. Purple is my favourite colour too.

Upstairs, I find Gabe sitting in bed, watching TV. Wordlessly, I crawl across the mattress and settle into his waiting arms.

He presses a kiss to the top of my head. "How did it go?"

"Good. It was...really good." I shift against him so I can better see his face. "I'm sorry I asked you to lie for me. I don't think I've properly apologized for that."

He shakes his head. "I knew what I was doing. Besides, there isn't much I wouldn't do for you, Foster."

"Because you love me?"

"Because I love you."

"Good," I say. "Because I love you, too."

FORTY-ONE

GABE

ABBIE RUNS AHEAD through the automatic doors, escaping the snow that is slowly starting to blanket the ground. With a week to go until Christmas, I figured we'd be having a green one, but we woke up today to a sea of white.

As I follow after my daughter, I envy how carefree she is. She's not nervous about this at all. Me, on the other hand? I'm trying not to sweat buckets.

"I found him, Daddy," Abbie says, pointing across the lobby.

Hallie's grandfather is sitting in a chair, playing checkers with another resident. He spots Abbie first, and then his gaze finds mine.

Pops grins. "I figured I'd be seeing you before long."

He excuses himself from his game, then leads us over to an empty seating area. Abbie plops down on the couch, and I sit beside her.

"Hello again, Miss Abigail," Pops says.

She beams. "Hi, Pops."

I smooth my hands over my thighs, suddenly nervous. "We came to see if you wanted to ditch this place for the evening."

"What's the occasion?" he asks.

"I—"

"Daddy got Grammy to call from Mexico and help him make *all* of Hallie's favourite foods," Abbie interjects, bouncing in her seat. "And he got her a ring that's *really* pretty. I helped him pick it."

Pops's brows lift, a knowing glint in his eyes. "A ring, eh?"

I swallow. "Yes, sir."

"Gabe, you've been in love with my granddaughter for the better part of your life, haven't you?"

I nod. There's no point in denying it. "I have."

He smiles. "Then it's about damn time," he declares, clapping his hands together. "I'm ready to get out of here when you are."

———

Back at the house, Abbie entertains Pops in the living room while I put the finishing touches on dinner. Hallie is still at the gallery, thanks to Carole's intervention. My mom's good friend already can't wait to brag about how instrumental she was in our *real* engagement.

That is, if Hallie says yes.

My phone buzzes in my pocket, and when I pull it out, I see Clara has texted in our newest group chat. This one includes our parents, Luke and Delilah.

Operation Make Hallie a Bowman

CLARA

How much are you sweating right now?

I bet it's a lot.

LUKE

I'll take that bet.

MOM

Stop being mean to your brother! This is important. It's normal to be a little nervous.

Thanks, Mom.

CLARA

Kiss-ass.

I laugh. Although they can be pains, I have to admit, the familiarity of their ribbing is making me feel better.

DAD

Why does my phone keep pinging?

LUKE

Because we're giving Gabe shit.

I wouldn't be so cocky, brother. I have a long memory. And one of these days, you'll be in my position.

CLARA

Ooooh. He's got you there.

DELILAH

Everything is going to go great, Gabe. She's going to say yes!

Thank you, Delilah.

See how easy it is to be nice? You two should try it sometime.

CLARA

Meh.

LUKE

No comment.

MOM

We love you, sweetie. Keep us updated!

When Hallie gets home a little while later, I greet her at the door. "Hey," I say. "I've got a surprise for you."

As soon as she sets her sights on her grandfather, her eyes brighten. "Pops!"

"My Junebug," he says.

"What are you doing here?" Hallie asks, leaning down to give him a hug.

"Gabe and Abbie invited me to dinner." He sends me a quick wink. "They figured I could use a change of scenery."

She smiles. "I'm glad you're here. I can show you the guesthouse after we eat!"

I breathe an almost silent sigh of relief. This is already going easier than I anticipated. I worried that having Pops here would be too suspicious, but luckily, she's just glad to see him. I make a mental note to have him over more often.

Once the food is finished, we all gather around the kitchen table. Hallie looks at me gratefully when she sees all the different vegetarian dishes on the table. I won't be giving up meat anytime soon, but I'll admit her food tastes good.

"Sorry I was late," Hallie says as we dig in. "I was talking to Carole about this idea I've had for a while. I wanted to run it past her before I got too excited about it."

"It's fine, baby," I assure her. More than fine, actually. "What's this idea?"

She takes a sip of her water. "Abbie was actually the one to give it to me."

My daughter perks up at that. "I was?"

Hallie smiles. "You were. That day you came home from school upset and we started painting, I thought about what it would be like to help other kids connect with art the way I did." She looks at Pops. "It gave me an outlet when I needed it. I want to do the same for kids like me."

"A wonderful idea," Pops says.

Pride shines on Hallie's face. "I was hoping Carole would be alright with me using the gallery as a meeting place. I want to set up art camps for kids, like during the winter break and March Break, when they're off school. We could do them in the summer, too."

Her passion radiates through her words, and I know, without a doubt, that she'll make this happen.

"I wanna come!" Abbie says. "Daddy, can I go to Hallie's camp?"

I laugh. "Let's give her some time to get set up first, Princess. But when she's ready, you can be her first attendee."

She nods. "And Sophia. She's gotta come, too."

Abbie launches into her plans to attend this camp, and Pops nods along.

Hallie turns to me. "You think it's a good idea?"

I take her hand. "I think it's a great idea, Foster. You love working with kids, and you love art. Seems like a no-brainer to me."

"I love you forever," she says, squeezing my hand.

"I love you, too."

When dinner is over, Abbie runs from the kitchen to collect the ring box we hid in her bedroom. As I wait for her to come back, my nerves return in full force. Pops catches my eye and nods reassuringly.

It isn't a secret that marriage is on the table for us. Hallie and I have both been honest about what we want our future to look like. Doesn't make me any less jittery, though.

When Abbie comes back into the room, she drops the square box into my hand.

"What's that?" Hallie asks curiously.

I open the lid, showing off the ring inside. As much as I loved her fake ring, this one is nothing like it. On a thin gold band lies an oval-shaped amethyst, with small clusters of diamonds on either side. The nontraditional stone is right up her alley.

But most importantly, I get to be the one to slide it onto her finger. If she'll let me.

Hallie claps a hand over her mouth in disbelief. She looks over to Abbie and Pops for confirmation. The latter gives her an encouraging smile, while the former dances on the balls of her feet, barely holding back her excitement. My daughter might almost be more pumped about this than me.

I push my chair back from the table, then lower to one knee in front of Hallie. As I look at her, all my nerves wash away. It's her, it's us. We're inevitable.

"Gabe," she whispers.

"Hallie, I've known for a long time that you're the one for me, and pretending to be engaged to you only solidified the fact that I want it to be real. That I would love nothing more than the honour of calling you my fiancée, and eventually, my wife. So what do you say, Foster? Will you marry me?"

She swipes a tear from her cheek with her sleeve. "Are you for real? God, Gabe. Yes. Of course, yes."

Rising to my feet, I crush her to my chest. I feel weightless. My dream girl—the woman I've been pining after for over a decade— just agreed to spend the rest of her life with me.

Our lips meet in a chaste kiss, suitable for our current audience. When I pull back, I have to concentrate to get my hand to work right, pulling the ring from the box and sliding it over Hallie's knuckle.

"It's beautiful, Gabe," she says, eyes shining. "I love it. I love *you*."

God, she could tell me that a million times and it still won't feel real.

Abbie wraps her arms around Hallie. "You make my dad smile really big. And me. You make me smile big, too."

Hallie hugs her close. "You and your dad are so special to me, Abbs. Thank you for letting me be part of your family."

"Does this mean you'll live with us forever?" Abbie asks.

Hallie nods. "There's no place I'd rather be."

EPILOGUE

HALLIE

EACH STROKE of my brush against canvas works to calm the thoughts swirling in my mind. Most of them are good, but there are a few that threaten to bring my mood down. Hence, the painting.

It was still dark when I slipped out of bed. Now the sun is steadily rising, and I know it won't be long until Gabe realizes I'm gone. He'll know I didn't go far, though. Just out to the guesthouse in the backyard, where I've been spending a lot of my free time since the weather turned warm.

Without us really discussing it, the guesthouse has become my studio. When I need to clear my head, this is where I come. Abbie joins me sometimes, and she helps me practice the kind of lessons I'll give during my camps.

We had the first one back in March, and although I was a ball of nervous energy the whole week, it went off without a hitch. And when we opened signups for this summer, parents were scrambling to add their kids' names to the list. I'm hardly the first person to think up a camp like this, but apparently, it was something Kip Island desperately needed. I'm more than happy to fill that void.

"Foster?"

Time's up.

I set my paintbrush down and swivel on my stool. "You can't call me that anymore," I say with a grin. I haven't officially changed my name yet, but we got married three days ago. As far as I'm concerned, I'm a Bowman now.

Gabe, however, doesn't take my bait. He crosses to me, worry in his expression. "How long have you been out here?" he asks.

"Um...two hours? Three?"

Based on how hungry I feel, probably longer. But as soon as I try to eat something, that craving will turn to aversion in the blink of an eye.

He grabs a second stool and sets it in front of me. Then he sits, arms crossed, and waits for me to elaborate. To tell him what's been going on with me the past few days. He's really got that stern dad expression down, which I imagine will come in handy in the coming years.

I can't blame him for worrying. We were supposed to leave yesterday for our honeymoon. It wasn't anything over the top— just a few days in a secluded cottage in the Muskokas—but I woke up too sick to travel anywhere. So instead, we've been stuck at home. I know he doesn't care about missing our trip, but I do feel bad he doesn't know why.

"One second," I tell him.

I stand and head into the small bathroom. Fixing the plumbing in the guesthouse dropped down the priority list when I first moved into the main house, but it has been fully operational for the past two months now. It's definitely more convenient to wash out my brushes here than lugging them all inside.

Nerves crackle and pop in my stomach. Grabbing the test off the counter, I take a deep breath through my nose, then let it out through my mouth. I've had to do a lot of that lately, trying to quell my nausea. It only works half the time.

Gabe is still sitting exactly where I left him. Not for the first time, I take a moment to appreciate him. My husband is *hot*. Especially when you consider the fact that, with the workout shorts he's currently wearing, you can clearly see the new tattoo on his left thigh.

If I wasn't already pregnant, I'd be demanding to be right now.

Hand at my side, I retake my seat on my stool. Gabe's knees bracket mine. As I raise my hand, holding it out to him, I don't take my gaze off his face. First, his eyes narrow while he processes what I'm giving him. Then they widen in surprise, followed by a shine I can only describe as pure adoration.

"Yeah?" he asks, taking the pregnancy test from me. Unlike the three others I took this morning, which only showed the two positive lines, this one spells out *pregnant* on the little screen.

I smile, my eyes growing misty. "Yeah."

Gabe looks from me to the test, then back again. "How long have you known?"

"I suspected at the wedding," I admit. I threw up a couple times before I could put my dress on, which was tighter in the bust than it should have been. "Clara dropped the tests off the day after, because I knew I wouldn't be able to go get them without you knowing, but I didn't take them until this morning. I was... scared."

He doesn't say anything, giving me space to collect my thoughts, but he holds his left hand out for me to take. The feel of his wedding band is something I'm still not used to, but it sends a bolt of giddiness through me anyway. Teenage Hallie would be flipping out right now.

"I want this with you, Gabe. *So bad.* But the minute I thought I could be pregnant, all those fears about turning into my mother hit me like a tidal wave."

I stopped taking birth control a couple months ago. We weren't trying, but we also weren't *not* trying. You just never know how long it might take, and I wanted more kids with Gabe. We wanted to give Abbie siblings. Only, I didn't expect it to happen so soon.

Now that it has, I'm kind of freaking out.

"You're going to be the best mom," he says. "Know how I know? Because you're already amazing with Abbie."

I shake my head. "I don't do much. That's all you and Larissa."

"You are an integral part of her life, and you share a special bond with her. It's different than what she has with me and Larissa, but it's no less important." He squeezes my hand. "So hear me when I say that you're ready. Okay?"

"Okay," I whisper.

Gabe lets go of my hand, only to grab me by the waist and tug me off my stool. He pulls me down onto his lap so I'm straddling him. I loop an arm around his shoulders to keep myself steady.

"I love you," he says. "Thank you for giving me this."

A tear slips down my cheek as he kisses me. It's gentle, a culmination of all the words swimming between us. All the quiet joy.

When we pull apart, I can't help but run a hand across the outside of Gabe's thigh. "Whatever workouts you've been doing lately, keep 'em up."

Gabe pinches my asscheek. "Behave."

I press a kiss to his jaw. "I can't help it. Must be the hormones." When I'm not feeling sick, I'm feeling *very* attracted to my husband. Which is unfortunate, because I haven't been able to do anything about it since we got married.

"Let's see if you can keep your breakfast down, then we'll talk."

I pout. "You're no fun."

But I know he's right. I can't exactly enjoy sex if I'm trying not to puke my guts out, which has been happening more often than not recently.

"I'm trying to take care of you, baby. Which, speaking of, you need to eat something."

My pout turns into a frown. "What time is it?"

"Almost eight-thirty."

Oops. I've definitely been out here longer than I thought. I'm not going to volunteer that information, though. I'll keep that to myself.

"Now that you mention it, I could probably use some food."

Gabe chuckles. "That's what I thought."

I slide off his lap, then reach for my brushes. I have to clean them before I can go anywhere.

"Oh! Bryan said he and his girlfriend will use the rest of our rental," I say. Since Gabe and I won't be using our cottage getaway this time around, we figured someone should.

My siblings and I have grown closer than I thought we would in the past few months. I wasn't sure what to expect when I fully decided to let them in, but it feels like I've known them my whole life, and they have totally embraced me as their younger sister.

Things with Kevin are a bit more complicated. Overall, we have a good relationship, but overcoming twenty-eight years of abandonment doesn't happen overnight. Still, I'm happy with where we are.

Kevin and Dana have been separated for the past five months. They tried counselling, but it was all too much for Dana to reconcile. Between Kevin getting sick and then him wanting to have a relationship with me, it's been a rough few years for her. She did reach out and apologize for the way she treated me, though. We won't be in each other's lives, but that's okay. I wish her nothing but the best.

"Clara will be disappointed," Gabe says. "She asked me an hour ago if it was still available."

I laugh as I turn the tap on, running the brush heads through the water. "*Please.* She'll be fine. Her man will just whisk her away to France or Italy for a few days instead."

For a woman who barely left the island her first twenty-eight years of life, Clara's brand new passport has been getting quite the workout lately.

Gabe rolls his eyes. "We can't all be worth millions."

I lean up and press a kiss to his lips. "I don't need millions. I just need you."

Once the brushes are clean and set out to dry, I move toward the door. Gabe's arms snake around me, tugging me back to my easel. One of his hands rests low on my stomach, right over where our baby is growing.

"Before we go inside," he says, "show me what my wife has been working on."

My wife.

The smile that stretches my lips is uninhibited. "I thought we could hang it in the baby's room," I say. I point to the blend of oranges and yellows on the canvas. "It's inspired by the sunrise this morning."

Gabe presses a kiss to my temple. "I love it."

I turn, looking up at him. "I love you."

So much of my life has changed since I came back home, but I truly couldn't imagine everything playing out any differently than it has. I fully believe that I was meant to end up right here, in Gabe's arms.

"It's always been you and me, Hallie Bowman."

And it always will be. Forever.

ACKNOWLEDGMENTS

This book has been a long time coming. I first began writing it the way I've written all my books—little snippets of random ideas at a time. The first words I wrote for Gabe and Hallie were in 2023. I was just starting on *The Edge of Summer* then, but I knew what their story would look like. Mostly.

I tried to jump into *This Kind of Forever* when I was done with book one in early 2024, but I quickly realized I was a touch burnt out. Now here I am in 2025. Writing a second book in an already established world proved more challenging than I was anticipating. It's been a long time coming, but I think the timing is just right. I put a lot of myself into Hallie (minus the best friend's brother who has been in love with me forever, unfortunately), and my hope is that she will resonate with some of you, too.

As always, though, this whole journey of mine wouldn't be possible without some important people in my life.

First and foremost, my family. You continue to be my loudest and proudest supporters, even though you embarrass the crap out of me. Really, though, we *don't* need to talk about my books. Please. But because I know you still will, I'm going to keep making fun of your grandma sweaters and find new ways to infuse some of our real life into my books.

To Karley. I remember sharing a very early snippet of this book with you when we first became friends, and you sent me a *very* panicked message wondering why Gabe had some girl's name tattooed on him that wasn't Hallie's. Safe to say, you've been Team H+G ever since. Thank you for listening to me ramble about these characters for almost two years now, and for putting up with me having an on again/off again relationship with finishing this book. I finally did it! Love you lots.

To my Menaci. Thank you for being there to commiserate with me as I set about buckling down and finishing this book, once and for all. And thank you for kicking my butt and yelling at me when my anxieties got in my way and I was being silly. I can't promise it won't happen again, though.

To my beta readers: Natasha, Ashley, Cait, Marina, Hunter, Paula and Bri. I feel like I've said this a hundred times now, but thank you. This book is so close to my heart for many reasons, and releasing it into the world has been a scary prospect. Your dedication to reading and giving me feedback, and your enthusiasm for my characters (despite the sometimes frustrating things they do) means more to me than you'll ever know.

Last (but certainly not least), my readers. It still doesn't feel real that people both read and enjoy my books, and I never want it to. Please know that I never take your support for granted. It's a privilege to be able to tell these stories, and I hope to continue telling them for a long, long time. Thank you.

ABOUT THE AUTHOR

Bobbi Maclaren is an indie author from a small town in Ontario, Canada. When she isn't writing, she can be found reading, wrangling her mischievous black cat or booking her next trip to a new country. She also loves fall, dresses with pockets, and her emotional support water bottle.

Find her @bmaclarenwrites on social media.